"Get the hell ou

yelled.

"Not on your life, buster!" she yelled back.

"I'm not joking, Kristine. I'm going to Chicago, but you're not. Don't you realize how dangerous the crime syndicate is?"

She looked him square in the eye. "Shouldn't we get going?"

Tucker jerked the door open and reached for her. She slipped her hand into his jacket pocket – the one with the gun in it.

"You don't know what you're doing," he whispered.

"I know, all right. I'm trying to stop a fool from making a mistake that might cost him the rest of his life."

Tucker clenched his jaw. She was just an added liability. But somewhere deep down inside, he wanted her with him. "All right, come on. But if you get caught up in something that's way over your head, well . . . you were warned."

Dear Reader:

We at Silhouette are very excited to bring you a NEW reading **Sensation.** *Look out for the four books which will appear in our new Silhouette* **Sensation** *series every month. These stories will have the high quality you have come to expect from Silhouette, and their varied and provocative plots will encourage you to explore the wonder of falling in love – again and again!*

Emotions run high in these drama-filled novels. Greater sensual detail and an extra edge of realism intensify the hero and heroine's relationship so that you cannot help but be caught up in their every change of mood.

We hope you enjoy this new **Sensation** *– and will go on to enjoy many more.*

We would love to hear your comments about our new line and encourage you to write to us:

Jane Nicholls
Silhouette Books
PO Box 236
Thornton Road
Croydon
Surrey
CR9 3RU

ANN WILLIAMS
Haunted by the Past

First published in Great Britain in 1991
by Silhouette Books, Eton House, 18-24 Paradise Road,
Richmond, Surrey TW9 1SR

ISBN 0 373 58269 2

18 – 9109

Made and printed in Great Britain

Another novel by Ann Williams

Silhouette Sensation

Devil in Disguise

For my parents,
Mr. and Mrs. William M. Price.
My thanks to Kevin Martin in Miami, Florida,
and Tim Hall in Pasadena, Texas.
Your help was invaluable.

Chapter 1

Tucker Winslow balanced the small, deadly looking pistol in his left hand, testing the weight and feel. It felt good. It felt right. It felt like just the thing to put a little round hole dead center in Jack Arnold's forehead.

"I'll take it."

Friendly Freddy, of Friendly Freddy's Fast Funds, smiled, nodded once and adjusted the thick-lensed, black-framed glasses on his chubby face.

Tucker watched as pale, sausage-like fingers slid a yellow sheet of paper across the counter toward him. A gold ring on the right pinky finger flashed fire as the light was caught and reflected back by the large blood-red ruby at its center.

Narrowing his eyes, Tucker ignored the paper for the moment, shifted the gun from left hand to right and asked, "How much?"

The little man, eyelids twitching, glanced nervously from the round black hole in the short-barreled gun to the man's cold silver eyes, and back. For an instant a bead of sweat glistened high on the sallow forehead, then slid along the bridge of his fleshy nose and disappeared into the bristles of his thick black mustache.

His answer, when it finally came, was considerably less than the original asking sum. He'd seen this man's kind before, dressed in their brand-new clothes and shiny new boots. They always spoke in short, terse sentences and harbored a shifty, almost paranoid expression in their remote eyes. They spelled trouble, and he wanted nothing to do with it—or them.

Licking his mustache, Freddy shifted his small feet in their too-tight boots and asked hesitantly to see the man's driver's license.

Careful not to touch him, Freddy took the small square of plastic and gave it a brief glance. Almost apologetically he inquired if the address was current. After being assured in short, clipped tones that it was, he began to make notes in a small, cramped hand on an official-looking document.

When Freddy had completed his part, he turned the paper around to face Tucker. "Over-the-Counter Firearms Transactions," Tucker read. Another stinking form to fill out. In the past couple of months, he'd read and signed all the damned forms he ever wanted to see for the rest of his life.

Their business transaction completed, Tucker pocketed the gun without further ado and turned toward the door. It opened abruptly, emitting a burst of frigid air, and another customer, a woman, entered the shop.

Behind the counter, Freddy straightened, focusing his black eyes on the young woman's face. He sighed beneath his breath. This one looked desperate. He'd seen her kind before, too; the city was filled with them.

Tucker glanced up indifferently, looked from the anxious white face to the tangle of wild blond hair, then looked away.

"H-hello," she said breathlessly, as though she'd been running. Her greeting included the silent man standing to one side of the counter, staring at a row of rifles, as well as the little fat man who seemed hardly taller than the glass case behind which he stood.

"Howdy do, miss." His earlier hardy manner once more restored, Freddy grinned, showing a wide gap between two large front teeth. "Can I help you?"

"Yes," she answered, drawing closer to where the man stood, shooting a quick glance back over her shoulder toward the large plate-glass window.

Reaching into the pocket of her red ski jacket, she withdrew a clenched fist. "I'd like to pawn this. How much can I get for it?"

A wide gold band mounted with a large square-cut diamond lay resting on her palm. Her hand shook. The ring fell abruptly onto the glass countertop, bounced twice, then came to rest against a miniature AM/FM stereo radio. Three pairs of eyes watched its progress, but only one shone with the gleam of avarice.

Kristine Stevens placed her hands in her coat pockets and prayed that Friendly Freddy was compassionate as well as friendly. She needed money desperately; as much as she could lay her hands on, as quickly as possible.

"How much can I get for that?" she repeated, her large dark eyes on the little man's ruddy complexion.

Freddy picked the ring up and looked it over without comment, hiding the excitement he felt, while Kristine stood looking on with suspended breath. Still without comment, Freddy reached a pudgy hand below the counter and picked up a small black jeweler's glass.

Placing the ring dispassionately on the first joint of a stubby index finger, and the loupe against the right lens of his glasses, he studied the cut and quality of the diamond. Both were excellent.

"Seventy-five—"

"Seventy-five!" the woman echoed, a stricken look in the huge rounded eyes. "But it must have cost more than ten times that brand-new. Please—I need the money," she stressed almost desperately.

Freddy shrugged. "Seventy-five," he repeated, pursing thick red lips. With this customer he had the upper hand. She'd beg for more, but in the end she'd settle for whatever he offered—and they both knew it.

After a moment, he added, "This ain't no charity establishment. You heard my offer, it's the only one I'm going to make. Take it or leave it." He shrugged as though it was of no consequence to him.

She couldn't stop the tears from gathering in her eyes, but she blinked quickly to hide them. She couldn't stay arguing with the man, not if she valued her life, and seventy-five dollars was more than she had right now.

Before she could answer one way or another, the other customer, silent until now, stepped up to the counter.

"You know Freddy, that looks like a pretty valuable ring to me. This lady just might decide to take it back and see what she can get for it at the next shop."

Oh, no, Kristine groaned inwardly, she'd already stopped at two other pawnshops along the street, and they had both told her they didn't want another diamond wedding band. If this interfering idiot ruined it for her—

Tucker knew he'd read the man correctly when he saw him lick his mustache and smooth an unsteady hand over the few strands of lank hair parted low on the side and combed upward to shield his balding pate.

Freddy's glance darted from the woman to the ring. He wanted it. It was an exceptionally flawless diamond, worth a lot more than the seven hundred she'd guessed. And diamonds were his weakness.

He didn't like the man with the gray eyes, and he wanted him and the woman out of his shop as quickly as possible—after he was in possession of the diamond.

Placing the loupe back to his eye, Freddy pretended to scrutinize the stone further. Anxious as he was to be done with the pair of them, he wasn't going to let the man have it all his own way.

"Yes." Clearing his throat, he nodded. "Yes, I think perhaps you're right. Two hundred—" He glanced furtively at the man, saw his slightly raised brow and added, "Fifty." Smiling expansively at the woman, he asked in falsely cheerful tones, "How's that, two-hundred and fifty dollars?"

Kristine would have liked twice that, but knew she would settle for the sum named. She accepted Freddy's offer with a slight nod, ignoring the other man altogether. She was embarrassed at having practically begged the shop dealer for more money.

Signing the pawn ticket in short, quick strokes, she put her half of it into her coat pocket and watched as Freddy counted out a pile of crisp bills. Just for a moment she envisioned the diminutive man cranking out the new bills in a room in the back of the shop only minutes before she had entered.

"Thank you."

She folded the money in half, flashed a short, perfunctory smile at each man, then backed away. After only a few steps she stumbled over a black-and-tan toolbox sitting half in the aisle. Regaining her footing, she moved toward the door. But instead of leaving the shop, she hesitated. Almost apprehensively she darted a look up and down the street before pushing open the door and leaving the comparative safety of the building.

Tucker Winslow watched the door slam shut behind the woman's slight figure before following in her wake.

It was cold outside, a blue-norther had moved into Dallas early that morning, bringing with it temperatures in the thirties and a windchill factor in the lower teens.

Tucker hunched wide shoulders against the cold, snuggling deeper into the sheepskin jacket as he sauntered toward the sleek black car parked at the curb. His left hand closed tightly around the .38 in his coat pocket. It felt reassuringly warm against his palm, almost alive. He was well satisfied with the results of the first part of his plan.

"E-excuse me."

Tucker paused reluctantly and turned toward the familiar tones. He didn't speak, but stood looking down at the woman from the pawnshop with what he knew was an intimidating slant to his thick black brows.

"I wondered if you might be headed out of town," she asked hopefully.

"Yeah, I am—so what?" The tone was a hair short of surly.

"Well, I am too—" Not normally a nervous person, Kristine was having a great deal of difficulty withstanding the impatient glare from the pale gray eyes. Deciding to jump right in, she asked, "If you're headed east, could I get a lift with you—at least as far as the interstate?"

"No." Turning away, he bent to the car door.

"Oh, but—please," she entreated, somewhat surprised by his unfriendly manner after his help with the money.

Her teeth were chattering with the cold, but nervousness had a big part in the act, too. Laying an icy hand on his arm beseechingly, she removed it almost at once as she felt the muscles tense and the arm stiffen beneath its light weight.

"I don't like to be touched," he muttered, jerking his arm aside. Women! They were all alike. They clung like leeches to any man who noticed them—until they were through using him that is. Tucker glanced down at the gold bracelet circling his left wrist. It was a constant reminder—one he wore deliberately so he would never forget about the one who had used him before moving on to greener pastures.

"Look, I didn't do that—" he motioned back toward the shop "—for you. Don't be mislead into thinking I did."

He'd seen plenty like Freddy where he'd come from. Men who profited from the suffering of others. Men who thought they could take everything away from him, strip him bare of his identity as a human being and make him docile—but they were wrong—dead wrong.

All it had done was made him mad, madder than hell—and strengthened his resolve to make *someone* pay for his misery.

The woman shifted her numb feet on the sidewalk, and the action focused Tucker's thoughts back into the present, away from the past and the future.

Giving her a cursory inspection, taking in her broad cheekbones and stubborn chin, he decided she would get by all right without his help. Some other man would come along and stumble all over himself to do her bidding.

"I make it a rule," he told her in a detached voice, "never to pick up stray dogs—or hitchhikers. Both are nothing but trouble."

He'd been planning this for five years—five long, humiliating years, having to fight every day for his sanity, to retain his identity, his dignity as a man. But the waiting was almost over. He had his freedom, a fast car, a gun and an address in Chicago. The sweet taste of victory was almost his. Nothing and no one would be allowed to stand in his way.

Sliding into the car without another word, he started the engine and pulled away from the curb.

Kristine watched him enter the flow of traffic smoothly, thinking what an unfeeling bastard he was. Obviously he'd never been in a position to need help from anyone else. Someday he'd learn what it was like—too bad she wouldn't be there to see it.

Shivering with a sudden chill, she shoved her hands deeper into the pockets of her jacket and looked quickly around her. Standing here was dangerous. She had to get out of town somehow, and right away. Her very life depended on it.

If only she dared to fly or to take a bus. But if there was one thing she was certain of, it was that *he'd* have all the public transportation terminals watched.

She already had the uneasy feeling someone had followed her from the courthouse. However, she'd transferred cabs so many times she was fairly certain she'd lost him. Now there was nothing left for her to do but hitchhike out of town.

On the outskirts of Dallas, Kristine was lucky enough to get a ride with an older man and woman who were headed home to Mount Pleasant. The couple had been visiting their daughter and her family in Dallas. They talked almost nonstop for the next three hours. All that was required of Kristine was an obliging nod of the head now and then.

It was late afternoon when she shouldered her knapsack, waved a last goodbye to the Cummings and began to walk at a quick pace along the interstate.

Maybe if she was lucky she'd meet up with another such pair. The worry plaguing her the most was that she might come across some of the dangerous weirdos she had read about in the newspapers or seen on TV.

As the minutes stretched out, her footsteps began to flag. Walking had never been her favorite pastime. As a nurse working in a hospital, she had gotten all the walking exercise she ever wanted, and then some.

The reassuring weight of the package strapped just below her breasts was both a blessing and a curse. Without it, she would be dead now. With it, she was a threat Vincent Spinelli couldn't afford to let slip away.

Up until now her safety had been assured, both because of the package and because Spinelli didn't want her dead body traced to him. It wasn't that easy to hide a body in the city—but on the open road—Kristine shivered again, though not from the cold this time.

He'd be coming after her, she knew it. Her only hope was to try to stay one step ahead of him—and she wasn't certain she knew how to do that.

The sun was setting in the west, the skies, already a dull gun-metal gray, hardly noted its passing. There would be no stars to light her path that night.

She really couldn't afford to spend the night in a motel, and yet she was afraid to spend it alone out on the road. What a mess! What were her alternatives?

Maybe she could give the package she carried to the first cop she saw. But Spinelli's influence was far-reaching—she knew that from experience. He had many contacts in the Dallas police force. He'd managed to get her fired from every job she could find—starting with her job at the hospital where she'd been working when she first met him.

Lord, if only people were all born with second sight. Then perhaps she would have been smart enough to run the first time she saw him, the night he'd come into the emergency room, where she was working, with a knife wound.

The sudden honking of a horn somewhere close by caused her to glance up sharply. A late-model white Mustang convertible was pulled over onto the shoulder up ahead. A ride. Off at a run, she slowed her eager steps before reaching the side of the car. She had made herself a promise. She would absolutely refuse to ride with anyone who looked like they belonged astride a chopper or as though they might carry a chainsaw in the trunk.

She needn't have worried. Two teenage girls sat in the front seat, dressed in purple satin jackets, with the name of their high school embroidered on their backs.

They were cheerleaders, they explained gaily, on their way to a football game. She was welcome to ride as far as they were going, which was only about thirty miles or so down the road to the next town. Kristine accepted their kind offer and climbed into the back seat.

For the next half hour Kristine learned all over again what it was like to be seventeen, crazy about football players and pizza, and to debate whether sex was *really* as important as boys seemed to think it was.

Mindy and Lou Ann let her out at a small restaurant with a Trucker's Welcome sign on a pole that was visible for miles down the road. Kristine wished them luck at the game and turned eagerly toward the half-filled parking lot of the restaurant.

* * *

Tucker wiped his mouth on a napkin and watched the tall man built like a wrestler, his black hair slicked back from a low forehead, pass from one table to the next.

When he stopped at Tucker's table, he stood for a long silent moment waiting for Tucker to look up and meet the almost invisible sneer in his dun-colored eyes.

Tucker obliged when he was ready, and they sized each other up, neither particularly impressed by what he saw.

The big man shoved a snapshot under Tucker's nose and asked in a deep, contemptuous tone, "You seen her?"

Tucker gave the picture a cursory glance. But his lips stayed firmly closed as his eyes traveled slowly upward over the fifteen-hundred-dollar suit. There was no question in his mind what this man did for a living—he was another of the familiar breed he'd come to know in the recent past.

"She's a runaway—my bride—" The sardonic grin on the wide lips made no pretense of being anything other than what it was. Both men knew he was lying.

After a moment the man shrugged broad shoulders and walked on. He knew from experience there weren't many women where this guy had recently been.

Tucker watched him saunter away, an icy sheen in the narrowed gray eyes.

The aroma of fried chicken caused saliva to fill Kristine's mouth. She was at the restaurant door when something cautioned her to scan the room before entering.

Two men blocked her view of the room as they opened the glass doors and exited the building. They both gave her a strange look when they held the door for her and she drew back instead of entering.

The smell of fried chicken became stronger, and Kristine clenched her jaws against the sudden pain of hunger.

She hadn't eaten all day, and her knees were beginning to feel wobbly.

When the two men had climbed into their pickup and driven away, Kristine once again leaned forward, peering through one of the windows into the lighted interior of the restaurant.

She was looking for a familiar face, one she dreaded seeing, because she knew that if Vincent had sent anyone after her, it would be Carl Morrell, his right-hand man.

There were about a dozen people sitting inside—two families with small children and several tables at which both men and women sat. She scrutinized them carefully, and to her tired eyes they all appeared to be normal, hungry people having a meal.

Feeling an almost overwhelming sense of relief, she stepped to the door and reached for the handle. A tall, broad-shouldered man dressed in a dark suit stepped into view from behind the wooden saloon-type doors that led to the rest rooms.

Kristine froze. With a sickening jolt she recognized the dark-skinned, pockmarked face. Carl Morrell smoothed a hand over black slicked-back hair and stopped to have a word with the young ponytailed waitress on his way to the door.

Kristine fell back, heart thudding in fear, eyes darting this way and that. What could she do? She had to think fast. A hurried glance told her there wasn't much of a choice—and *he* was almost at the door.

She had to hide, but where? One of the cars—but what if she picked *his* car? Scrambling behind the nearest automobile, she waited and watched, praying the man would come outside, climb into his vehicle and leave.

But Morrell was smarter than that. He began a quick yet thorough search of every automobile and truck on the parking lot. He opened those he could and inspected the front and back seats. And he checked the interiors of those that were locked, by shining a flashlight through the windows.

Kristine was near one of the first cars he'd looked over, and while he was peering beneath a tarpaulin covering the back of a pickup, she tried the car's door. Finding it unlocked, she slithered from the ground to the space behind the front seat and made herself as small as possible on the floor. Her right hand slipped inside her jacket pocket and gripped the thick Swiss army knife she had begun carrying for protection when she first started working nights at the hospital.

A few minutes later she heard the sound of a car nearby start up and pull out of the parking lot, its tires spraying gravel. Wiping an unsteady hand over her damp brow, she drew a shaky breath and started to raise her head to peer outside.

Suddenly she heard the sound of masculine voices in conversation and dropped back down onto the floor. What if it hadn't been Morrell she'd heard leave? What if the man was hanging around outside, waiting for someone—waiting for her.

Maybe she should stay where she was a while longer to be perfectly safe. She'd wait until she heard a couple more cars leave, and then she'd take a chance and look. If he was gone, then she'd go inside and get something to eat. Her stomach began to protest her change in plans, but she ignored it as best she could and settled down as comfortably as possible to wait.

She had no idea how long she'd been in the car. Ten minutes, twenty, an hour? Sometime during her wait, she had apparently fallen asleep. She recognized the steady hum she heard beneath her ear as the sound of a car's engine, and the rhythmic slapping noise was tires rolling over wet pavement. Wet pavement?

Raising her head cautiously she peeked over the back of the seat. Headlights from oncoming cars showed her the steady back-and-forth movement of windshield wipers. With a panicky feeling she realized she had no idea in which direction the car was headed. She could be on her way to anywhere—even back to Dallas!

Should she tell whoever was driving that she was in the back? What could she say? *Pardon me, but while hiding from someone who might possibly want to kill me, I climbed into your car. I have no idea where you're going, but if it's in the direction I'm headed, do you mind if I just ride along with you?*

Fat chance! Whoever was driving would probably tell her in no uncertain terms to get her rear out. Perhaps she could keep her mouth shut and wait until he stopped for gas or something and then slip out of the car without his seeing her.

The car gave a jerk, and the decision was abruptly taken out of her hands as Kristine was thrown against the back of the front seat. Hearing muttered curses, she felt the car slow, its rocking sensation jarring the teeth in her head, until it came to a dead halt.

There was an ominous silence from the front seat. The only sound that could be heard was the whooshing noise of other cars as they passed the stopped vehicle.

"Okay, whoever the hell is in the back—show yourself—now."

With a sinking sensation, Kristine pushed herself up from the floor and slid onto the back seat. The interior light came on as she looked directly into the angry face of the driver.

"You!"

"You?"

They spoke in unison.

"How the hell did you manage to follow me?"

"I don't know—I mean—I didn't—I didn't know it was you."

They stared at each other with open animosity, the lights from passing vehicles playing eerily across their faces.

"How did you get in?" he asked stonily. "And when?"

"Back at the restaurant. I was tired from walking," she lied. "I couldn't go any farther on foot. I took a chance the car I picked would be going the same way as me, and—" she shrugged "—I opened the door and climbed inside."

"I told you back in Dallas, I don't give rides to hitchhikers. And that's what I meant. Out!" He lifted a thumb and jerked it toward the door. The overhead light glinted on the gold bracelet as it slid down his bony wrist.

"Aw, come on. It's cold and wet out there. And take a look—" she motioned outside the car "—there isn't a house or building in sight. Just give me a ride to the next town—please." It galled her to have to say that to this unfeeling oaf.

"I don't believe in charity," was his unbending reply.

"I'm not asking for charity." What luck—of all the cars, she had to pick the one belonging to the good Samaritan here.

"Look, you don't like me and I don't particularly like you, but I need a ride—and I'm willing to pay," she added for good measure.

She didn't have much money, but then he knew exactly how much she did have—maybe he would be satisfied with a little to help pay for the gas. She could do without food if she didn't have to trudge through the cold rain and mud tonight.

"How much?" he asked dispassionately.

"Ten?"

His unblinking eyes held hers.

"Twenty?"

"Ten will do." He turned around to climb from the car. "And you can help change the tire," he added.

"W-what?" she asked in surprise.

Help change the tire? In the cold rain? For a moment she sat stubbornly unmoving. Whatever happened to the knights on white chargers who rode in to rescue the maidens in distress? Now it was pay your way or else.

"Come on." He opened the back door and motioned her from the car. "Here." He flipped her the keys. "Get the spare while I remove the hubcap." Taking a tire iron from beneath the front seat, he moved around to the side of the car.

Kristine looked down at the keys she had automatically caught in her right hand. She'd never changed a tire before in her life. Thank God, he'd said *help*. She pulled her backpack off her shoulders, put it on the seat and began to climb from the car.

"You going to sit there all night?" Tucker asked. "It's getting colder, and from the feel of this wind, I'd say snow was definitely on the way."

Kristine moved around to the back of the car, fit the key into the trunk and opened the lid. She found the jack under the spare tire in the tire well. By the time she lugged the jack to the far side of the car, the hubcap was lying on the gravel.

Kristine adjusted the jack into place, and her knight errant pumped the car up off the ground. In a matter of minutes he had the lug nuts and the tire off.

Sitting back on his heels, he stared up at her in the light from a passing car and muttered, "Well?"

Kristine gave him a look from watery eyes, wiped her nose on the sleeve of her jacket and glanced from him to the empty tire hub. What was she supposed to do now?

"The spare tire, damn it," he prompted, "I need the spare tire." Blowing on his cold hands, he rubbed them together, clenching and unclenching the numb fingers.

Feeling like a fool but annoyed at the same time, Kristine managed to get the tire out of the trunk while he crouched there watching her struggle in unbending silence.

Taking the tire from her grease-stained hands without comment, he fit it into place, added the lug nuts to hold it on and tightened them by rote.

Kristine stood back, watching him work, her cold hands tucked into the opposite sleeves of her jacket. Staring down at the top of his dark head, she wondered what kind of a person she had stumbled upon. He was a complete enigma to her. When she hadn't wanted his help, he had jumped right in, yet when she asked for it, he denied her. Who could figure men?

He knew she was short on cash, yet he was willing to take her money for a lift of only a few miles. Kristine sneezed. And he had made her get out in the freezing rain to help change a flat. She'd never met anyone so perverse—that is, unless you counted Vincent— "Damn!" Falling back onto his heels with a curse, Tucker put a finger to his mouth.

"What is it?" she asked anxiously, taking a quick step closer.

"Nothing, not a damned thing," he answered tersely. He finished fitting the hubcap into place and stood up.

"Come on, get this stuff in the trunk so we can be on our way."

As he spoke, the sporadic patter of rain became a cloudburst. Kristine returned the jack to its proper place in the tire well, but had to have help lifting the now-flattened tire into its snug resting place.

Handing her a piece of greasy blue rag, he wiped his own hands on its twin then threw them both into the trunk and slammed the lid shut.

"Let's go." Rain had already soaked his hair and ran in rivulets down his unshaven cheeks.

Kristine wiped a hand over both sides of her face, inadvertently leaving a dirty trail along one cheek. Afraid that he might leave her on the roadside in the pouring rain, she hurried around the car to the passenger side and opened the door determinedly.

Tucker glanced at her with a raised brow as she slid into the bucket seat across from him. But he started the car without comment, letting it warm up before moving out onto the black ribbon of wet highway.

Kristine breathed a sigh of relief once they were finally under way and whispered a silent prayer of thanksgiving. After a slight pause she added a brief postscript about God making the next town several hundred miles down the road—please—and ended it with a fervent amen.

Resting her head back against the seat, she unzipped her damp jacket and pressed a reassuring hand to the area below her breasts. Everything was still in place, so she could relax. Taking a deep breath, she basked in the warm air blowing from the heater.

Turning her head, she looked toward her unwilling host, but his features were hard to make out in the muted light from the dash. Remembering their unwelcoming harshness, she decided perhaps that wasn't such a bad thing after all.

"You didn't ask where I was headed," she spoke abruptly, shattering the stillness.

"No, I didn't," was his uncompromising answer.

So, he wasn't interested in her destination. Fine, but she was interested in his.

"What about you?"

"East."

"Are we still on I-30?"

"Yeah."

They were traveling east on Interstate 30. That meant she was on her way home—or at least in the general direction of the town that was once her home. There wasn't much family left there now, just an odd cousin or two. But it was still home—familiar—safe?

"You have a name?" she asked, trying once again for a more friendly note. They wouldn't be together for long, but she saw no need for the hostility she felt bubbling below the surface.

"I have a name," he agreed stiffly, offering nothing more.

When the silence had stretched a few miles, Kristine asked, "Is it a big secret? Or are you just funny about people knowing it?"

He spared her a glance, his strange-colored eyes catching the light in a manner that caused them to appear to glow for a moment. Kristine's stomach muscles tightened in apprehension. Who was he? And for a moment she wondered, *what* was he?

His answer, when it came, didn't surprise her, though it did relieve her mind a bit. It sounded very human.

"It's no secret, I'm just choosy about who I give it to. And I don't much like questions—especially from strangers."

That put her very thoroughly in her place. Releasing a pent-up breath, she snuggled into the corner of the seat and closed her eyes. If he got off on keeping an air of mystery about his identity—then let him.

As long as he was in no way connected with Vincent Spinelli—and she felt confident that he wasn't—he could be as mysterious as he liked.

The blast of warm air from the car's heater first warmed her and then made her drowsy. The steady rhythm of the tires on the road and the swishing sound of the windshield wipers moving back and forth lulled her into sleep.

Tucker glanced her way and saw the gentle rise and fall of her breasts. She'd loosened her jacket in the car's warmth, and a patch of the sweater she wore beneath it was visible. It was impossible to distinguish its color in the muted light from the dash, but for some reason he remembered it as sunny yellow from seeing her in the pawnshop.

She sighed, turned her face on the seat, squirmed for a more comfortable position and pressed her back against the door.

Forcing his eyes away from the sight of her smooth cheeks, the one nearest to him marred by a greasy black streak, and the full, slightly parted lips, he reached for the automatic door lock. He told himself his concern was merely in seeing she didn't fall out of the car, thereby creating an accident that would delay him, and had nothing at all of any personal nature to it.

Nevertheless he was determined to put her out at the first opportunity. He had to admit she was a plucky little thing. She hadn't turned a hair when he had agreed to accept money for the ride, even though all indications pointed to her having little of it. And when he'd insisted she help with the flat, he'd expected her to tell him what he could do with his ride.

His eye was momentarily captured by the glitter of gold on his left wrist. Then he glanced back at his sleeping companion's blond shoulder-length curls. She looked nothing at all like Sylvia, the statuesque brunette who had given him the bracelet he wore. But they were all sisters under the skin, he reminded himself sharply; conniving, deceitful, always looking for a way to further their own ends.

He forced his attention back to the road. He still had a long way to go, but at the end of this trip he would finally be able to cauterize the wound that had been festering inside him for the past several years, eating away at his soul.

The first thing Kristine became aware of was the silence, then the cessation of movement and then the cold. She opened her eyes, and twisted toward the sound of soft snores emanating from the man beside her. But all she could see was the back of his head, the short dark hair cut away from the collar of his jacket and the glass fogging beneath his forehead with each exhale.

Raising a hand, she wiped the mist from the window beside her and looked outside. They were pulled into a rest park and sitting at the very end of the parking area. A short distance away, she could see the concrete building that housed the rest rooms and information center.

Realizing all at once that she needed to visit the bathroom, she glanced over at the sleeping man, eased her hand onto the door handle then hesitated. What if he awakened and made his getaway in her absence?

For some untold reason he hadn't put her out of the car as he'd threatened—maybe because she'd been asleep. Somewhere under that rough exterior there was a spark of human charity after all.

In any case, the decision had been taken out of her hands; nature called. Racing along the sidewalk, she was glad her companion's prediction of snow hadn't materialized. At the lighted glass-encased map in front of the building, Kristine stopped long enough to see how far they had traveled from Dallas. With a jolt of shock she noted that they had passed out of Texas and across the border into Arkansas.

Her spirits leaped as she darted into the toasty warm interior of the building. She was almost two hundred miles out of Vincent Spinelli's reach.

A few minutes later, while making her way from the building, her attention was drawn to a man moving stealthily down the line of parked vehicles. Pulling back into the shadows outside the entrance, she waited and watched.

He was systematically shining a flashlight into each vehicle as though searching for something—or someone! He passed under a light and Kristine got a fair look at his face. It was Morrell!

Falling back against the building, her pulse rioting out of control, she panicked. What should she do? Hide? Where? Staring around in the dark at the bushes flanking the building she was leaning against, she wondered if they might give her enough cover until he'd made the rounds and left.

But what if he didn't leave? She would never be able to make it back to the car without his seeing her.

Should she glide through the dark to the road up ahead and hitch another ride? Her knapsack! It was in the car. And all her money was hidden inside it. Damn! How dumb! She should have carried the money with her.

Morrell was getting closer. If she didn't make a decision soon, he'd see her. She didn't have much choice, she would have to hide in one of the rest rooms. Obviously he hadn't searched them yet or he would have found her.

Waiting until his back was turned, Kristine darted to the door and into the building. She hesitated for just a moment. If she hid in the ladies' room, he'd find her for sure. But would he search the men's room for her? It was a chance she would have to take, there was nowhere else to go.

Hoping there would be no one inside, she opened the door, keeping her eyes closed. "Hello," she called tentatively. "Is anybody there?" No one answered, so she opened one eye and peeked around. Opening the other eye when she saw that the room was apparently empty, she slid inside and closed the door softly behind her.

There was nowhere to hide! All but one stall was open, and should Morrell come seeking her here, there was no possible way he'd neglect to look behind that one door. It was hopeless.

The door behind her suddenly swung open, nearly hitting her. She drew back in alarm. With eyes as big as saucers, she stared up into the face of the man giving her a disparaging glance from cold gray eyes.

"Here, put this on—and make it snappy," he told her impatiently.

Her rescuer, the man who kept his name a secret, threw a hat and a pair of coveralls at her.

"How did you know I'd be in here?" she asked in surprise.

He gave her a look that spoke volumes. "Leave the coat on underneath," he directed as she began to unzip her jacket.

Kristine didn't question his instructions. Slipping the coveralls over her clothes, she piled her hair up under the cowboy hat and turned to smile at him.

"All set."

Tucker spared her a slightly less critical look, but gave no indication that he approved of either the speed or the silence in which she had complied with his terse directive.

"How do I look?" she asked as they passed through the doorway into the open hallway.

"Like a female trying to look like a man," he answered darkly. "Come on." Grabbing her hand, he pushed her behind him. "Don't say a word. No matter what I say or do, or what your friend out there does, just keep your head down, your mouth shut, and head for the car. You got that?"

Kristine nodded and, head down, paced swiftly at his side. Once they were outside the building, the man beside her began a conversation about transmissions, manifolds and exhaust systems.

Kristine didn't understand a word of what he was talking about, but she nodded and grunted a time or two while surreptitiously keeping an eye on the man trying to look inconspicuous at the other end of the car park.

They had it made, both were at opposite ends of the car, reaching for door handles, when a strong gust of wind whipped the hat from Kristine's head. She gave an involuntary cry as pale blond strands flew about her head and began slapping at her startled face.

As she whirled to run after the hat now sailing across the tarmac, she glanced up to see Morrell watching her.

"Get in the car!"

Kristine twisted her head in her companion's direction. "But—"

"Get in the damned car—now!" Shooting a glance past her shoulder, he jerked his own door open and fell inside.

Kristine peered behind her and saw Morrell start to run in their direction. The car door unexpectedly banged back, almost knocking her to the ground.

"Come on!"

The engine was revving when she dropped down onto the seat and slammed the door, locking it for good measure.

In seconds they were speeding out of the park, heading down the ramp and back out onto the road. For the next ten or fifteen minutes neither said a word, but both kept close watch on the rearview mirror.

"I guess we aren't being followed," Kristine spoke first.

"Nope, doesn't look like it."

"I wonder why," she asked, puzzled at their comparatively easy escape. That didn't sound like the type of man she knew Morrell to be.

"Because," her companion answered matter-of-factly, "unless he steals a car, he's got to change four flat tires before he can go anywhere."

"What?"

"You heard me." His glance met hers, causing goose bumps to ripple along both arms before he looked away.

"How did you know to come after me?" she asked suddenly. "How did you know it was me he was looking for?"

"I'm a very light sleeper." That was only one of the many things his recent past had taught him. If you wanted no unpleasant surprises performed behind your back, you kept one eye and both ears open all the time.

"And you forget," he continued, "I was inside that restaurant where you decided to force your way into my car. That guy was showing a picture of you to everyone who'd look at it."

"He was telling some cock-and-bull story about you being his runaway bride—"

"Why didn't you believe him?" There was a minute grain of truth somewhere in that story.

"I've seen his kind before, and learned to recognize them for what they are—human predators."

He concentrated on his driving. She couldn't see his face, but she knew that grim, stony look would be in his gray eyes.

"Where?" she asked softly. "Where have you seen his kind before?"

"In the joint—prison," he clarified.

Kristine slumped slowly back against the plush suede seat covers. Prison? Her mouth felt suddenly dry, and she was having difficulty keeping the breath from lodging in her throat. All she could think of was the irony of it all. She had run away from a man who wanted to kill her—into the arms of a man who'd been in prison.

Questions darted through her mind. How long had he been out? What had he done to be put there? Had he escaped or been released? And what might he do to her?

Chapter 2

"You want to tell me what he's after?"

"You want to tell me why you were in prison?" she countered, a stubborn tilt to her chin.

Tucker removed one hand from the steering wheel, bunched up the knapsack that was lying between them and threw it onto her lap.

Kristine stared down at it in silence, seeing the snaps hanging open and the zippered compartments all exposed. Apparently she'd made a big mistake in thinking she could trust this man. And she had even begun to like him.

"You went through my things."

There was disbelief in her voice. And try as he might, Tucker couldn't help but feel a twinge of guilt at his actions. He knew what it was like to be betrayed by a person you thought you could trust. But he hadn't asked for her trust, he insisted silently, perversely. And she had no business trusting a stranger, anyway.

"What does he want?" he asked in inflexible tones. "There's nothing in that—" he indicated the bag on her lap "—to make a man chase you halfway across Texas, and then some."

Sliding her hand inside the small hidden compartment in the lower corner pocket, Kristine felt for the tight wad of money.

Glancing at her from beneath furrowed brows, he bit out, "I didn't touch the money—I'm not a thief—or a liar." There was a bitter edge to the words. "Are you?"

He didn't have to remind her that if it hadn't been for him she'd have considerably less than the amount now resting against her palm—or perhaps nothing at all.

Kristine ignored his question and stowed the money safely in the pocket of her jeans. Hugging the bag to her with both arms, she stared mutely out the window.

It wasn't the scenery that drew her attention; it was too dark to make anything out, except for the occasional lighted windows of a house in the distance or the gleam of a security lamp casting a glow over a farm and its outbuildings. She was trying to deal with the sudden sense of loss at having been betrayed by this man.

It was unreasonable, she knew, to expect anything like friendship or faith from a stranger. But somehow, she'd thought that despite his words to the contrary, they had forged a foundation for joint trust when he helped her just now to escape Morrell's clutches.

"I'm not a very patient man." He further shattered that false assumption. "And I'm waiting for your answer. Is he after you because you stole something from him—like maybe that ring you pawned?"

The irony of being thought a criminal, when she was running from men who made their living as such, almost made her smile. But her situation was no laughing matter.

Kristine drew her dignity around her like a shield. She didn't have to answer to this man. He was only giving her a ride, and that didn't give him the right to question her about the past any more than she had the right to question him. Apparently his ban on questions extended only to *his* business—and not to hers.

"Maybe I was wrong back there, maybe he is chasing a runaway bride."

Kristine's glance jerked from her clenched hands twisted together on her lap to his inscrutable face.

"Are you running from a husband?" he persisted.

"No," she denied vehemently. "I'm not married—he wants something I have—but he isn't going to get it."

That was all she was going to tell him. He could either settle for that or put her out, it was up to him. And at this point in time, she didn't care which he did.

If she told him what he wanted to know, no doubt he'd put her out for sure. Someone like him, just out of prison, wouldn't want to get mixed up with the likes of Vincent Spinelli, not unless he wanted to make prison his life's career. Besides, it was safer for *him* if he knew nothing.

Tucker expected more from her than stubborn silence. He knew he should let it go, but— "I don't know what you're running away from—or who—but it must be damned urgent for you to get out of Texas if you'd sneak into some stranger's car to do it.

"Don't you read the newspapers or watch TV? It isn't safe to hitchhike these days. You could meet up with all kinds of freaks on the road. Even I know that, despite where I've been."

Kristine couldn't resist the shot in light of his recent actions. "You're right," she agreed, surprising him, "a person might even end up accepting a ride with an ex-con—one who has no compunction in violating their privacy. I'll be more careful in the future."

Tucker's jaw tightened, he knew it was retaliation for him going through her things. "We'll leave it for now, but I *will* have an answer about why you're running—later."

"Does that mean you aren't planning to put me out?" she dared to ask slyly. He might not be the best choice as far as traveling companions went, but right now he was her only one, and despite her previous thoughts to the contrary, she didn't relish walking alone after dark.

"All it means is that you've got a ride—for now," was his uncompromising reply.

The car slowed as Tucker spotted red-and-blue flashing lights in the distance. Red flares spluttered in the rain, marking the trail to an accident. As they drew closer, they saw the twisted wreck of a tractor-trailer that had apparently skidded on the increasingly slick road and jackknifed, blocking two lanes of the four-lane highway.

"The road's getting dangerous," Kristine murmured with a shiver.

The man beside her only grunted but reduced his speed. An accident could cost him more than a few hours' delay, it could cost him the whole game. If Arnold learned he was out of prison earlier than expected, it was a good bet he'd make tracks for parts unknown, and Tucker wasn't about to lose him—he'd waited too long.

The lonely highway, a never-ending ribbon of black, stretched out before them. Kristine was uneasy knowing she had a ride only as long as her companion was feeling magnanimous. He appeared to be a moody person, and she feared his attitude could change at any moment. Did prison life do that to a man? And she still didn't know what he'd been sent to prison for.

A sudden chill snaked down her spine at the thought of being isolated in the car on the lonely road with him at night. But an even deeper chill caused her to quake inside at the thought of being alone and on foot in the deteriorating weather with Carl Morrell somewhere close behind. Especially when she had always gone out of her way to avoid the man even in a room full of other people.

Tucker caught the shiver and, misinterpreting its source, reached to turn up the heat. Kristine glanced apprehensively at his hand as it moved into the light from the dash, then relaxed when he only switched the heat up higher. Her attention centered now on the hand. She noted that it was large and powerful looking, the palm wide, the fingers long and tapered, the square nails cut short and scrupulously clean.

The skin covering the back of it looked pale. Was that prison pallor? It made the black hair showing from beneath his jacket cuff and sprinkled on the backs of his fingers appear darker by contrast. It was altogether an attractive hand, the kind she could readily envision holding a woman close with just the right amount of strength and ease. And passion?

Still smarting from his treatment of her, she pushed that unwelcome thought aside and once more turned her attention out the window. There was nothing, not one blessed thing, about him she wanted to find attractive. He was a prime example of a male living in a male-dominated world. He was right and she was wrong. He kept his secrets while she was expected to bare her soul for his enlightenment.

A green road sign flashed by, capturing her attention, and she saw that they would soon reach Little Rock, Arkansas. She was getting closer and closer to home—closer and closer to safety?

"Did you steal the ring?"

"No, I did not!" The abrupt question startled her into answering him truthfully. "It belonged to me."

Catching her breath, she glanced furtively at him from beneath half-lowered lids. What would he make of that? She had told him she wasn't married.

When he didn't question her any further but concentrated instead on his driving, she relaxed in relief. The silence between them stretched out, and she let her mind drift with it until the steady rhythm of the car lulled her again into sleep.

Tucker couldn't resist glancing at her from time to time as they sped along. She was a woman full of contradictions—and she was beginning to fascinate him. With her, he was already learning, despite their brief acquaintance, to expect the unexpected. And after years of soul-diminishing sameness and the seemingly never-ending hours of boredom of prison life, her liveliness was bewitchingly refreshing.

Questions about her kept him occupied as the distance steadily increased between them and Texas. Who was this character chasing her? What was he after? She said it wasn't *her* he wanted, but something she had in her possession. Looking at her, at the beauty of her face and figure, he found it hard to believe the man chasing her could be interested in anything but that.

A warning signal went off somewhere inside his brain at the thought. He could not become involved with her. It would be the height of foolhardiness to become embroiled in her problems. He had more than enough of his own, and besides, there was no room for her in his plans, in his life. His course was unequivocably set and could not be altered by anything or anyone.

He should have put her out when he'd threatened to. Why hadn't he? And why hadn't he left her when he'd awakened at the rest park and found her gone from the car? Why had he stared uneasily around in the dark, a sixth sense he'd developed while in prison telling him all was not right? And seeing the man arrive, why didn't he simply make tracks? No, he had to play the hero, he condemned his actions now. When would he learn?

Shrugging mentally, forcing his attention onto the road and the increasingly hazardous driving conditions, he leaned forward to turn the radio on, searching for a station giving weather information.

The rain had mixed with sleet and finally turned to snow. An announcer's voice on the radio predicted that the temperatures would continue to plunge steadily and an ice storm would hit the area sometime in the early morning hours, making driving nearly impossible.

As time passed, Tucker noticed that the moisture on the windshield had begun to freeze. And he knew that if he couldn't outdrive the weather he would be forced to stop someplace for the night. But that was something he didn't want to do, not even for safety's sake. He didn't want to lose the travel time, and he didn't want to spend any more time than was absolutely necessary in the company of the woman sleeping peacefully at his side.

They were on the outskirts of Little Rock when the car hit a patch of black ice and went careening across the road toward the median. Easing his foot off the accelerator, Tucker fought the wheel, trying to do as he'd once been taught and turn into the skid.

The car made a complete three-hundred-and-sixty-degree turn, before he got it under control and stopped finally at the side of the road. Tucker sat for a moment with his forehead against the steering wheel, listening to his heart drumming out of control in his ears. Taking a deep, steadying breath, he turned his head and met his passenger's wide, anxious glance.

"Are you hurt?" she asked, eyeing him intently.

She had awakened abruptly as the car went into its wild dance. Managing to raise her head and get her bearings well enough to take stock of the situation, she had seen her companion slumped over the wheel, and fear had knifed through her. There was genuine concern for his safety both in her eyes and in her voice.

For some reason her caring left him speechless, and it was several long moments before he could respond.

"I'm fine," he managed gruffly. "You?" he added reluctantly.

"Just a little shaken up." She grinned. "That was the wildest merry-go-round ride I've had in years."

There was no answering grin on his dour face. The light gray eyes continued to hold hers, a bleak expression showing in their depths. However, another emotion, one she couldn't quite define, also peeked out at her from further back.

But though she couldn't put a name to it, something inside her responded instinctively. It made her long to smooth the lines of care from the corners of his weary eyes and say something to bring a smile to the grim, marble-like lips.

Before she could act on such a foolish notion, he pulled his gaze from hers and sat up straight in the seat.

"I'll see if there's any damage to the car before we get under way."

Tucker climbed quickly from the car, the open door admitting a blast of damp, chilly air into the warm interior.

Kristine pulled her jacket closer around her and shivered. She wasn't certain which had been colder just now, his eyes as he yanked them from hers or the sound of his voice when he spoke. The winter weather outside was by far the warmest of the three.

Twisting the radio dial, she turned into a station giving an updated weather report as he opened the door and got back inside.

"A winter storm warning has been issued by the National Weather Service for the north and central parts of Texas, and the whole of the states of Oklahoma and Arkansas.

"Freezing rain, mixed at times with snow, is expected to blanket the area, and the temperatures are going to plunge to around twenty degrees. In some areas, with the windchill factor, temperatures could drop as low as eight to ten degrees below zero.

"Travelers are advised to seek shelter and to call ahead for road and weather conditions before starting out again."

"Damn!"

Slamming his palm against the steering wheel, Tucker switched the radio off and sat for a moment, staring at the large flakes of snow dancing before the twin beams of the headlights.

"I guess that means getting a room somewhere," she murmured into the turbulent silence.

He glanced her way momentarily before maneuvering the car back onto the road. It was an hour and thirty miles later, on the far side of Little Rock, when they came across a sign advertising the Hide-a-Way Motel, Restaurant, Gas Station and Convenience Store.

Taking the exit ramp, Tucker edged cautiously up the hill. In a few minutes they sat in the lighted parking lot of the motel, staring at a sea of vehicles. If their number was any indication, he knew they'd be damned lucky to get a room for the night.

Kristine started to follow him from the car, but he told her to stay put. When she looked up at him indignantly, he added that it was warm in the car, he'd left the key on and the heater running, and there was no need for the both of them to freeze to death.

The glass doors of the office were locked, and only a night-light remained on inside. There was a buzzer on the door and a sign below it that read Ring after Ten P.M.

Tucker punched the buzzer and stamped his feet against the cold. Hunching his shoulders, his hands in his pockets, he peered through the glass to the office beyond.

A few minutes later, a middle-aged man wearing a heavy bathrobe over pajamas, his thinning hair standing on end, moved into view. After shuffling slowly toward the door, he unlocked it and stood back to allow Tucker inside.

Kristine watched him stamp the snow from his feet onto the welcome mat before entering the carpeted office. Somewhere, sometime, a woman had taught him to do that, she thought to herself with a slight grin.

While he was gone, she stared at the interior of the car, turned the radio on and off and found her eyes drawn repeatedly to the glove compartment. Curiosity about the man was driving her crazy—his name, that's all she wanted to know, just his name. And surely it had to be somewhere in there, on a car registration form or an insurance card, something.

After all, she excused her curiosity, he'd rifled her personal possessions. Why shouldn't she peak inside? Glancing up and through the lighted office window, she saw him take up a pen and bend over the reservations desk. Good, that meant they had rooms. But he'd be back in a few minutes. It was now or never.

Taking one more quick look at the office window, she pushed the button on the compartment latch and opened the small door on the dash. She picked up the pile of papers secured in a clear plastic wrap and emptied them into her hand. There was a bill of sale for the car—he'd paid for it in cash? What did he do for a living—rob banks? There was also a registration form, an insurance card and a receipt for the car license. And all were made out to Tucker Winslow.

Kristine looked through the papers while still cautiously maintaining a watch on the motel office. His place of residence was listed as Dallas, Texas. There were other things, like a social security number, but nothing to tell her anything about the man, nothing she didn't already know. He'd done time in prison, but he could afford to purchase in cash an expensive car shortly after his release. Who was this man?

Stuffing the papers back inside, she folded her hands on her lap and watched as he left the motel office. Slipping and sliding on the slick parking lot, he made his way to the car.

Tucker, she thought, giving him a sidelong glance as he climbed inside. Somehow, the name fit him. Without speaking, he started the car's engine and drove past the rows of parked vehicles and around to the back of the two-story building.

He led her to a corner room on the backside of the building. Kristine stood beside him, huddled in her coat, hopping back and forth on numb feet, while she waited for him to fit the key into the lock and open the door. Inside she threw her bag on the bed and began searching for the heater. The room was like ice.

It was a typical motel room. The carpet was threadbare, a dark gold in color, the walls a pale green. A television was mounted in brackets on the wall across from the bed. There was a picture of a mountain stream hung on one wall and a picture of an abstract bouquet of flowers on the other.

The headboard to the bed was attached to the wall, and the bedspread was flowered in shades of green, brown and gold. There was one straight chair sitting before a dressing table with drawers, and across the room to the left of the door were two heavier, more comfortable-looking chairs, placed one at either side of a small round table.

Kristine paid no attention to Tucker, assuming he would leave her the key and go on to his own room, presumably one close by. When the door finally slammed shut, she had found the heater and turned it up full blast. Detouring around the corner to the bathroom, she switched on the light and peered inside.

Good, a shower and a tub. The room was hardly big enough to turn around in, but that was fine with her as long as there was plenty of hot water for a good long soak.

Unzipping her jacket, she turned around and stopped dead in her tracks.

"What are you doing?"

Tucker Winslow looked up from his suitcase opened in the middle of the only bed in the room. Quirking a dark brow at her, he continued with what he was doing. "What does it look like? I'm getting something to sleep in before I take a shower. What are you doing?"

Not bothering to wait for an answer he obviously didn't give a damn about, he removed a pair of dark blue sweats, a clean pair of white briefs and a pair of black socks.

Kristine folded her arms across her breasts and stiffened her spine against the wall. He thought he was staying here in her room? Boy, had she read him all wrong. Well, no way, José, as the saying went.

"Look, I intend paying you—in cash—for my room—"

"And I intend accepting it," he agreed, cutting her off while at the same time moving around her stationary figure toward the bathroom door.

"Wait!" She grabbed at his arm as he passed her. "Where do you think you're going? Why don't you shower in your own room?"

"This is my room," he answered, carefully removing his arm from her touch.

She'd forgotten that he'd said he didn't like being touched.

"*Your* room? But I thought this was *my* room."

"It is. It's *our* room," he stressed as he entered the bathroom and closed the door with a snap. In a few moments, sounds of the shower drifted through the door to the woman leaning against the wall in shocked silence.

Tucker entered the room a short while later, dressed in the form-fitting sweats, his hair bristling damply on his head. Still wearing her jacket, Kristine was sitting, in one of the two imitation-leather chairs near the door. Every light in the room blazed brightly.

Tucker permitted her a swift glance before moving about the room, turning off lights until only one remained on—the one slightly swaying above the statuelike figure of the woman whose eyes had followed him, as though drawn by a magnet, while he moved from light to light.

Dropping down onto the corner of the bed nearest to her, Tucker folded his hands across muscular thighs and fastened those unusual eyes onto her face.

"Okay, out with it. What's the problem, kid?"

She was nowhere near to being a kid, but calling her that put a bit of distance between them, and right at this moment he needed all the distance he could muster.

"This." She spread her hands, ignoring, for the moment, the irritating and inaccurate title, "kid." "I thought we were getting two rooms. One for you, and one for me."

Sighing heavily, brushing at the tendrils of wet hair sticking to his forehead, he shrugged massive shoulders.

"There was only one room to be had. This one. One room, one bed. That's all the man had to offer. And I took it—" he paused "—for both of us."

"I see." She swallowed. "You expect me to share that—" she gestured toward the bed where he sat "—with you."

A cold glitter entered the eyes that up until now had been neutral.

"I leave that decision entirely up to you. You have my permission to do so, if you choose—as long as you stay on your side of the bed. On the other hand, if you prefer the floor or the chair, so be it. In either case, let me assure you, you couldn't be any safer than with me."

"Listen, Winslow, I'm not naive. I know men—they're always interested in—sex."

Climbing to his feet, he fastened his suitcase and moved it to a corner of the room. So she knew his name, that made them even now. Folding back a corner of the blankets on the side of the bed nearest the door, he faced her and informed her coldly, "You don't know this man. As I said, I'm not interested."

Still meeting her glance, he could see the new and totally inaccurate idea forming behind the expressive dark eyes. Like all women, she needed an explanation for his not being interested in sex—in her. Something that didn't reflect badly on her own charms.

He'd already told her he'd been in prison, therefore she had put two and two together and reached a totally erroneous conclusion. Well, let her, she didn't matter enough for him to worry about correcting the idea—that he preferred men.

After folding the covers back to his satisfaction, it took him exactly ten seconds to make himself snug in the bed with his back turned toward her.

Kristine stared speculatively at him. She was wrong, she had to be.

So far he had managed to make her feel a whole range of emotions, anger and frustration among them, but he also made her feel all woman. And none of the homosexual men she had worked with had ever made her feel that way before.

Therefore, her conclusion had to be that he was trying to mislead her into thinking him something he wasn't—in an attempt to deter her from making unwanted advances—to him?

Well, fat chance! She wasn't interested in men, either, and especially not in him. Vincent Spinelli had cured her of the disease of finding dark, brooding men attractive. A dose of Spinelli was better than any vaccine known to modern medicine.

But she was here, she couldn't change that, so she would just have to make the best of a bad situation. Climbing to her feet, she switched off the light and, taking her knapsack with her, walked past the bed toward the bathroom. He'd left the light on in the tiny room, and the illumination guided her progress.

Tucker followed her figure with his eyes. Again he asked himself, what difference did it make what she thought of him?

He knew his tastes hadn't wavered through the long, frustrating years of the forced monastic-like existence. Days when he prayed to go to sleep at night and never to awaken. Days when the sight of bars, the thought of another day spent like the last one, and the one before that, made him break out into a cold sweat and gnash his teeth together to keep him from screaming and continuing to scream until the nightmare came to an end.

First had come the days, then the weeks of waiting, expecting that one important visitor, the one face that stood out among the crowds. The one person he was positive would come to him, tell him it was all a mistake and that he would soon be a free man. But the weeks turned into months and the months into years without him ever receiving a visit from Sylvia. Hers was the face he watched for, and she was the reason he couldn't afford to feel anything now—not for any woman.

The only emotion he could allow himself was hate. That's what had kept him going for the past five years—hate—and the desire for revenge. Soon, soon, he knew, it would all be over. And when it was finished, then, as now, nothing else would matter.

Tucker slipped the gun, warm from contact with his body, from the waistband of his sweats and placed it under the pillow. His fingers moved against the hard, smooth metal almost caressingly. This piece of machinery, this weapon would help him to find peace and justice for the wrong that had been done to him.

Did Illinois have the death penalty? He didn't know. But whether it did or not, it wasn't relevant to his plans. Once he'd accomplished his goal, the death of Jack Arnold, his own end wouldn't matter. And what of Sylvia? That was a question he still couldn't answer—not yet.

The bathroom door opened with a squeak, and Kristine stood silhouetted against the light. Tucker blinked and stared, swallowing dryly. The light behind her turned her gown into gauze and left nothing to the imagination.

He couldn't seem to get his eyes to move in any direction except upward, over trim, smooth calves, to long, shapely thighs and beyond. And when she turned to pull at the door, his eyes were riveted by the revealing sight of firm, high breasts free from any restraint.

Feeling a sudden wrenching in his gut and a powerful stirring in his lower body, Tucker snapped his eyes shut and rolled over onto his stomach. There was no place in his life for a woman, he reminded himself strongly. And tomorrow he'd have to get rid of this one once and for all.

Kristine left the bathroom light on and pulled the door almost closed. Dropping her knapsack onto the floor beside the bed, she drew her jacket on over her gown. Her money was safely hidden inside a small zippered pocket on the inside of the lining.

Standing with bare toes curled against the drafty floor, she looked from the figure huddled beneath the covers to the two chairs placed beneath the wide-curtained window. The curtain swayed abruptly as a swift gust of winter wind slammed against the building.

Kristine knew there was no choice between the chairs beside the drafty window and the warm, inviting bed. She was cold, tired and sleepy. And the man lying on his stomach beneath the covers could have been twin to the wolf man for all she cared at this moment, because she was sleeping in the bed. She was paying for half the room, and that meant half the bed, as well.

Lifting a corner of the blankets gingerly, she climbed onto the bed, settled down against the pillows with a soft sigh and crossed her arms over the covers outside. After a moment, she glanced at the bed's other occupant. Mindful of him not liking to be touched, keeping her body well away from contact with his, she leaned toward him.

"Hey—Winslow," she whispered loudly, "I think people who sleep together should at least know each other's name. Mine is Stevens, Kristine Stevens."

He gave no indication of having heard her, but nevertheless she was satisfied to have had the last word. Dropping back against the pillows, she closed weary eyes with a sigh.

After a while, Tucker turned his head and glanced at her profile. Thank God, she was asleep at last, now maybe he could get some rest, too.

Wrapping his hand around the handle of the gun beneath his pillow, he grinned slightly and closed his eyes. She was a real scrapper, he acknowledged to himself, and a small part of him couldn't help but wish he'd met her a long time ago—before all the trouble—before Sylvia.

Chapter 3

Kristine opened her eyes slowly and stared through the gloom at the luminous numbers on the clock radio. It was only six o'clock, but she was wide-awake. Careful not to disturb the sleeping figure at her side, she crawled from the bed and tiptoed to the window. Drawing back the curtain, she wiped away the moisture and peered outside.

The sight that met her eyes caused her to gasp softly in delight. Like a winter wonderland, everything in sight was covered with a layer of snow-covered ice. It looked like a scene from the past, from when she was a child growing up on a farm in Illinois. Nostalgia for times gone by brought a lump to her throat and the sheen of tears to her eyes.

Her childhood was a warm memory, blighted by her parents' deaths when she was a senior in high school. She put that particular sadness behind her now and let the curtain fall back into place. Hearing a soft grumbling sound, she lay a hand against her middle, deciding that food was the first order of business for the day.

She dressed quickly, but once outside, stood for a long moment staring at the fairyland around her. Everything was dressed in a sparkling white shell that dazzled the eyes. She realized all at once the world seemed unnaturally still even for six-thirty in the morning. Her eyes drifted toward the road, easily visible from where she stood. There was no traffic moving on it, none at all. Looking around her, she saw that all the vehicles from last night were still parked in the spaces before their rooms.

Snuggling down into her jacket, her breath forming a cloud around her head, she moved toward the restaurant. She hoped, hungrily, that those who worked there either lived on the immediate premises or within walking distance of it.

About twenty minutes later, juggling containers and sacks filled with hot food, she managed to open the motel door and slip inside. Placing her burden on the small round table, she looked toward the bed. It was empty. Sounds from the bathroom told her her roommate was at his morning ablution.

The food was arranged on the table, two settings complete with folded napkins and white plastic utensils, by the time he emerged amid a cloud of steam.

"So that's where you went," Tucker commented, catching sight of her immediately.

Was that disappointment she heard in his voice? Because she had returned?

He leaned casually against the wall, bare from the waist up. A white towel draped around his neck covered his shoulders, but the blue sweatpants riding low on narrow hips left little to the imagination.

Kristine quickly averted her eyes, remembering her thoughts the night before concerning the question of his masculinity. It seemed so ridiculous this morning. At the moment there was no question in her mind about the man's virility. It was staring her in the face.

And besides, surely a man doesn't call out a woman's name, call her "darling" in his sleep, unless he's emotionally involved with her.

"I was hungry," she murmured, hiding the questions she wanted to ask by keeping her eyes on the food. "I thought you might be, too."

There was another purpose for keeping her glance focused on the food. It was the only way she could stop her eyes from wandering over his body. From following the line of black hair as it narrowed just below the spread of his chest and arrowed down the narrow waist to disappear beneath the tie string of his sweatpants.

Still shirtless, Tucker took his place at the small table across from her and helped himself to hot coffee. He wasn't particularly pleased to notice she looked more appetizing this morning than the food. The trip to the restaurant in the cold air had put color into her cheeks and a sparkle into her dark eyes.

Feeling a tension building between them, she tried to dispel it by acting as though it didn't exist. Taking a hurried sip of hot coffee, she choked. Hard fingers pounded her back. Eyes watering, she met his sardonic glance before looking hastily away.

Clearing her throat, she tried a bite of food, but all she could think about was the powerful shoulders intruding into her line of vision. Why was she suddenly so aware of this man's body? She didn't even like him, and the naked male body was no novelty to her. How could it be, after years in nursing—and then there was Vincent.

Hoping to dispel the feeling of intimacy and tension, she began to speak about the lack of traffic on the interstate.

"Do you suppose we'll be stuck here for another night?" she asked when she'd told him it looked as though no one was going anywhere, this morning at any rate.

"Lord, I hope not," was his cursory reply before grabbing his coffee cup and returning summarily to the bathroom.

Stung by the sharp retort, she cleared the table of the uneaten food and switched on the TV. Maybe the news would mention the state of the roads and give travel information.

The prediction was for clearing skies and warmer temperatures, but travel was not advised for at least another twenty-four hours. The road crews were out doing their jobs, but unless it was an emergency, driving was still too dangerous for the masses.

Great! Well, she considered her case to be an emergency. It was urgent that she get as far from Texas as possible—and she was beginning to fear it was just as urgent that she get away from Tucker Winslow, as well.

"The bathroom's all yours."

Kristine jumped guiltily and whirled to face him. His glance followed her curiously as she grabbed her knapsack and hurried past him to the obscurity of the bathroom, slamming the door in her wake.

What had he done now? Was she teed off because he hadn't eaten? Or because he hadn't taken advantage of the invitation evident in her sidelong glances and demurely downcast eyes? Women, who could figure them?

When Kristine emerged a long while later, rubbing a towel over wet hair, she noted with relief that the room was empty. Good, now maybe she could relax for a little while. His presence was starting to make her nervous. And she couldn't make up her mind whether it was because she didn't like him at all, or because she was beginning to like him very well indeed.

Half an hour later the bed was made and the room straightened to her satisfaction. With that done, she turned on the TV and stretched back on the spread to watch a movie that she had missed when it was on at the theaters. It didn't take long for her to become completely embroiled in the tragic love affair of a woman who could never have the man she loved, not in this life.

Tucker returned to find her lying on her stomach, a towel covering her head, her chin propped on her hands, staring intently at the screen. He glanced from her to the figures on the TV and found himself feeling uncomfortable at the blatant sexuality being displayed.

Television hadn't been this daring five years ago, and it hadn't interested him while in prison. Pulling his eyes in embarrassment from the passionately entwined couple, he looked around the room and then couldn't help glancing back at Kristine's face.

She was perfectly well aware of his presence, had been since he'd first entered the door, and had ignored it as best she could. But as she felt his glance come to rest on her, she knew that her enjoyment in the movie had been ruined. Now she viewed the lovers on the screen with a detachment she donned as a shield against the man sitting staring at her from across the room.

"What in sweet hell have you done to yourself," he inquired suddenly in amazement.

Kristine had forgotten all about her change in appearance. A hand flew toward the towel, but the towel had slid unnoticed to her shoulders. She knew he was seeing the new chin-length cut of her hair. Hair now a deep blue black in color, instead of the naturally light champagne blond.

"I figured that it would be harder for—anyone—to recognize me when I was on my own again, if I changed the way I look—"

"I told you you had a ride," he interrupted impatiently.

"For now," she reminded him. "You said, for now. Well, I don't know how long 'for now' is, and I can't take the chance of Morrell catching up with me."

"Are you ready to tell me what it is you've got that he wants?"

"It doesn't concern you," she answered stubbornly. "And you as much as told me you didn't like people, especially strangers, prying into *your* business—well, the same goes for me."

Pushing to his feet, grabbing the door key angrily, Tucker stomped out of the room. To hell with her. He didn't know what made him more angry, her for not telling him what he wanted to know—or himself for feeling the need to know it. And her hair—damn—what she had done to her hair!

The day passed slowly, with Tucker in and out a lot of the time. Kristine didn't know what he did when he was gone. Maybe he drank a lot of coffee at the restaurant, or maybe he was a health freak and wanted the exercise after being confined first in the car and then in the motel room with her. From the look of his muscles, he liked to keep himself in shape.

Whatever his reasons for staying away, she was thankful for them. When she was removed from his disturbing presence, her thinking about him became more clear. It was only when she was around him that she felt the pull of his attraction. And, she could admit only to herself, she was beginning to find it difficult to fight it.

Her one thought as the afternoon and then evening dragged by was that, thank heaven, tomorrow they could be on their way. One more day of being closed up with her silent, morose companion and she would go stark raving mad.

Kristine spent over an hour that evening in the bathroom after they'd eaten a meal of sandwiches and French fries in their room. When she came out, Tucker was watching a western on TV. He'd changed into the familiar sweats and was comfortably ensconced on the bed, ankles crossed, hands linked loosely over a flat abdomen.

Kristine took a seat by the window and wished that she still smoked. At least he hadn't referred to her hair again. And after all—she touched it self-consciously—it was none of his business what she did to her hair.

As the minutes passed, her eyelids dropped shut and her head slowly tipped forward. The man on the bed, his attention focused more on her than on the rather boring, predictable western, knew the instant she fell asleep.

He wanted to shake her every time he looked at what she had done to her beautiful long blond hair. And when she had insisted upon staying as far from him as possible all evening, jumping every time he moved or cleared his throat, he'd wanted to throttle her.

He was having a hard time accepting the fact that he was coming to care about what happened to her. It wasn't something he welcomed, this feeling of responsibility for her welfare. But he had to admit he didn't want to see the Morrell character get his hands on her.

His eyes followed the gentle rise and fall of her breasts beneath the thin flowered gown. Tonight she hadn't bothered to put the jacket on over it. He wished she had.

Dark curls hid her sleeping face from view, but in his mind's eye he could see the chocolate-colored eyes going round with alarm if she knew the thoughts that were filling his head at the moment. Any errant questions she might still harbor about his virility would be explicitly answered if she could read his mind.

Knowing he shouldn't, telling himself he was a fool for not throwing a blanket over her and leaving her to sleep where she sat, Tucker moved off the bed and crossed the room to her. He lifted her in gentle arms, his nostrils filled with the pungent scent of the hair rinse she'd used. Stopping at the bed, he laid her carefully down on the sheets. As he pulled the covers up to her hips, his hands lingered at her waist. A slight bulge that shouldn't have been there captured his attention. Pressing light fingertips against the soft material of her gown, Tucker felt the hard ridge beneath. The first thing that popped into his mind was a money belt.

But that was ridiculous. Hadn't he seen her practically beg the little creep at the pawnshop for more money. Hadn't he watched her carefully count and then hide her money more than once in the past twenty-four hours? What could she be carrying that was so valuable she wouldn't allow it off her person?

And then his mind put two and two together and he knew. It was what the man Morrell wanted from her, badly enough to take by force if necessary. For a moment he was tempted to lift the gown and discover for himself what she had hidden. But caution stayed his hand, and, remembering his vow of noninvolvement, he moved reluctantly away. The secrets she kept hidden beneath her gown were hers, he wanted no part of them.

And that was a lie, he admitted mockingly to himself. Since she'd stood silhouetted in the doorway to the bathroom the night before, all he could think about was what lay hidden beneath her gown.

Taking a seat in the chair still warm from her body, Tucker put his feet up on the bed and crossed his arms over his chest. Forcing his attention onto the TV screen, he knew beyond a shadow of a doubt that it was going to be a long, long night.

Sometime during the dark, silent hours between midnight and dawn, Tucker crossed the invisible barrier he'd placed down the length of the bed. His head moved from his own pillow onto the pillow beside him, and his face became buried in the soft, damp curls spread over its surface.

Before long, his restless hand found its way to her soft curves, gentle fingers slowly cupping a small, rounded breast.

Kristine murmured in her sleep, turned slightly and pressed against the warmth radiating down the length of her left side. Licking dry lips, she moved her head across the pillow, moaning slightly at the sudden, sharp pain in her head. Opening heavy lids, she blinked groggily and gazed at the dark head lying next to hers on the pillow. Without fully gaining consciousness, she settled her head back onto the pillow and returned to sleep.

Hours later, soft light filtered into the room, sunlight reflecting off the melting snow and ice. Kristine turned her head and felt a slight tug on her scalp. She opened her eyes and almost screamed at the sight of the man's face so close to her own. Stifling the sound, she stared instead at the long, thick lashes fanning hard masculine cheeks, so close she could see the individual hairs in each lash.

Her eyes moved over his face and head. The dark hair wasn't really black, she noted. Up close it was a deep rich, dark brown, and it was threaded with strands of silver. Looking closer, she saw a small star-shaped scar at the corner of his left eyelid. It was hardly noticeable mixed in with the tiny lines denoting him as past first youth. He was probably somewhere in his late thirties or early forties, she guessed.

A heavy shadow of a beard masked his lower face and upper lip. The hard line of his mouth looked younger in repose and more innocent, stripped of its sardonic curl. It wasn't until he stirred restlessly and moved a leg over both hers that she realized he held her breast trapped beneath his hand. Hot color flooded her cheeks. How had she come to let him take such liberties with her person?

Feeling indignant and embarrassed but very conscious of the heat being generated by that hand, she began slowly to withdraw from him an inch at a time. Pressing his leg away from both of hers, she then encircled his wrist with the fingers of her right hand, aware of the cold touch of the metal bracelet, and lifted it lightly, determinedly, away from her breast.

Tucker moved in protest, and his body pressed closer. Kristine's other hand, buried beneath the covers between them, all at once became intimate with his lower body. Muttering beneath his breath, only one word clear to her, he rolled away onto his back, thereby freeing her.

Kristine scurried quickly from the bed, the name "Sylvia," once more ringing in her ears. Twice now he had called the woman's name within her hearing.

Who was she?

Dressing quickly, she grabbed the room key from the table and let herself out into the bright sunlight. Who was Sylvia? The question followed her as she crossed the motel grounds and entered the restaurant. Whoever she was, the man she'd left sleeping in Room 120, appeared to know her intimately.

When she left the restaurant a short while later, knowing they would be leaving soon because traffic was beginning to move once more on the interstate, she decided to take a short walk. There was very little exercise to be had when closed up in a vehicle traveling across the country.

And, too, it gave her a chance to think about Tucker Winslow and the unwelcome emotions she was starting to feel toward him. Her situation was not an enviable one, with Carl Morrell following her, and the idea of becoming emotionally involved with a man of Tucker's background was as foolish as her getting mixed up with Vincent Spinelli had been. But right at the moment she hadn't much choice if she wanted to stay one step ahead of Morrell.

As she made her way back toward the buildings, she glanced up through the trees and spied a long black Cadillac pulling to a stop before the motel office. A frighteningly familiar figure made its way to the office door while Kristine stood, turned to stone, hardly daring to breathe.

Morrell! He'd found her again! Her first instinct was to run back the way she'd come. But she'd have to reach the road to get a ride, and once he'd left the motel, she'd be able to put precious little distance between them on foot before he caught up with her. Obviously Morrell hadn't seen her, or he'd be after her now, not in the office looking for her. Her only hope was Tucker; he'd have to get them out of there, and fast.

Reaching the door to Room 120, Kristine darted swift, fearful glances behind her as she wrenched at the lock, opened the door and fell headlong into the room. After slamming the door, she clicked the lock into place and fastened the chain. Then, for good measure, she dragged the room's one straight-backed chair across the floor and shoved it under the door handle.

There, no one could get inside now. Her eyes flew across the room and were immediately ensnared by two chips of ice in a face devoid of all expression.

"What was that all about?" Tucker asked softly, arms folded across his broad chest.

Unable to speak for a moment, she shook her head, panting. Finally, after taking several deep breaths, she was able to articulate.

"Morrell—he's here. He's at the office right now, probably going through the guest register."

"So?" he asked calmly.

"He'll find out I'm here—"

"No." He shook his head. "He won't."

"B-but—"

"You didn't sign it, I did. Mr. and Mrs. Tucker Winslow from Houston, Texas. How could he know you're the implied 'Mrs.' from that?"

He was right. There was no way Morrell could identify her from the ledger. Thank God she hadn't signed it. Dropping down onto one of the two large chairs, she rested her head in her hands and closed her eyes. She could still feel the terror of almost stumbling unexpectedly across the man's path.

Breakfast was skipped because Morrell had gotten a good look at Tucker, too, and would no doubt recognize him and possibly his car, also. They took as little time as needed to get their things ready in preparation for leaving, with Kristine jumping at every sound coming from outside as other stranded travelers prepared to continue on their way.

A little while later, while Tucker was in the bathroom, making certain he'd left nothing behind, out of habit Kristine began to straighten the room. She was making the bed when she pushed her hand up under the pillow, the one Tucker had used the past two nights, and it bumped against something cold and solid. Curious, she pulled the pillow off the bed and gasped at what she saw. Mesmerized by the sight of the small, wicked-looking gun, she leaned forward, one hand reaching toward it.

"What the hell are you doing?"

The harsh, grating voice coming so abruptly from behind caused her to scream and spin away from him, the bed and the thing lying dark against the sheet.

Tucker took her place, grabbed the weapon and tucked it quickly out of sight into the pocket of his sheepskin jacket. Throwing his suitcase onto the bed, he furiously began to cram his things into it. When it was full, he slammed it shut, locked it and, without a glance in her direction, made for the door.

Her thoughts in a whirl, Kristine watched him go, followed him to the door and quickly fastened the chain into place. Leaning back against the door, she stared at the floor, seeing instead the small deadly looking object lying against the white sheets. A gun, he had a gun. Why? Was it only to be used for protection while he traveled? If that was the case, then why had he been so angry when she found it? Why hadn't he simply explained?

She had to admit the knowledge of his past—his having been in prison—made her feel doubly uncomfortable about his having a weapon in his possession. Wasn't it illegal for an ex-con to carry a gun?

If it hadn't been for the knowledge, or incomplete knowledge, she had about his past, would the fact that he carried a weapon be so upsetting to her? She didn't think so. It would have made her uneasy, perhaps apprehensive, but given her present situation with Morrell on her trail and the fact that Tucker had helped her escape him already, she might have felt comforted by the weapon's unexpected presence.

However, whatever his past, Tucker had proved to have her best interests at heart. And who was she to tell him what he could or could not have in his possession? And, too, what she kept hidden on her person was every bit as dangerous as the small gun Tucker carried in his coat pocket.

Once over the shock of her discovery, she gathered her things together and made ready to leave the room. Despite his obvious anger at her, Kristine expected Tucker would be back any minute. Thinking he'd gone to check on the road conditions and to pay for the added night in the room, she sat down to wait.

A few minutes later, a sound at the door alerted her to his return. The key lay where she'd left it earlier, and she hurried to remove the chain and let him in.

Kristine threw the door wide and felt the welcoming smile freeze on her face.

"No!"

Shoving with all her strength, she tried to close the door on the man pushing from the other side. But Carl Morrell was a big man, and his strength more than equaled her paltry efforts.

After a few futile moments, Kristine fell back and Morrell entered, closing the door firmly behind him.

"Well, here we are, face-to-face at last. You didn't really think I'd be so easy to lose now, did you?"

For the moment he stayed where he was, leaning casually against the door, a wide smile stretching his thick lips. The look in his eyes made her skin crawl. She had never been comfortable in this man's presence, even before she found out exactly what he did for his boss, Spinelli.

"I'd get out of here while I still could, if I were you." Kristine stood her ground. "My—traveling companion isn't happy about the fact that you've been following and harassing me. And he can be pretty mean when he's unhappy."

"Is that so? Is he the tall guy driving the black Trans Am?" He shook his head in mock sympathy. "You just can't trust anyone these days. Your boyfriend was pulling out of the driveway as I came around the corner. Looks like he's left you high and dry, sweetheart. Maybe you made *him* unhappy—" he took a step in her direction "—just like you made the boss unhappy."

Kristine backed away. He was lying, he had to be, Tucker wouldn't walk out that way and leave her—would he?

Well, why not? She was nothing to him. Just an unasked for and unwanted encumbrance. A stowaway. One he had threatened to get rid of on numerous occasions during the past forty-eight hours.

"How did you know I was here?" She didn't have to pretend curiosity. "There must be an awful lot of motels along the stretch of highway between here and that rest park."

She was stalling for time, giving Tucker the benefit of the doubt. He'd be back any minute now, she kept telling herself with sinking spirits as the minutes dragged by.

"Pure luck, with a little help thrown in by Mother Nature," Morrell answered without hesitation. He had her right where he wanted her, and this time she wasn't getting away. "The storm stopped most people in their tracks, but not me. I kept going as long as I could, and this morning I started out again at the first opportunity.

"I followed right behind the road trucks as they cleared the road, and stopped at every motel I came to until I finally found someone listed on the register from Texas. Then I had a little look at their car. It wasn't all that hard to spot your boyfriend's."

His eyes traveled to her new hairstyle and color. "You didn't really think that would make any difference, did you?" he asked derisively.

Kristine kept him talking, hoping he wouldn't notice she was edging closer to the bathroom door. If she could make it inside and get the door locked, maybe she could climb out the bathroom window before he had time to break the lock off the door.

"Why doesn't Vincent just leave me alone? He has my word that I won't say anything to anyone about him as long as he doesn't bother me." Another yard and she'd be home free—she hoped.

"He'd be a whole lot more willing to believe you if you returned that little package you took from his desk."

Kristine feigned ignorance. "What package is that?"

Morrell laughed. "Good, baby, but not good enough. You know damned well what package. And your husband—"

"Ex-husband," she corrected him sharply.

The big man shrugged broad shoulders and nodded. "Okay, ex, then. The boss wants his property back."

The grin was gone all at once, and there was a dangerous gleam in the cold eyes focused on her face.

"Look, I'll send the package back to Vincent once I get where I'm going," Kristine lied. She knew that small bundle was the only thing keeping her alive. And when it left her hands it would go to the authorities, someone she knew she could trust; otherwise, she was still as good as dead.

"I won't even open it," Kristine said. "All I want is some insurance to see that I get where I'm going without incident. Surely you can understand that?"

"Oh, sure," he agreed with her, the smile on his lips never reaching the chilly, narrowed eyes. "I understand that real good." He advanced a step closer. "But it's Mr. Spinelli who doesn't understand. He thinks his word should be good enough for you."

Shaking her head, Kristine suddenly grabbed the thick telephone book that was lying on the table beside her and threw it at his head. He ducked and she ran.

She barely had time to slam the door and lock it in place before his weight crashed against the wood panels. The hinges protested under the force of the blow.

While he pounded and cursed, Kristine was hitting the window lock with the heel of her hand. It appeared to have been painted over a number of times, and it wouldn't open easily. The door continued to protest loudly as Morrell slammed his shoulder against it again and again. Cracks began to appear in the cream-colored paint, and she knew if she didn't get out of there soon, the wood would splinter or the lock would give under the repeated heavy punishment.

Finally the window latch twisted in her hand, and she raised the window as high as it would go. Standing on the toilet seat, she shinnied through the tight space. Falling to the ground, hands and knees stinging from rough contact with the tarmac, she spared one glance over her shoulder as she heard wood splinter and the door crash back against the wall.

Thank God, he was too big to get through the window. But that only gave her a few minutes at best to make a decision about what to do next, where to go. Gaining her feet, she glanced this way and that, then scurried around the building, across the parking lot and directly into the path of an oncoming car.

Throwing her hands up instinctively for protection, the car's grill filling her vision, Kristine halted abruptly, both feet frozen to the pavement.

Chapter 4

The black Trans Am came to a screeching halt inches from Kristine's stationary figure.

Tucker stuck his head out the window and yelled. "Get in the car! Come on—hurry it up, damn it," he added, when she continued to stand unmoving, as if hypnotized by the car's shiny black hood.

Then she blinked and, shaking her head lightly, rounded the front fender and reached for the door handle. Conscious that Morrell might be right behind her, she threw herself inside. The car was moving even before the door closed. Kristine twisted in her seat and peered through the back window. Morrell was a big man, but he moved swiftly.

Sure enough, he was hot on her trail, but came to a pounding halt when he saw Tucker turn onto the down ramp to Interstate 40. Kristine watched him slap his fist against a powerful-looking thigh in frustration before turning away. Facing the road again, she took a deep, unsteady breath and looked at the calm face of the man beside her.

"You rotten bastard!" she panted. "You ran out on me! You left me at the mercy of that—that Neanderthal. How could you?

"And why, because I found your gun? Big deal! What did you think I was going to do? Call the cops and tell them all about you?"

With his eyes focused straight ahead, stern jaw set and hard hands gripping the wheel, Tucker refused to make comment on her angry accusation.

Damn her! Damn her for thinking he had run out on her, and damn her for making him feel responsible for her. He'd been mad, sure, mad as hell when he'd left the motel room, but his anger had been directed toward himself for leaving the gun where she could find it. And he hadn't run out on her. He would never run out on someone who was counting on him in a tight situation.

For the next hundred miles they didn't speak at all. Tucker concentrated on his driving, suiting the car's speed to what the road conditions would allow. And the closer they came to West Memphis, the better the driving conditions became.

The weather had warmed considerably. The hot sun beating down on the pavement, and the tires on the road had created a sea of dirty gray slush where once there was snow and ice. Travelers who had been forced to stop because of the weather were trying to make up for lost time, and the flow of traffic was heavy.

Kristine sat stiffly beside him, fuming at the imagined injustice of him running out on her. Admittedly he had the right to leave her if he wanted, he was under no obligation to her. But she would have expected him to have at least told her before doing so. To just run out like that, leaving her at the mercy of Morrell—when she'd told him the man was there—it hurt, perhaps more than it should have.

That was it, wasn't it? She was more hurt than angry. She'd thought he was better than that. So what if he'd been in prison? He had admitted that to her—and he didn't have to, either, she wouldn't have been any the wiser if he hadn't. But that didn't change the fact that he had walked out and left her. There was no denying that—or the pain she felt at the knowledge.

Tired of staring unknowingly at the countryside, she began watching for and counting license plates from different states. She counted fifteen before she got bored with the game. No matter how hard she tried, she couldn't keep her glance away from the man and finally gave up trying. She took to discreetly watching him from the corner of her eyes. He was so very good-looking in a hard, uncompromising sort of way. She couldn't deny his attraction, but knew too that something was missing.

She could detect no evidence of softness in the strong chin and stern mouth. A man needed some softness somewhere, some kind of vulnerability to make him human. And the only softness she'd seen in him had been when he was asleep. There was a permanent crease in the center of his forehead, breaking the long black line of his brow, making it appear as though he frowned a great deal of the time.

The more she looked at him, the more she wanted to forget her anger and ask him why he found the world such an unhappy place to live. What—or who?—had taken away his joy in life?

Tucker shifted restlessly in his seat and reached for the radio knob. Did she have to look at him so damned accusingly, with that hangdog expression in those big brown eyes? Didn't he have the right to pick his traveling companions? And besides, he hadn't been leaving her behind anyway, though he knew she wouldn't believe him if he told her so.

She didn't trust him. And why not? Hadn't he kept her safe this far? What did she expect from him?

Then again, what did he expect from her? Wouldn't he have figured the same thing if he'd been in her shoes? After all, he was in the car when she came across him, and it did appear as though he was heading away from the motel. And didn't he know from experience that you couldn't trust anyone—

No, that wasn't quite true. He trusted Bob, his brother. Bob had proved himself more than once in the past five years. Hadn't Bob stood beside him when Tucker had been accused of fraud, tried and convicted?

There was still no reason for *her* to think he'd betrayed her trust in such an underhanded fashion. He'd never run out on her when her defenses were down and her back was against the wall. Damn it, she ought to know that by now.

Kristine's eyes fell on the heavy gold ID bracelet at Tucker's wrist. She strained her eyes and managed to make out four intertwining initials carved on its shiny gold surface in fancy script. T.W., Tucker Winslow, and S.R. *S*? Sylvia? The name he had moaned aloud twice in his sleep?

She turned back to the road, not liking the feelings surfacing with the question of the woman's identity. She resented the man beside her and felt an intense dislike for the unknown Sylvia. Who was she? Had he run out on her, too?

Tucker hooked a left a few minutes later, and they pulled into the parking lot of a restaurant.

"Lunch," was all he said as he climbed from the car and waited for her to do the same.

The place was small, a roadside café frequented by truck drivers, she guessed from the number of tractor-trailers in the huge parking lot. And that's when she came up with the brilliant idea to leave Tucker here and let him get on with his trip and his life the way he liked it—alone. It should be easy to get another ride here.

The meal was an uncomfortable one. She was too nervous, thinking about how to go about leaving him, to even make a pretense at enjoying the meal. She failed to notice the raised brow and questioning looks he shot her as the tension between them grew to impossible proportions.

They didn't take long with the meal, as though in silent agreement that Morrell wouldn't be far behind. And when Tucker stood up to pay, Kristine excused herself to go to the ladies' room.

She took a long time in there, hoping that when she came out he would miraculously have left without her and she would be spared the necessity of having to make an excuse for leaving him. She was also afraid she would lose her nerve when it came right down to walking away.

Kristine couldn't help that her heart gave a tiny leap at the sight of him as she moved out to the parking lot. He stood leaning against the car, his forearm on the roof, his eyes on her lagging figure.

"I was beginning to think you had fallen in," he commented sourly, denying the small twinge from somewhere deep inside his chest as she moved into his line of vision.

"I'm not going on with you," she began. "When I came out of the rest room just now, I heard two truckers talking. One said he was heading to Illinois," she lied. "I spoke with him and found out he's passing within a few miles of my hometown. He's agreed to give me a lift."

The words came tumbling out. And with every one she uttered, her spirits plummeted deeper as, hoping against hope, she looked for a sign that her leaving meant something to him. She didn't know what she expected, perhaps for him to tell her in his gruff, impatient voice not to be ridiculous and to get into the car.

"Where's your knapsack?" he asked expressionlessly.

"I left it back at the motel," she answered, fighting sharp disappointment.

"Your money?"

"It's in my pocket."

Without another word or a glance, he climbed into the car, started the engine and pulled off the parking lot and onto the road. Kristine watched him go with mixed feelings and almost ran after the car's disappearing taillights as he sped down the access road and onto the highway.

When she could no longer see the black Trans Am, she turned a wretched face toward the door to the restaurant. What was she going to do now?

"'Scuse me, little lady," a voice spoke from directly behind her.

"Yes?" Kristine turned in its direction.

"Where you headed? You needin' a ride?"

He was short, dressed in a striped western shirt, jeans, run-down boots and a baseball cap with the words Truckers Do It on the Open Highway emblazoned on it. He looked good-natured, uncomplicated and just a little bit like the boy she had grown up next door to in Illinois.

"I'm going back home to the Midwest—Illinois, as a matter of fact. And yes, I do need a ride."

They had been on the road for almost an hour when he propositioned her. For a moment she didn't know what to say. There was no finesse involved with the query, he simply asked her if she was interested, and when, with a wary glance, she shook her head no, he smiled, shrugged beefy shoulders and nodded. The subject was never brought up again. His manner became almost brotherly after that.

He told her it wasn't safe to accept rides with just anybody, even some truck drivers weren't to be trusted. Then he began to regale her with tales of what life on the road was really like. Some things had her laughing uproariously, and some made her feel sad, but he managed to make her forget her problems and even to push thoughts of Tucker from her mind for a little while.

During the ride, he'd asked questions about her hometown and her finances. She was reluctant to discuss either with him until she realized he was really only interested in her welfare. And when he asked her exactly how she was set with money, she admitted she hadn't much in the way of ready cash. He then offered to lend her the money for a bus ticket to take her the rest of the way home.

But she declined his generous offer, assuring him that she could afford the price of a bus ticket. That's when he told her apologetically that his route took him north at the next interstate they came to. With her approval he called ahead on his CB radio, contacting truckers who were more knowledgeable about the immediate area, to learn if there was a town near his turnoff with a bus station.

The trucker received word that there was one at Blytheville. He let her out there with a few last words of caution about hitchhiking and, waving goodbye and good luck, moved out of sight.

The bus depot was located in the corner of The Steak Place, a restaurant that advertised having the best steaks in the state. Kristine entered the building and was immediately assaulted by the appetizing aroma of mesquite-broiled steak and fresh-baked bread.

Swallowing a mouthful of saliva, she dared to take the time to get something to drink, then turned determinedly toward the small window marked Bus Terminal. Approaching the elderly man stationed behind it, she asked when the next bus to Danville, Illinois, would leave.

From out of nowhere came the unbidden question of where Tucker Winslow was and if he had given a thought to her whereabouts since they had parted. And suddenly she wondered where Carl Morrell might be right about now. Far, far away, she hoped.

As though her thoughts might have conjured up the man, a firm finger abruptly tapped her on the shoulder. Kristine's heart stopped for an instant. Morrell—he'd found her again. She turned slowly to face her nemesis.

"What are you doing here?" Was that her voice sounding so high and squeaky, so eager?

Tucker raised a brow and gestured over his right shoulder. The large, unmistakable figure of the man she'd been dodging through two states was making his way across the parking lot.

"Oh, no!"

Tucker grabbed her arm with hard fingers and pulled her away from the small teller's window.

"Lady! Lady," the stoop-shouldered, gray-haired man behind the window called, leaning forward, trying to keep her in sight. "Do you want this ticket, or not?"

"No!" Tucker answered for her, not stopping until they had passed down a short hall where the rest rooms were situated side by side and entered a door marked No Admittance—Employees Only.

Kristine found herself standing in a storage closet in pitch-blackness, her front pressed up against the rigid muscles of Tucker's back. Hardly daring to breathe, her heart thumping madly, she waited for the door to suddenly burst open and for them to be confronted by the triumphant grin belonging to their wily pursuer.

The seconds ticked by, the only sounds from outside the airless room were those of people going into and coming out of the rest rooms. The tiny enclosed space became warm, and Kristine began to perspire beneath the heavy sweater and ski jacket she wore.

An itch developed somewhere in the center of her back, caused undoubtedly by the scratchy wool of the sweater and a trickle of sweat sliding down between her shoulder blades. She shifted her weight from foot to foot, wishing she could scratch the irritating spot.

"Will you stand still!" the man in front of her hissed over his shoulder.

Kristine stilled instantly, once again unconsciously holding her breath.

"You can breathe, damn it, just don't wiggle about."

His words created a sudden tension in the air, different from the dread of discovery. The heat all along her front, where her body pressed against his, suddenly became a scorching inferno, threatening to ignite the layers of clothing separating their bodies.

Trying to put a little space between them, she pressed back against the boxes stacked behind. They gave way with a suddenness that surprised her, and she felt herself falling backward.

A startled cry left her lips before she could stop it. The man before her twisted around and clapped a hard hand over her mouth, stifling the sound. His other hand grasped her shoulder, pulling her toward the solid wall of his chest. They stood, blinded by the darkness, pressed tightly together, neither daring to breathe, listening to the silence and waiting.

"Please," she mumbled after a time against his hard palm, "you're hurting me."

The hand over her lower face relaxed slightly, and she worked her stiffened jaw experimentally before licking dry lips and tasting salt—salt from *his* skin, she thought with a tiny, unexpected thrill.

Making a second pass over stinging lips, the tip of her tongue slid across the center of Tucker's broad palm. She felt his hand jerk and heard his immediate short, indrawn breath.

They stood once again with neither daring to move, hardly daring to breathe, both unwilling to acknowledge the flood of emotions that her simple accident had unwittingly spawned. The very air around them seemed to pulse as though electrically charged.

Kristine opened her lips to say something, anything that would break the awful disquiet that held them bound tightly together yet separate. But before she could speak, his hand moved, and she couldn't still the spasmodic trembling within her. His fingertips lightly touched her bottom lip, gently traced its fullness from one side to the other, then drew reluctantly away.

She closed her eyes, surrendering to the magic of his touch. And when he drew back, she had to fight an overwhelming need to lean in to him, to experience the heady sensation once more.

After a moment, she felt his touch on her cheek. It slid, feather light, to the narrow bridge of her nose, then back, to smooth the damp hair at her temples away from her hot face. Kristine felt her knees shake, and the hands hanging at her sides until now moved up hesitantly to his waist. She was at once captivated by the feel of the lean masculine planes and hard muscled ridges beneath her fingertips.

The hand at her shoulder tightened before sliding toward the edge of her jacket. Tucker explored the delicate bones of her neck, then burrowed questing fingers beneath the band of her sweater, his touch setting her aflame. Suspended somewhere between disbelief and enchantment Kristine felt herself flowing toward him.

Was this the same man who could still a heartbeat with his cold glance?

One of his hands became tangled in her soft hair. He bunched the short mass in a powerful fist, exerting pressure to raise her up onto her toes, bringing her lips to within his reach. His head lowered unerringly in the darkness, and he could feel her warm breath feather his skin. He just had time to ask himself what he was doing before his head descended and his lips took hers in a hard, passionless kiss.

Kristine felt the bruising force of his mouth take possession of hers with a shock. Her lips had parted softly, waiting to receive his first kiss. But this was no passionate salute, no testament to recently discovered warm and tender feelings.

As his relentless mouth ground her soft lips bruisingly against her teeth, she knew without a doubt, it was a punishment he bestowed on her. One she had not earned, but bore the brunt of nevertheless. Sylvia—the name slithered through her mind.

Wrenching her mouth from his, Kristine pushed against the rigid wall of his chest with determined hands, drew her stiffened body from contact with his.

Feeling all at once ashamed, Tucker let her go but knew he could not take back the kiss. Telling himself it was her fault for instigating it he covered his shame with anger.

Wiping the back of one hand across her lips, tears of anger beading her lashes, she whispered one word. "Why?"

He didn't answer, but she felt the tension seep out of the small space like water leaking through a sieve. Turning away from her, Tucker grabbed the doorknob and twisted it savagely. That one softly spoken word did more damage to his self-respect than any harsh epithet she could have uttered.

Kristine looked on in silence as Tucker opened the door and peered outside. After a moment he widened the opening and slipped through, pausing long enough to whisper that she was to stay put. And then he was gone.

She waited anxiously, trembling with every sound from the outside hallway. And after what seemed like hours, the door opened and Tucker stood there, motioning for her to follow him. Without a word she complied and in minutes found herself at the back of the building, running across a muddy field to a destination only the man keeping pace beside her knew.

"Where are we going?" she panted, slipping and only just keeping herself from a nasty fall.

Feeling a sharp pain in her left side, she glanced up from the ground to tell him she couldn't go a step farther. That's when she saw the black Trans Am ahead, parked in a thick stand of tall trees.

She fell against its mud-splattered side, gasping for breath, waiting for him to unlock the doors. Once he had, she slid inside, dropped her head back against the headrest and closed her eyes.

"How—did—you—know—where I—was?" she panted, turning her head to look at him.

She had to pretend the incident in the storage closet hadn't occurred, otherwise she would be screaming at him in anger. And she couldn't afford to let him know how deeply his act of vengeance had affected her.

"Simple," he replied, appearing to be unaffected by the run or what had preceded it. "I followed you."

"Why?"

His silver glance met hers, and she wished she could interpret the varied emotions she saw there, before, eyes shuttered, he glanced away.

"I feel responsible for you. Don't ask me why. Believe me, I know it sounds crazy, but I didn't believe you when you said you had gotten a ride with a trucker—even after I saw it was true." He shrugged. "I followed you, and that's how I spotted Morrell."

Meeting her eyes, his thoughts concealed once more behind a wall of blankness, he asked, "Are you ready yet to tell me why that character is chasing you?"

Here he was, doing the very thing he'd warned himself against—trying to get information out of her, getting himself more deeply embroiled in her problems. But he felt he owed her something, something for what he'd done to her back in the closet. She hadn't deserved that, and he knew it. He saw the slight swelling of her lower lip and realized he'd marked her. Branded her with his own hate, he couldn't help thinking.

Kristine saw his glance move over her face, touching and lingering on her mouth. She moistened her lips, feeling their soreness, and saw something flare briefly in his eyes before he looked hurriedly away. Could she trust him? There was so much she didn't know about him. Like where he was headed, what he was running to—what he was running from. Why he carried so much hate around inside him. And why he was packing a gun.

On the other hand, he'd stuck by her even when she had left him. And without his help, she'd surely have been caught by Morrell just now—perhaps even be dead.

Something inside told her the man following her would get a whole lot more desperate in the next few hours, especially as she got farther from Texas and closer to help. She wanted to trust the man at her side. It would be such a relief to have him know the whole story, to know just how dangerous this man Morrell and the absent Spinelli really were.

But how much danger would that knowledge bring to him? And was she willing to accept the responsibility for his possibly dying on her behalf? Then again, wasn't she bringing him closer all the time to such an end, the longer she relied on him to get her out of Morrell's way? She was very confused, but ready to trust him with her secrets if he showed the least sign of being disposed to trust her with his.

"Are you ready to tell me why you carry a gun?" she asked softly.

"I guess you still don't trust me. That's okay," he added after a long moment, "for now. I'll tell you what, I'll make a deal with you. I'll see you get safely to—"

"Danville, Illinois," she supplied.

"No questions asked—as long as you do the same. And when we part company, that's as far as we go."

She knew there was a double meaning to his words. He was telling her the incident in the closet was to be forgotten. And any romantic illusions she might have developed from it, if she was foolish enough to do so, were strictly her own.

"Once we say goodbye," he continued, "we're quits. From that moment on, it's like the other never existed." Catching her eye, he asked, "Deal?"

"You mean, you're willing to deliberately put yourself in the path of a man like Morrell for me?" Frowning, she searched his face, saw him shrug. "But, why?"

"You're placing too much emphasis on the personal aspect of the whole business. What I'm doing isn't for you, any more than what I did in the pawnshop in Dallas was." Did he really believe that? Could he, in all honesty, tell himself that he was as uninvolved with her as he would like to be and believe it?

"What I'm doing, I'm doing for me," he continued. "I can't explain my motives, they're personal, but they are mine," he emphasized.

What could she say? She needed help, his or someone like him. And as strange as it might seem to others, though she knew her companion hardly at all and he obviously wanted to keep it that way, she hadn't felt this safe in almost six months. Not since the night she had inadvertently overheard Vincent Spinelli's plan to murder a Dallas city official because the man intended to block his bid to construct a building on a sight the official felt was unsafe for such construction.

"It's a deal," she answered finally. And in a few minutes they were on the road once again headed east.

Kristine crossed protective arms over her chest, feeling the hard ridge beneath her jacket just below her breasts. As long as the package was safe, so was she. With that thought in mind, she closed tired eyes and slid into exhausted sleep.

Bright light against her closed eyelids awakened her. It was dark now, the brightness was coming from lights stationed above a row of gas pumps. Tucker walked out of the gas station and moved into view.

"You awake?"

Sitting up straighter in the seat, she nodded, rubbing gritty eyes.

"Hungry? There's a restaurant across the street. We can't stop for long if we expect to keep ahead of your friend Morrell, but long enough to grab a quick bite, I guess."

"He isn't my friend," she bit out quickly.

Tucker leaned his elbows on the window, eyeing her. The question, "What exactly was Morrell to her then," on his lips. But he only shrugged, murmured, "Sorry," and got into the car.

They ate quickly, and near the end of the meal, Tucker told her he'd been thinking about their situation. Staying on the interstate, though unquestionably the quickest route, was also the most dangerous. It made it too easy for Morrell to follow them. They could take a side road running parallel to the interstate and be safer, but it would take longer to get where they were going.

Kristine gave it some thought and after a moment agreed to the change in the route. Tucker brought out a map for them to study and they pored over it, finally settling on the route they wanted to use. After that, the meal was finished quickly and they left the restaurant. Going outside, they saw that it had started to rain.

"Great weather we're having," Kristine commented, shaking her head as they climbed into the car.

Neither she nor her companion noticed the black Cadillac parked behind the Dumpster, the rear bumper barely visible in the darkness.

Carl Morrell grinned and licked his lips in anticipation. Miss Nurse Stevens thought she was so smart. He patted the CB radio with a wider grin and shook his head at her stupidity. Trailing her was a piece of cake compared to other jobs he'd been on. She was very predictable, and so was her boyfriend.

He'd always wondered what it was about her that had first attracted his boss. She was good-looking, sure, but so were a lot of women, women who knew how to make themselves even more attractive to a man like himself.

Wiping the screwdriver he held on a rag, he marveled at how easy this all really was. In a little while he'd have them in the palm of his hand. And then he'd discover firsthand exactly what it was about her that had tied Vincent Spinelli up in knots for so long.

And he'd know all about her traveling companion in short order, too. Information was only a telephone call away. And Mr. Spinelli had this guy's number, his license plate number, thanks to him.

He laughed out loud, started the car and pulled out behind the Trans Am. Close, but not too close, he wasn't ready to let them know he was there, not just yet.

"Well, I'm no longer hungry, thirsty or sleepy. How about you?" Kristine asked Tucker.

He agreed that the food had hit the spot all right. He gave no thought to the fact that part of the pleasure he'd taken in the meal was the companion he had shared it with.

"Do you think Morrell is still on our trail?" she asked apprehensively. The man had somehow managed, so far, to anticipate all her moves.

Tucker shrugged. "It would be a miracle if we lost him for good that last time. He's pretty adept at what he's doing," he added almost admiringly.

"Thanks, you're great for my morale. Just don't break into song if he pulls up beside us, will you?" she muttered sarcastically.

Sneaking a look at him, she saw him grin. He was laughing at her—but what caught and held her attention was the dimple in his right cheek. The sight of it—and his smile—the first one she'd seen on his face since they'd met—plucked at her heartstrings.

"You're laughing at me," she accused in a soft, quivery voice.

"Am I?"

Tucker took his eyes off the road long enough to spare her a brief glance. She was staring at his mouth. His grin died instantly, and his lips became at once the too familiar uncompromising slash across his lower face.

There he was again, letting her get beneath his guard. When would he learn? Wasn't it enough that she'd made him feel responsible for her, so that he'd chased after her to keep her from getting caught? Did she have to make him *like* her, too?

He took the next curve too fast, and the tires skidded on the wet pavement, throwing Kristine painfully against the door handle.

They traveled in silence for several miles, the air fraught with an unbearable tension. She was confused and hurt by it. What had she said? She had only been enjoying a little humor. Didn't he at least want to be friends?

Finally, unable to stand it a moment longer, Kristine asked if she could drive. Maybe he'd go to sleep, and then she could regroup her defenses against him. And beat down the growing attraction she didn't particularly want to admit to feeling.

"Please, I'm a good driver," she assured him. "Really, I am. And you could get some sleep."

Hoping he was doing the right thing, Tucker let her persuade him. He could go to sleep and then he wouldn't be so aware of her shapely thigh only a few scant inches from his own. Somehow she had divested herself of that awful smell from the stuff she had used on her hair, and the scent of the perfume she used, or maybe it was only her personal body scent, was driving him crazy.

Without another word, Tucker pulled over to the side of the road and got out of the car. Kristine did the same. As they passed, her ankle turned on the uneven ground, and with a startled cry she pitched sideways.

Tucker caught her, steadying her while she regained her balance. The bones of her shoulder felt small and delicate beneath his large hands. He knew he should release her at once, but his hands lingered, tightened almost of their own accord. His eyes were drawn to her mouth. He'd tasted it once in anger, what would it taste like without the anger? He could feel himself weakening—

Kristine read his indecision. She tried to throttle the dizzying current racing through her at the thought of his lips on hers. Could she withstand another such demonstration as the one she'd experienced earlier at his hands? Or would it be different this time? Should she let him kiss her or not? The decision was taken from her abruptly.

The headlights from a car cresting the hill fell on them, and Tucker wrenched his gaze from her lips. Releasing her quickly, he waited until she took a couple of steps, to be certain she hadn't injured her ankle, then turned away.

A few moments later, under his steady gaze, Kristine pulled too quickly onto the highway and spun the tires on the loose gravel. Tucker didn't say anything, but she could sense his disapproval.

Feeling the response of the sleek automobile under her hands, she began to relax and gain confidence. She was a good driver, and as soon as Tucker went to sleep and quit watching her with that unwavering silver-eyed stare, she'd be just fine.

The road was only two lanes, but there were few other vehicles on it. When she slowed to allow a car behind to pass before reaching a No Passing zone, she noticed the brakes felt somewhat odd. Thinking perhaps it was because she wasn't used to the car, she didn't say anything, only reduced her speed and continued following the path the headlights carved out of the darkness.

She'd been driving for perhaps twenty minutes, Tucker slumped down against the seat, eyes closed, head against the door, when she realized something indeed was wrong—very wrong.

She had no brakes! They weren't in real trouble yet, the road was a bit hilly but nothing too steep, and the curves weren't very sharp. But the idea that she was driving without brakes began to frighten her. All kinds of possibilities came to mind, like something being in the road up ahead or a car pulling suddenly from out of nowhere directly into her path.

She was becoming panicky, it was time to awaken her companion.

"Tucker! Tucker!" In her growing anxiety she didn't notice her use of his first name. "Wake up! Wake up, damn it, something is wrong with the brakes!"

Tucker jumped as the peaceful silence was abruptly shattered by her alarmed cries. Bumping his head against the door window, he shouted, "What the hell's going on?"

"That's what I've been trying to tell you!" she shouted back. "Something is wrong with the brakes—we don't have any. I don't know what to do!"

Chapter 5

"Throw on the emergency brake."

Kristine took her eyes off the road long enough to give him a look of grudging respect. He sounded so calm and reasonable that she found herself thinking, of course, why didn't I think of that.

Tucker concentrated on the road up ahead. In the glow from the headlights he could see a clear stretch where the shoulder widened, giving her plenty of room to maneuver the car to safety.

"Now—push down on it, now," he directed.

"Where?" Kristine asked, beginning to sound desperate again. She couldn't find the blasted brake. "Where is it?"

"On the floor," he answered. "To the left—you'll have to lift your foot high to reach the pedal." His glance flew from her nervous face back to the road.

Kristine located the pedal at last, pushed down solidly with her foot and felt the car instantly slow. However, the pavement was slick with rain, and she congratulated herself too soon. She didn't see the jog hidden in the road up ahead.

"Watch out!" Tucker shouted.

Too late, Kristine responded to his urgent warning. If the road had been dry—if she'd been paying more attention to what she was doing—if *he* had been driving—all these thoughts spun through her mind as the car skidded over the pavement's wet surface and onto the grassy verge.

Momentum drove the vehicle across the slick grass and down the embankment. Kristine held on to the steering wheel, thankful for having had the foresight to fasten her seat belt into place after taking the wheel, a thing she was guilty of not always doing. She could hear her teeth rattling together inside her head.

As soon as Tucker saw they were going over the side, he grabbed for his seat belt and clicked it into place. In the dark he couldn't tell how far they were likely to go before reaching the bottom, if they went all the way.

Jarring its occupants, the car bumped and rattled over the uneven ground, crashed through a string of barbed wire used to keep cattle from wandering out onto the highway and came to rest solidly against the trunk of an old oak tree.

Tucker shook his head, rubbed at a knot forming on the side of it where he'd hit the window and turned to look at Kristine.

"You okay?" he asked sharply. The lights from the dash showed him her figure slumped sideways in the seat.

Kristine put a hand to her forehead and felt the moist stickiness of blood. She'd been fine until the tree had gotten in the way of the car's hood, and then her forehead had cracked against the steering wheel as it came to a crashing halt. "I'm fine, how about you?" It was bad enough she had wrecked his car, she wasn't going to tell him he now had an injured woman on his hands.

"Yeah," he answered bitingly, "I'm great, just great." Opening the glove compartment, he took a flashlight from it and shoved a shoulder against the door beside him a couple of times until it opened. Climbing outside, he moved around the car, assessing the damage.

"Is it bad?" Kristine asked tentatively. She had followed him after a moment spent in getting her bearings and wiping the blood from her face with the rag he kept beneath the driver's seat.

"Not if you have a spare radiator somewhere on your person, and a new tie-rod," he answered in a controlled voice.

He should have known better than to let her behind the wheel. It was all he could do to keep his hands balled into fists at his sides. If he let go of just a fraction of the anger building up inside, he'd strangle her. She had said she was a good driver. If this was an example of her driving skill, God help everyone else on the road at the same time as her.

"I'm sorry," she apologized. "It's all my fault. I should have awakened you immediately, back there when I first noticed the brakes going bad—"

"What do you mean, 'going bad'?" Tucker gripped her arm tightly. "They didn't go all at once—like something just gave?"

"No-no—they felt strange, a little mushy at first. It happened gradually— What is it?" she asked when he pushed her almost roughly away with a curse and turned to glance up at the road.

"Morrell," she heard somewhere in the string of curses that followed.

"I don't understand."

"The brakes didn't just fail—I suspect your friend Morrell had a hand in helping them reach that end."

Looking puzzled, she moved around to stand in front of him. "How? How could he do that?"

"It's simple, you just punch a little hole in the brake line. Every time the brakes are used, a little brake fluid is pumped out. Before you know it, it's all gone—and so are your brakes."

"But how?" she protested. "When could he have gotten to them? Wouldn't that take some time to—"

"At the restaurant," he interrupted her impatiently. "It's the only possible explanation. The brakes were fine when I drove. And you took over right after we stopped for our last meal."

The words sounded almost prophetic. Kristine looked up at the incline down which they had traveled only minutes before. "We could have been killed—" She glanced to the frustrated man standing silently beside her. "You could have been killed—" she added softly.

And she would have been responsible for his death, because she had involved him in this mess even before he had consented to help her. It was becoming too real for her. This was no game. Morrell was after her to get what she'd taken from Spinelli—whatever the cost to her or anyone helping her. She was under a death sentence and—because he was with her—so was Tucker.

Wiping the rain from his face with the back of one hand, Tucker pivoted to look at the twisted wreckage of his car. Playing the flashlight beam back and forth, he clicked his tongue in annoyance and shook his head.

"Come on, let's go."

"Go? Where?" Kristine lagged back.

"Away from here," was his short, testy reply.

"Look, Tucker," the name slipped easily from her tongue. "I'm sorry—for all this—" she gestured around them. "By helping me, you've gotten mixed up in something lethal. I appreciate what you've done for me. But—"

"There's no time for that now." Tucker grabbed her by the wrist, the sound of his name spoken in her soft, throaty voice ringing in his ears. "Morrell has got to be right behind us. We've come far enough from civilization for Morrell to make his move. It's what he planned all along.

"And by taking the back roads we've played right into his hands. We've got to make tracks, and fast."

"Make tracks?" she sounded incredulous. They were both shivering in the cold rain. The temperatures couldn't have been much above freezing, barely enough so that the moisture was falling as rain and not snow. And her head was splitting from the blow to it she'd received in the accident. She doubted she could go a few yards, much less the distance it would take to get them out of here before Morrell came upon the scene.

"We haven't got a hope in hell of outdistancing him on foot," she reminded him in exasperation.

"You're right," Tucker unexpectedly agreed with her. "But maybe, just maybe we can outsmart him," he added thoughtfully.

She doubted that. She had been trying to outthink Morrell for a long time, and he always seemed to be there waiting for her next move.

"Look," she began in a matter-of-fact tone, all at once giving in to the inevitable. "I appreciate what you've done for me. But I've gotten you into a bad situation. Just take a look at your brand-new car.

"I'm truly sorry about that, and I think perhaps it's time I faced Morrell and gave him what he wants. None of this has anything to do with you. He won't bother you once I'm out of the picture.

"Why don't you just go on alone, find a phone and get your car fixed so you can get on with whatever it is you're on your way to do? I'll stay behind, reason with Morrell, he'll listen when I—"

"Don't be an idiot," he interrupted her harshly. "The man's a killer. Do you really think he's going to let you walk away? You can't possibly be *that* stupid."

"Now, look here, Winslow, I'm only trying to save your worthless hide."

"That's what I figured," he responded in a calm voice. "Well, thank you very much, Miss Fix-it, but I don't need your gesture of self-sacrifice."

Morrell had become for him a composite of all the men he'd had to deal with in the past few years—none of them of his choosing—and all of them bad. He wanted Morrell for himself, perhaps even more than he wanted to get him for her.

"I'm a part of this now, whether you like it or not. It doesn't matter how I got to be a part of it—it's a fact. And I'll be damned if I let that bastard get away with this—" His hand swept toward the remains of his car. "So stop spouting drivel and let's get on with this farce. I have a life to lead, too, and as you said, you've held me up long enough," he finished sardonically.

Drivel? Kristine was hurt beyond words. She'd been trying to keep the arrogant so-and-so from getting killed—and he accused her of spouting drivel. And hadn't she just told him to leave?

"What are you going to do?" Kristine gave in without a fight. Though his words and tone infuriated her, she was secretly relieved that she wouldn't be facing Carl Morrell alone.

"I heard a car pass by on the road a few minutes ago, going real slow. I suspect it was Morrell looking for us. He knows we wouldn't have gotten far after he fixed the brakes. When he doesn't spot the car on the side of the road up ahead, he'll be back."

"Right now he has all the balls in his corner pocket, but maybe we can even up the score a bit."

"How?" she asked skeptically.

"I need something sharp," Tucker muttered, searching through the trunk.

Kristine felt for the knife she still carried in her jacket pocket. "Will this do?" she asked, holding it in the beam from the flashlight.

"What's that for?" Tucker asked after a moment, looking from the knife to her and back.

"A woman needs protection when she's traveling alone," she informed him almost defiantly.

"Yeah, well, put it away, it won't do for what I need," he answered before going back to his searching. After a moment, he drew the tire iron from the trunk, felt the sharp end and nodded to himself. This would work.

A few minutes later, Kristine stood looking back over her shoulder at the small blaze that would soon ignite and destroy what was left of the car, along with all evidence of their occupancy.

Tucker's idea was to make Morrell think they had been trapped in the car when it wrecked, that it caught fire with them still inside, and burned—killing them both.

"But won't that draw him to where we are," she asked.

"Yeah, it will. But he's bound to find us soon anyway. At least the fire may slow him down a bit, while he checks to make sure we were inside."

"By the time he discovers we aren't, maybe someone else will have been drawn to the area by the explosion. Somebody coming to investigate the fire, and finding him at the scene, would delay him even longer, giving us time to get away."

"But what about your car," she asked. Such willful destruction of an expensive piece of machinery was beyond her comprehension. "The insurance company will investigate, and when they discover the fire was deliberately set, they won't pay you a dime," she admonished him.

But her dire predictions fell on deaf ears. Tucker shrugged broad shoulders, folded the map he'd taken from the seat of the car before setting the fire and stuffed it into his pocket. Then, directing the flashlight beam onto the ground ahead, he continued on without a backward glance. He knew something she didn't. He wouldn't be collecting the insurance money. He had no need for a fast car—any car—where he was headed.

They had gone about a quarter of a mile, Kristine fighting dizziness every step of the way, when they heard the sound of the explosion. Whirling around, they saw the yellow-and-orange fireball shoot into the night sky and fall immediately back to earth.

"What about a fire?" Kristine asked, out of breath, trotting along at his side. She remembered seeing pictures of the destruction left after a forest fire. Acres and acres of blackened debris where once there had been green growing things.

Tucker wiped a hand down his cheek then rubbed it over one of hers. "Does that feel like anything will burn for long? And look at your feet, aren't you standing in ankle-deep mud?"

He was right again, nothing would burn for long in this rain and mud. How she longed for the time before Vincent Spinelli's advent into her life. For the peace and quiet of her life back in Dallas, the comfort of her own apartment and the warmth of her own bed.

"Do you think Morrell might think we perished in the fire?" she asked suddenly, trying to take her mind off her physical discomfort.

Her hands were balled into fists in the pockets of her jacket for warmth, but she couldn't feel her toes any more in the wet sneakers. Her jaws ached with the effort at clenching them to keep them from chattering in the piercing cold, and from the throbbing pain in her head. With her luck, she was probably suffering from a concussion.

"I doubt it," he answered honestly. "Whatever else Morrell might be, he isn't stupid. I never actually expected to fool him into believing we were dead. I figured to slow him down a little while he checked for the remains—"

"What—" Kristine stopped abruptly. "You *knew* he wouldn't buy our being in the wreck? And you destroyed your car just to slow him down?" she asked incredulously.

What kind of man paid cash for an automobile and then casually destroyed it without any hope of recovering his money?

"I don't understand—"

"You don't have to," he told her succinctly. "Just keep moving. It won't take him long to find our trail in this mud."

Kristine wanted to protest, to ask any number of questions, but she knew this wasn't the time or the place. She started walking again, angry at his nasty tone. True, she hadn't been very forthcoming about her past or the reason for Morrell's pursuit of her. But by comparison, he knew twice as much about her as she knew about him.

Her right ankle twisted as she inadvertently stepped into a hole of some kind, and, unable to regain her balance, she pitched forward. Head over heels, she tumbled down a small hill and landed with a splash in a stream of icy water.

Tucker made a quick grab for her, but his fingers only brushed against the material of her jacket as she disappeared from sight. Taking a giant step, the flashlight directed on where she had disappeared, he fell into space. He came to rest on his backside in freezing water, somehow managing to keep hold of the flashlight. Sitting up, he played the beam around and discovered they were sitting smack-dab in the middle of a small creek bed. Without knowing it, they had been traveling by its outer banks all along.

"Ugh!" Kristine sat up, pushed streaming hair out of her eyes and wiped a sleeve across her face. She hadn't been as fortunate as Tucker; she had landed facedown in the muddy water.

"You all right?" he asked, hiding a smile at her obvious disgust.

"Just great!" she spluttered hostilely. She was wet, dirty and frozen. She was on foot miles from civilization in the middle of winter with a killer chasing her, and he wanted to know if she was all right. And this made twice in one night that she had nearly had her brains knocked out.

Getting to his feet in one fluid motion, Tucker reached out a hand to help her up. It was time they headed back the way they had come.

"Come on, let's double back a little and see if we can spot Morrell. We've been walking about an hour, and though I've kept a sharp ear out, I haven't heard anything that sounded like another human being on our trail."

"Double back!" Kristine repeated in alarm. "But what if we stumble on him? Shouldn't we just keep going?"

Tucker wasn't an expert on hypothermia, but he knew that if the two of them didn't get in out of the cold, especially now that they were soaked, they both would be in serious trouble. He had hoped that by taking off across country they would come across a farmhouse or an abandoned building where they could shelter for the night from the inclement weather.

What had seemed like a good plan at the time had turned into serious trouble for the two of them. They would have to go back. They had been heading across country and away from the road, now they would have to take their chances with Morrell. The highway offered the slim chance at a ride, but the probability of their surviving this night as things now stood was less than nil.

Tucker felt the heavy weight of the gun resting against his hip. If they did meet up with Morrell, there was always that alternative. He felt certain Morrell was the kind of man who would understand the business end of a .38.

They hadn't gone far when Tucker finally had to admit to himself that they were lost. The fall must have thoroughly confused his sense of direction. As they had left the scene of the accident, he'd marked certain things in his mind, keeping them as landmarks. But using the flashlight, he realized nothing he saw now looked in any way familiar.

Sensing something, Kristine asked, "What is it?"

There was no use pretending, "We're lost."

"L-lost?" she asked numbly, as though she couldn't quite comprehend the meaning of the word.

"Yeah, I don't know where in the hell we are."

"Well—look at the map," she told him in exasperation.

"This map is a road map," he stressed, "not a topographical map."

"Wonderful—so what do we do now?" She was shivering so badly that she could hardly speak, and the word *hypothermia* loomed darkly in her thoughts.

"I guess we just keep walking," was his surly reply.

Coming to an abrupt halt, Tucker peered into the distance. Kristine, walking with her shoulders hunched and her head down watching the ground as best she could, stumbled into his back.

"I don't believe it," he muttered abruptly.

"W-what?" she asked in apprehension, wishing she dared to snuggle up to his warmth for even a few moments.

"It's a farmhouse and a couple of outbuildings. We've found shelter. Come on."

Running, stumbling, falling down, they got up to run again. In a short span of time they were just outside the circle of the illumination cast by the security light Tucker had spotted in the distance. As they drew even with it, Tucker halted Kristine with a hand on her shoulder.

"I'd better take a look around first," he whispered softly. "You stay here."

He stationed her behind an old pickup truck parked at the edge of the clearing where the farm was situated. Pulling the gun from his pocket, he made his way through the shadows at the edge of the light's glow and into the yard.

At first he worried that Morrell might have found the place before them. Then he considered the possibility of the farmer owning a dog. But quiet reigned. No dog and no Morrell—so far so good. He bypassed the two-story farmhouse, keeping his distance. He didn't want to awaken anyone inside and have them find him armed and nosing around their property this late at night. That was a surefire method for someone to get hurt.

There were two other buildings—a long, white chicken house and a two-story barn. He left the chickens alone, he didn't want them creating a ruckus that would bring the farmer running with a shotgun to see if a fox was after them.

Inside the barn, he gave the place a quick once-over, found the hayloft, and figured this would be the best place for them to shelter for the night. It seemed to be a fairly new barn, and there was enough fresh straw in the hayloft to keep them warm for the night. Before he left the building, he also found a lantern full of kerosene and ready for use.

Coming out of the building, he ran straight into Kristine, who was peering around the edge of the barn doors.

He gave a start, his finger tightening on the trigger reflexively. When he realized who it was, he wanted to throttle her for the second time that night.

"Damn it! Don't you ever do what you're told? I could have shot you just then."

"It was dark, and I—thought I heard something—" she retorted in self-defense. "Why do men always tell a woman to stay put anyway? What makes you think I'm safer all by myself in the dark than following you?"

Ignoring her indignant question, Tucker pulled her inside the barn, warning her to keep her voice down.

"Everything looks peaceful, and the barn is clean and dry. Even though there's a strong horse smell, I haven't seen anything that looks like a horse. I don't know about you, but I'd just as soon not awaken the people who live here tonight. Maybe in the morning we can get one of them to take us to the nearest town where we can rent a car."

Kristine agreed with him. If Morrell did show up, as frightening as that sounded, it would be best if the farmer and his family were left out of it. She didn't want any more innocent bystanders involved in what was her own personal battle with the mob.

She wandered around inside the barn, checking out the horse stalls and looking for anything she thought they might be able to use for warmth that night. Though the barn wasn't warm and toasty inside, at least there wasn't a bitter wind with the threat of snow in it howling around their ears.

Kristine learned that there were four horse stalls in all. And, as Tucker had said, they were all empty. But she discovered a couple of well-worn saddles and all the paraphernalia needed to care for the animals.

"Look what I've managed to locate," she called suddenly in delight.

Tucker pivoted on his heel and strode toward her. In her hand she clutched two striped blankets. Horse blankets. He wrinkled his nose at their scent.

"Beggars can't be choosey," she told him defensively. "And at least we won't freeze tonight. We have blankets and a light. Now all we need is a bath—" she sighed longingly "—and something hot to drink."

What a pathetic creature she looked with her dyed black hair hanging in wet, muddy clumps around her small pale face. Dark circles ringed her eyes, and her lips were pinched blue with the cold. But as Tucker's eyes took all of that in, he felt something in his stomach curl into a tight ball and found that he could not sustain her glance.

"I can't provide either the tub or the hot drink, but I can make us up a place to sleep in the hayloft," he answered thickly.

The loud clatter of rain on the roof drowned out any reply she might have made. With the flashlight clutched in one hand and the blankets in the other, she watched him move to the ladder.

"Are you coming?" He paused halfway up to look down at her. She was standing half-inside one of the stalls.

"Not just yet," she replied. "I refuse to sleep in this grime."

"So what are you planning to do? Take a shower in the rain?"

"Not quite, but close." She flashed him a grin over one shoulder and called out, "Leave me one of the blankets, please."

Tucker shrugged and tossed one down to her. If she was crazy enough to attempt bathing in these freezing temperatures, it was none of his business. And in any case she wouldn't have listened if he had tried to talk her out of it.

When he was out of sight, Kristine took the bucket she had found in one of the stalls and opened the back door to the barn. She knew better than to attempt a full bath in these circumstances and in freezing temperatures. But a little wash wasn't out of the question. She proposed catching enough of the rain falling outside in abundance to remove at least a part of the accumulated grime from her hands and face. Then she discovered a tall rain barrel full of water, sitting outside against a corner of the building.

Kristine laughed to herself gleefully. She remembered using rainwater as a child back in Illinois to wash her hair in because it made it soft and shiny. It appeared as though perhaps someone still used it these days despite the fear of whatever pollution there might be scattered about in the air to contaminate it.

Dipping her bucket into the barrel, she went back inside and closed the door. It could hardly be called a bath—without benefit of soap, washcloth or towel—but at least she would feel cleaner. And the cool water on her bruised forehead would help to relieve some of its soreness.

When she was finished, she made her way carefully up the narrow wooden steps to the loft. There she found Tucker still bent to his self-appointed task, though he appeared to have finished, from what she could see as she stepped from the top of the ladder and into the loft.

She kept her presence a secret for a few moments longer and watched as he sat back on his heels to admire his handiwork. She saw that he hadn't taken the time to rub the rain from his hair and it had dripped down his back, making a dark wet stain on his jacket.

As her eyes traveled over his form, she realized, with a little shock of surprise, that he had taken the time to remove his boots and socks. And then she saw why. She wasn't the only one sporting a souvenir from their jaunt in the wilds of Illinois. There were red, raw places worn on the heels of both of Tucker's feet.

Her glance covered the long bony feet and high, narrow arches. She had never before thought of feet as being sexy. But a funny little bump at her insides made her reevaluate that opinion.

"I spread one of the blankets over the straw," Tucker spoke without turning around. "Because it's itchy next to the skin. You can put the other blanket over you and pile the straw on top of that for added warmth."

He paused a moment as though considering his next words, or their effect on her. "We'll have to share again, since there are only two blankets. I hope that won't be a problem—" His voice faltered abruptly as he turned and his eyes fell on her figure.

Kristine stood, holding the lantern in one hand and her jacket in the other. A yellow-and-green-striped blanket was wrapped around her middle, leaving bare shoulders to rise alluringly from its top edge. Long, shapely calves and thighs angled up from the other edge of the blanket, making it obvious that she wore little or nothing beneath its folds.

"I washed some of the mud off," she explained, feeling awkward under his unblinking stare.

"There's a rain barrel out back of the barn—the water was cold—but I feel better now. You should try some of it on your sore feet. . . ."

Tucker turned abruptly back to the pallet, staring at the blanket's blue-and-green design. But all he could see were Kristine's shapely shoulders, appearing creamy yellow in the light from the lantern, their beautiful contours exposed to his hungry gaze.

"You can keep both blankets," he muttered. "I'll be perfectly fine with my jacket."

"Oh, but—" Kristine protested. He was as wet and bedraggled as she had been. "I'll put my—"

Tucker got to his feet, his head almost touching the loft ceiling and pushed quickly past the startled woman.

"Where are you going?" she asked as he started down the ladder toward the lower barn.

"To soak my feet in cold water, and my soft head, as well," he muttered half beneath his breath. He'd asked for this. He'd accepted the responsibility and all it entailed by agreeing to help her. "Get some sleep. It must be morning already, and we need to be out of here at first light," he reminded her tersely.

With an unhappy knot in the pit of her stomach, Kristine watched his head disappear. She had thought they'd made some progress in their relationship, but he was proving her wrong. Just once she wished they could talk about things, get whatever it was that bugged him about her out in the open and discuss it. Maybe then they could approach something like understanding—even friendship.

After he left, she tried lying down in the one blanket she had wrapped around her and leaving the other for Tucker when—if—he returned. But the straw poked and scratched at her skin, making her itch all over. She tried wearing her jacket, but it was too damp and clammy. It made her feel as though she were wrapped in wet cotton and caused her to shiver continuously.

Finally she tried lying on the other blanket, as Tucker had advised, and putting the straw over the one wrapped around her otherwise naked form. But that proved to be no better. She came to the conclusion that she must be allergic to straw.

Sitting on her knees, diligently picking straw off the blanket covering her, a sharp sound alerted her to the fact that she was no longer alone. She glanced up and over her shoulder just as Tucker spoke.

"Here." He held a soft blue bundle out to her. "I forgot all about this until I opened my jacket downstairs and there it was. I stuffed a couple of shirts and a pair of jeans from my suitcase inside my jacket before setting the fire," he explained.

Kristine reached for the shirt, but pulled back as the blanket around her began to slip. Silently Tucker moved to stand over her, offering his assistance. Bending slightly at the waist, he held the shirt for her to slip her arms into.

First one, then the other arm was covered in soft blue chambray. The air in the loft was heavy with a silence Kristine could feel beating against her eardrums. She kept her eyes lowered, but when he didn't immediately let loose his grip on the shirt's collar at either side of her chin, she couldn't keep from looking up into his face.

As their eyes met, she saw the battle being waged inside him. His jaw worked, his hands tightened on the shirt. She thought she could detect a light sheen of perspiration on his upper lip—or perhaps it was moisture from his bath.

Her heart stilled, lurched, then began beating at an alarming rate. He appeared almost angry about something. Was he angry with her because of this night's happenings? The ever-present specter of Vincent Spinelli loomed over them. Could she ever blot his memory from her mind?

The chill air around them began to vibrate with a static electricity. She watched him warily as he hardly seemed to breathe. Kristine moved uncomfortably under the silver-gray eyes, knowing she—and not he—would be responsible for the outcome of the next few minutes. There was a darkness in the expression on his face that she read without difficulty. He wanted her. Would he take her without her consent?

In her agitated state, Kristine forgot about the blanket loosely tucked beneath her arms. She shifted beneath his gaze, knowing what was going to happen if she didn't put a stop to it. The blanket came loose, preempting whatever she had in mind to stop the proceedings. The extraordinary eyes above her began to blaze and then glow as they followed the blanket's slow descent past the tips of her breasts down to her waist.

Tucker lowered to his knees, still gripping the front of her shirt, drawing her slowly to meet him. His gaze traveled her face, across her cheek and chin, settling on her mouth. He remembered its softness and warmth, its tentative invitation. And he remembered too how he had rejected it earlier that day, promising himself he'd never get that close to her ever again.

Wrenching his eyes from her lips, they moved downward to the creamy valley between her full, rounded breasts. Without planning it, his hands began to move, drawing the shirt back, slowly exposing the pale, smooth flesh to his avid gaze.

"No," Kristine's hands covered his, halting their progress.

Tucker's hot eyes jerked to her face. Their glances met, locked and did battle.

"Why not?" he asked in a deep, dark voice. "Isn't this the natural, foregone conclusion to this night? Isn't this why you came up here naked except for the blanket?"

With each word, his fists bunched tighter on the shirt, drawing her a fraction closer to his heaving chest.

"The only foregone conclusion I know is that if you don't let go of me, you're going to be sorry. I wore the blanket because my clothes were wet and covered in mud," she said angrily. "Now take your hands off me."

"And if I don't," he countered, "what will you do? Slap my face?"

"No," she whispered, "I'll use this."

Tucker felt the cold shock of sharp steel against the unprotected flesh of his ribs. His glance dropped quickly to the knife she held firmly in one small, determined hand, then traveled back up to meet her stormy dark eyes.

Leaning forward, his flesh pressing tautly against the knife point, his breath fanning her face, Tucker whispered, "Use it if you dare. It won't be the first time I've felt the bite of steel between my ribs."

The words brought to mind a vivid picture of what prison life must have been like. And suddenly she knew she couldn't use the knife. She didn't want to hurt him. But she held on to her resolve for a moment longer, knowing only that she wanted the violence to end. What she needed this night was understanding, sympathy, comfort—

Love? It had nothing at all to do with what she wanted from him. She liked him well enough, she told herself, then qualified it with—sometimes. What she needed, what they both needed right now was comfort from each other.

The knife grew heavy in her hand. The glitter in the gray eyes holding hers became the glitter of cold fire. Her wrist drooped, the knife lowered. Tucker took it from her unresisting fingers and threw it away from them into the straw.

With deliberate slowness, he slid the shirt from her shoulders, touching soft, moist lips to her skin. He felt the slight shudder she gave as she raised her shoulder for his touch, and the slight moan his kisses drew from her lips fired his loins.

It had been so long—too long—since he'd touched a woman in this way. Too long since he'd felt the need. His mouth scorched a path up her shoulder to her long slender neck, his tongue tasting the dewy softness of delicate skin. He pressed closer. Lord, it had been so long he'd forgotten the taste, the scent, the sound of a woman as she gave in to a man—and met him passion for passion.

Wrapping a hand in the tangled curls, pulling her head back, he looked into her face. Her eyes were closed, but there was an expression there he recognized. She wanted it, too. She wanted all he could give her. And he was about to give her his all.

Capturing her mouth beneath his, he drank of her sweetness; sweetness that if given time might have replaced the bitterness inside him. Her body vibrated like a finely tuned instrument in the hands of a master musician. And he knew he'd play this melody to its bittersweet end.

Tucker lowered her back onto the blanket, eager to know her in the fullest sense of the word. Easing himself down on top of her, his hip bones grinding gently against hers, a low groan escaped tight lips. A thirst had been growing inside him, he admitted to himself, since he'd first laid eyes on her, a thirst for release from his own self-imposed celibacy.

Kristine drank in the comfort of his nearness. She felt wrapped in an invisible warmth, and the building emotions, wrought beneath his lips and hands, melted her resolve to seek only comfort. She couldn't miss the musky scent of him as he moved over her, his weight a welcome burden creating a hot ache low in her body that grew steadily to insurmountable proportions.

Trailing kisses over her face, down one bare shoulder to her breasts, Tucker paused to take the puckered nipple of one soft globe into his mouth. His tongue slowly tantalized the bud that had swollen to its fullness, while at the same time he removed the blanket from between them. Kristine lifted her hips to assist him, feeling the rough dampness of his jeans against belly and thigh replace the coarse fibers of the blanket.

Tucker's fingers moved unsteadily to the snap at the top of his jeans. He quivered at the sudden touch of cold fingers alongside his and stayed his own hand. His breathing became ragged as he felt Kristine unfasten the first button on his jeans.

Neither of them was prepared for what happened next. His body stiffened abruptly, shuddered once and then went still.

A rough masculine cheek lay against the softness of one breast. No one moved, hardly seemed to breathe, for several long, taut moments. And then Tucker pressed away from Kristine and sat up. He couldn't look at her, so he turned his body stiffly aside and stared down at the flickering glow of the lantern's flame.

Kristine watched his averted profile with sympathy. Obviously his need had been great. Being a nurse, she knew it wasn't unusual in cases such as his, when there had been a prolonged period of abstinence. Surely he realized that. She also knew instinctively that he wouldn't appreciate her comments or understanding about his problem just now.

Perhaps there was one way to ease the tension between them and prove to Tucker she too was human. And like all human beings she made mistakes, but her last one had been a real whopper.

"About a year ago I was working nights in the emergency room of a hospital in Dallas. One night a man was brought in suffering from a knife wound to the chest. I was the first one to attend him.

"He was bleeding profusely, and he was frightened but trying not to show it. I thought he was being brave. I stayed with him until he went to surgery. He was conscious most of the time, and once he asked my name." Kristine paused, but Tucker gave no indication that he was even listening. She continued.

"After he left my immediate care, I never expected to hear from him again. Patients are like that. They form a quick attachment to anyone who helps them, but quickly forget it once they're out of danger. That's the way it should be. It's something everyone who works in the medical field expects and understands.

"But this particular patient began to send me flowers and little gifts. I sent everything back except the flowers. And then he called and asked me out. At first I declined, though I was flattered. But he kept on calling, and the gifts kept on coming, becoming more expensive all the time.

"Finally I consented to go out with him. I figured, one time and he'd be over his infatuation. But as the evening progressed, I found that I enjoyed his rather dry wit and gallant manners. We had a good time together. I accepted another date, and another, until I was spending all my spare time with him.

"He flattered me very chance he got, and told me how much he admired and envied my ability to save human life. I was very stupid—I believed what he told me—believed in his naïveté and in his awe for my profession. And ultimately, I made the biggest mistake of my life and believed in his professed love for me.

"It wasn't until later—much later—that I realized it was only because I'd helped to save *his* life that he felt so indebted to me. He felt he owed me something. And he once told me that he always payed his debts—all of them—even the bad ones."

She hesitated, this next was hard for her to admit, but she was going to be honest with him.

"I was blinded to his true nature by the money he lavished on me. I guess I wanted my share of the good things in life and didn't want to look too closely at where they were coming from. When I finally took the blinders off, it was too late."

Kristine touched gentle fingers to the hard ridge of Tucker's spine. She felt him quiver ever so lightly, but he didn't move away from her touch. After a moment, she brought her story to its unhappy conclusion.

"I married him." She waited for a reaction, but Tucker maintained his stony silence.

"Within a short few weeks, I knew without a doubt that the man I had married was a gangster." She laughed without humor. "I don't know if that's the correct term for them these days." She shrugged to herself then continued. "Anyway, Vincent had his finger in every dirty deal going in the city. I learned more than I ever wanted to know about the Dallas branch of the family, and how they operate.

"By that time I just wanted out—that's all—I wasn't looking to see Vincent pay for his crimes or anything noble like that. I just wanted out. Does that make me a wicked person?" she asked all at once. "I don't think of myself as being bad or wicked. Anyway, he wouldn't let me go. He said no one walked away from Vincent Spinelli—and lived to tell it.

"I had been told Carl Morrell was Vincent's bodyguard. But he's more than that—he's Vincent's own personal method of revenge. Morrell began following me everywhere I went. I was told by my supervisor at the hospital that they no longer needed my services. My friends began crossing the street to keep from passing too close to me.

"I knew I had to get out—and I knew the only way would be to make Vincent let me go. So, one night when he was gone from the house, I broke into his locked desk and I took some—things."

Tucker pivoted slowly to face her.

"Morrell is after what I took from Vincent's desk. It's my insurance—to see that I make it back home—alive."

"You stole from a Mafia kingpin? And you expected them to just let you go?" he asked incredulously.

"No." She shook her head, shivered and pulled the blanket up around her shoulders. "I just didn't think it would be that hard to get away from them. When I had time to look over the papers I'd taken, I realized what a really evil man I'd married, and I decided it wasn't enough to just get away—he had to be made to pay for what he's done, what he'll continue to do if no one stops him.

"I tried to give the information to one of the cops at the police station in Dallas. He phoned Vincent, with me sitting right across from him. He said a wife couldn't give evidence against her husband, and he pretended to think I was neurotic or paranoid and needed psychiatric help.

"But I managed to get out of there before Vincent arrived. And after that, I stayed away from the cops, because I didn't know which one I could trust. That's when I decided to go back home, to the midwestern town where I was born, to people I could trust."

"You know," Tucker spoke suddenly, "the cop was right. You can't testify against your own husband in a criminal case—"

"He isn't my husband," she assured him hastily. "That's why I couldn't leave town right away. I was getting a divorce. It took sixty days—and Vincent didn't even have to appear in court.

"Which he didn't in any case—but Morrell did. I thought I'd lost him by the time I got to the pawnshop. I guess I was wrong—or else *he* outguessed *me*."

Meeting his eyes, eyes a little less distant than when he'd first turned to look at her, she added, "You know something? I really did get into your car by chance. But knowing what I know now—I'd do it again—only this time on purpose."

He didn't realize he was reaching for her until he felt the smooth softness of one cheek cupped in the large rough palm of his hand. He could offer her nothing of himself—he had nothing left to give. It had all been burned out of him by hate. But she was one gutsy lady, and for what it was worth, she had his help as long as she needed it, along with his undying respect.

Chapter 6

Carl Morrell stood looking at the footprints in the glare of the flashlight. Smoke from the smoldering car hung in the night air. It was a damned foul night. He hated cold weather and he wasn't particularly fond of rain.

Flashing the light around the immediate area, he saw nothing but emptiness in every direction. They could be anywhere. But he couldn't take the time to look for them even if he had been so inclined. The sound of the explosion might bring others to investigate. And he couldn't take the chance on the cops showing up and asking questions.

Besides, he didn't have to chase them down. He knew they were headed north. And in a little while, Mr. Spinelli would be contacting him with the information he'd gathered about the guy Kristine was traveling with. Either she was going along with him to his destination or the guy was taking her to hers. One way or the other, his boss had things covered.

Someone was already waiting for Kristine in her hometown. And all he had to do was to wait for the dope Mr. Spinelli was ferreting out on the guy with her, and he'd know everything there was to know about him right down to the color of his underwear.

Giving a last look over his shoulder at what was left of the car, he grinned. It looked like this guy, whoever he was, liked to play hardball. Well, that was okay with him—he liked a good fight.

"Wake up." Tucker gave Kristine's shoulder a little nudge. His arm had gone to sleep hours ago, but he'd ignored the sensation and let the exhausted woman sleep.

She had given him a lot to think about with her story. They weren't dealing with just an angry ex-husband here, or even a small-time crook. This Spinelli character had the whole crime syndicate and their resources at his disposal. And this man Morrell who was following them was every bit as bad as he'd had him pegged to be. He was a Mafia hit man, without a doubt.

"Hey, come on, it's time to get a move on." He shook her shoulder again, causing the hair lying across her forehead to bounce. He would have liked to stay where he was, basking in the warmth of her body. But that idea was dangerous, too, as he well knew from last night's fiasco. It was a good thing, he suspected, that they hadn't actually made love. Because if he ever did make love to her, he feared it would quickly become a habit, one he'd find very hard to break.

Tucker watched as Kristine lifted a negligent hand and pushed at the hair on her forehead. Opening her eyes slowly, she glanced in surprise at his face so close to her own, then remembering, smiled. Blinking sleepily, she gave a mighty yawn and groaned.

"What time is it? It feels like the middle of the night."

"I don't know exactly, but I heard the rooster crowing in the chicken house across the yard. It must be about five-thirty or six, I guess." He saw the cut and bruise above her right eye and asked, "When did you do that?"

She touched the area lightly, winced and explained. "In the accident, when we hit the tree. It's all right," she assured him, seeing the concerned look on his face.

"You know, you just may have a shiner by the end of the day," he murmured thoughtfully, seeing how the bruising extended down below her eyebrow and across her eyelid.

"I've never had a black eye before. I hope I like it." She grinned widely. And for a second she thought he'd flash her an answering smile, but he sobered immediately and, rolling away from her, sat up.

Kristine jerked the blanket more firmly around her and darted a bleary-eyed look at her surroundings. The flame in the lantern was still burning brightly. A couple of hay forks hung side by side in brackets on the wall, and a pair of worn work gloves lay on top of a pile on the straw. All at once she was overcome by a feeling of panic as thoughts of the package came to mind, and then she relaxed as she remembered. Her clothes were spread out to dry over the rails of one of the stalls downstairs. And the package was safely hidden.

Tucker moved away from where Kristine lay and, placing hands on hips, bent from side to side, then back and forth. The night spent on the hard floor, even with the straw to cushion it, had made his bones ache and brought home to him the fact that he was no longer the skinny, homeless kid who had spent many a night sleeping under the stars after climbing outside whatever place his present foster parents had stuck him in to sleep at night.

It had been years, too, since he'd shared a bed with a woman, holding her as he'd held Kristine during the night. That thought brought to mind pictures created by his unsatisfied longings and caused the normal male reaction. Embarrassed to have her know what was happening to him, especially after his faux pas of a few hours ago, he stepped hurriedly toward the wide double doors that opened outside to allow the dropping of hay down to the animals below. The blast of cold air flowing over his tall frame as he opened them instantly cooled his ardor.

Taking a deep breath, he looked up at the sky. It appeared as though the rain had passed for now at least. The sky was an allover gray, but in the east, it appeared lighter. Maybe, if luck had decided to finally smile down on them, they might even see a little sunshine later in the day.

A light going on in one of the upstairs windows of the house across the yard drew his attention. The farmer and his family were beginning to stir. Good, they could get on with their travels earlier than he'd hoped. Morrell would no doubt be lying in wait somewhere along the road, but if they got an early enough start, they might be able to slip past him without him knowing it.

"I've been thinking," he spoke without preamble, startling Kristine into a fuller awareness by the serious sound of his voice.

"Yes." She sat up straighter, feeling chilled by the cold air pouring in from outside the big double doors at which he stood.

"I think you should get rid of that package you have as soon as possible. While it's in your possession, your life isn't worth a plugged nickel, considering who wants it." He wondered where it was at the moment? He knew for a fact it wasn't on her person.

"Right," she agreed with him. "So what do you suggest I do with it?"

Her joints were stiff, and her whole body felt like one massive bruise from the accident and her tumble into the creek. Her mind just didn't seem to want to function this morning. She gave a convulsive shiver. She couldn't ever remember feeling as cold as this, as though the cold originated in her bone marrow and spread outward from there.

Tucker closed the heavy doors and barred them before answering. "I think you should let me have it."

"No way." She shook her head vehemently, very much alert all at once. "It's my responsibility—I'll see that it gets into the right hands—"

"You didn't let me finish." All at once he was on his haunches beside her, hard hands gripping her stiff shoulders. "You don't understand, my brother is a cop. He'll see that it gets to the proper authorities."

Kristine digested that piece of surprising information for a moment in silence and then asked, "Where? Where is he a cop?"

"St. Louis. And in case you're wondering, he's honest."

Kristine met his glance head-on. "If he's your brother, I trust him."

"He's my foster brother actually." He saw the question in her dark eyes and added, "But that's another story. If you agree, I could be in St. Louis in a couple of hours."

"How? Have you forgotten you don't have any transportation?"

"I haven't forgotten anything. But, somehow, I'll see that the package gets there undamaged and into my brother's hands."

"All right," she agreed, "under one condition—I go, too. I have to see you put it in your brother's hands."

Tucker's fingers tightened on her arms. His eyes searched her face. "I thought you trusted me?" She had told him her secrets in the night. Was she regretting those confidences in the light of day?

"I do," she said. "I do trust you. But it's still my responsibility. I won't rest easy until I know—I see that it's placed in the right hands."

"Okay." He gave in without a fight. Kristine eyed him with one raised brow. That was unlike the man she was coming to know.

"We go as far as St. Louis together," he continued. "After that, the deal we made is still in effect. We part company, no strings attached. I have some business to take care of—alone. My brother will see you get home safely from St. Louis."

"Your business—does it have anything to do with that gun you carry?"

Tucker let her go abruptly and got to his feet. "And no questions asked. That's part of the deal—take it—or leave it."

With his back facing her, he waited for her decision. He wouldn't admit even to himself that he could accept only one answer. He knew he wouldn't walk away and let her try making it on her own. Because he knew how far she'd get.

"Deal," her voice came softly from behind.

Tucker pivoted slowly to find her standing a few inches away. Their eyes met, and he wanted very badly to say something, anything to make her understand that he would take good care of her—see she stayed healthy until this was settled. But there were no words, none he cared to speak.

Pushing past her, he muttered harshly, "Get dressed. I'll go introduce myself to our hosts and see if we can get a ride into town."

After he'd left her, Kristine stood for a moment, thinking about all that he'd said and what had not been said. He was still determined to keep his secrets from her even though she had laid her own soul bare for him.

She had, however, gathered one new piece of information that she hadn't known before. He had a brother—a foster brother—a cop, one who lived in St. Louis. Perhaps after meeting this brother of his, she would better understand the man, a thing she was finding increasingly important to do.

Tucker was nowhere in sight when she descended the stairs from the loft and found her clothes. They were stiff with the cold and mud. It was all she could do to force herself to don the jeans. She left the sweater where it was. The shirt she had slept in, the one belonging to Tucker, would do nicely with her jeans. And when she was dressed, she removed the package from its hiding place and anchored it beneath her breasts as before.

Tucker and the farmer came looking for her a short time later. She was introduced to Silas Nickols, a friendly man who appeared to be somewhere in his late fifties or early sixties. He told her his wife was fixing a hot breakfast and she had best come on into the house and get the chill out of her bones before she turned plumb blue with it.

Inside the kitchen of the house, Ida Nickols stood at a big black-and-white gas range. She was turning slices of ham with a large pronged fork, but stopped to smile at Kristine during the introductions. A large motherly woman with gray hair piled in a bun atop her head, she clicked her tongue as they told her they'd been in an accident and lost their car. She told Kristine they should have awakened them in the night, and they could have had a nice warm bed to sleep in instead of that drafty barn.

Kristine's mouth watered as she watched the woman lift fluffy brown-topped biscuits from the oven. Taking the cup of coffee Mr. Nickols offered, she sipped it slowly, savoring its warmth both inside and out.

While Silas kept watch on the food, Ida took Kristine upstairs for a hurried shower and to find something for her to wear while she threw the sweater and jeans into the washing machine. When they came back downstairs, Kristine saw Tucker was wearing a pair of faded jeans a size too small and a pair of brown house slippers his host had lent him. She tried, but found it difficult to keep her eyes off the way he filled the jeans.

When they were all seated around the oval-shaped wooden table and grace had been said, they heaped their plates high with the mouth-watering food. Kristine had never been a breakfast person. When working nights, she tried not to eat before going to bed because she didn't think it was healthy. But her plate was as full as Tucker's when she finally began to eat.

Once the edge had been taken off their hunger, Tucker got her attention and began to speak.

"Mr. Nickols has kindly offered to take us into town after breakfast. He says there isn't anywhere to rent a car, but he knows someone who might sell us one."

"What about the old blue pickup out in the yard," Kristine asked, accepting a second cup of coffee from the older woman.

Tucker raised a brow and looked across at the other man. "What about it, sir? Is it for sale?"

"Well, I don't know—"

"Oh, go on, Pa, you know Davey wants to get rid of it," his wife encouraged him. "Our son is in the air force," she explained to Tucker and Kristine. "And he's over in Germany right now. Gonna be gone for two years. And I know he won't want that old thing when he gets back."

Her eyes widened, and her hands fluttered. "I don't mean the truck don't work good. I just know Davey was talking about getting one of them new sporty cars before he left, that's all."

Kristine looked at Tucker. *What do you say,* her eyes asked. He gave an imperceptible shrug and turned to ask the other man a few questions about the truck.

A couple hours later, Kristine and Tucker waved goodbye to the Nickols. A container of hot coffee rested on the seat between them. And at Kristine's feet sat a box of sandwiches and fruit, along with the biscuits and ham left over from breakfast.

"Those are good people," she commented as the older man and woman faded from sight.

"Yeah, it seems there are a few left in the world, after all."

"You really think this idea of going to your brother is a good one?" she asked into the silence that fell after his cynical observation.

Tucker stared out the window without answering. He had more than one reason for wanting to go to St. Louis, though originally he hadn't intended going there at all. This might be the last chance for him to spend any time with his brother. And he wanted to hear firsthand everything Bob could tell him about what Jack and Sylvia had been doing over the years.

Bob had followed the couple when they moved to St. Louis shortly after Tucker's trial, his purpose being to keep an eye on them and to try to find any new evidence that would prove Tucker innocent of the fraud charges. He'd kept track of them when they'd later moved to Chicago, and hopefully he would ultimately be able to place the blame for what had been done where it really belonged, on Jack Arnold's shoulders.

"I think it's the only thing you can do," Tucker answered slowly. "Have you considered the possibility that Spinelli might have connections in the town where you grew up?"

Taking his eyes off the road, he cast a quick glance in her direction, meeting the stricken look in her large brown eyes. Evidently that possibility hadn't occurred to her at all. She still didn't comprehend the magnitude of what she had done—who she had taken on, when she took on a man who made his living in organized crime.

Kristine saw a hint of something in the gray eyes she had never thought to see there. Fear? For her? Because she was naive enough to believe that the people she had known as a child would be honest and have no part in Spinelli's type of activities?

With her eyes focused outside, she pushed all thoughts from her head except one. It was almost over. Soon she would be able to live a normal life like everyone else. She wouldn't have to constantly peer over her shoulder, expecting, fearing, to see Carl Morrell's ugly face leering at her.

Her eyes became heavy, and as she drifted in the twilight between sleep and wakefulness, she recalled last night's happenings. She'd wondered if she and Tucker would ever make any progress in their relationship—at least toward friendship. Well, she had her answer now. Tucker wouldn't have offered to see her to safety and involved his brother in doing it if he still thought of her as he had in the beginning.

Sneaking a peek at him, she hid a slight smile and relaxed back against the seat, closing her eyes. He might not know it yet, but he was beginning to care about her. He probably wouldn't admit it if confronted, but all the same it was true.

A flash of memory of what it was like to feel his lips on hers, sliding down the naked expanse of her shoulders and across her breasts, made her squirm in the seat. Friendship—was that enough for her? Then why did she burn at the thought of his kisses? And long to feel his arms around her even now, to hear words of love being whispered in his deep, velvety voice next to her ear?

Carl Morrell listened to Vincent Spinelli explain exactly what he wanted him to do and murmured his understanding.

Replacing the car phone, he started the powerful engine and pulled onto the road. So, St. Louis, that's where they were, no doubt, headed. It didn't matter that he had no idea when they had left or how they were getting there. He had a name and an address, and that's all he needed.

It seemed Tucker Winslow had a brother living in St. Louis, a cop. It figured he'd head in that direction, especially if Kristine had spilled her guts to him. And knowing the stupid bitch, she would. Well, no matter, he sure as hell wasn't afraid of a cop. Cops could be had, like hookers, for the right price.

Somehow he hadn't been surprised to learn that Winslow had done time in the joint. And in some small way, it made Morrell think a little more of him. It certainly made him more of a challenge. But one he was confident of being able to handle.

And as far as Kristine Stevens was concerned, he smacked his lips in anticipation. She was all his, once the merchandise had been taken care of. He'd take his time with her, let her know what it was like being with a real man for a change, enjoy himself thoroughly before he disposed of her once and for all.

Chapter 7

Two hours later Kristine straightened in her seat and stared out the window at the St. Louis arch, the Gateway to the West. They were on the loop that circled the downtown area and were passing right beside it.

They had traveled the last ninety-five miles in total silence, perhaps because they were both beginning to realize that their time together was drawing to an end. Once the package of information was turned over to Tucker's brother, Kristine would be going home to Danville, and he would be on his way alone.

Kristine glanced at Tucker's wrist. The bracelet on it was gleaming brightly in a shaft of sunlight. Did the woman Sylvia have anything to do with the business he said he had to take care of? Did the gun?

She knew it was none of her business, but she couldn't help wondering if it had anything to do with his recent stay in prison. Even though he was helping her and though she

Silhouette Sensation
KRISTIN JAMES
Worlds Apart
Silhouette Sensation
ANNE STUART
Rancho Diablo
Silhouette Sensation
NORA ROBERTS
Tonight and Always
Silhouette Sensation
ELDA MINGER
Spike Is Missing

had shared a bit of her past with him, Tucker Winslow was still a complete enigma to her.

On the edge of the city, Tucker stopped at a phone booth to place a call to his brother. Kristine watched him hunch his shoulders against the cold as he talked on the phone. She could see his face, and the controlled joy expressed there made her chest feel tight and achy.

It almost seemed as though he was afraid to allow himself to feel anything, even though he and his brother evidently shared a special bond. She found herself envying the other man. Anyone on the receiving end of Tucker Winslow's love was a very fortunate individual indeed, she had come to realize. He was a man who wouldn't give his love lightly, but once given, she was certain it would last for a lifetime.

The idea made her sad, because it meant that Sylvia would be assured a permanent place in Tucker's heart, as well as his thoughts.

"Bob didn't have much time to talk," Tucker said as he entered the car and took his place behind the wheel. "He was on his way out on a call; he works the homicide division. But he asked us to have dinner with him this evening." Sensing something in the atmosphere, but unable to put a name on it, he continued, feeling somewhat uneasy.

"If it's all right with you, I think we should get a room somewhere and get some rest. I could use a hot shower and a few hours of shut-eye."

Kristine nodded her agreement without speaking. There was a very large lump in her throat just now. She was discovering that she didn't want to say goodbye to this man, not in a few hours' time, not in a day or two—not at all. She'd grown used to being with him, and she knew from experience that she could depend on him to watch out for her, to see her through the rough times. He gave her a feeling of security, and that was something she had had too little of recently.

Even though he had taken her emotions on a roller coaster ride that veered from anger to empathy and finally to love, she had done the second most idiotic thing she'd ever done in her entire life and fallen head over heels in love with the man. First a gangster, and now an ex-con. Maybe she really did have a death wish.

Unaware of the turmoil of thoughts running through his silent companion's head, Tucker drove down a tree-lined road west of the city. They passed a couple of motels—similar to the one in which Kristine had been cornered by Morrell—and came to a gravel driveway down which were a group of scattered cabins. Tucker took the turn and stopped before the cabin marked Office.

Kristine waited in the truck while he went inside and paid. All at once she felt nervous and anxious about spending more time alone in his company. She might have realized her feelings for him were deeper than she'd imagined, but Tucker was nowhere close to feeling anything like love for her—or was he?

Tucker came out, climbed into the truck and drove them down the lane that led to the very last cabin, set off by itself. The rear of it faced an empty field.

"I figured it might be wise to keep a low profile even after we get rid of the stuff," he explained, in case she had any questions about his choice of accommodations.

"Right," she answered, climbing from the truck and following his tall figure inside.

Her eyes darted around the room but kept coming back to the one thing in the room that she couldn't ignore. The bed. One large, empty bed. Was he expecting her to share that with him? Or had he decided to stay with his brother while he was in town? It was a logical assumption to make, since apparently he and his brother hadn't spent much time together in recent years.

"If you don't mind," Tucker spoke from close behind, startling her. "I'll take my shower first, while you look around." He kept his eyes directed somewhere above her shoulder as he spoke. But even after he finished speaking, he made no move to follow through with his plan.

A certain tension had been building between them all day, and now the room rang with a silence that stretched taut nerves to the breaking point. The air inside the small cabin became thick. Tucker wondered if it was him? Was he the one stirring things up because he had begun to feel the bonds between them growing tighter, despite his trying to beat them down with logic?

Again he reflected upon the fact that the wise thing would have been to put her out when he first found her in his car. That would have ended it then and there. But deep down inside he was glad he hadn't, though he still wanted—needed—to believe that he could walk away from her—when the time came. He had to, if he was going to carry through with his own plans. And in order to do that, he'd have to keep his distance from her, no more letting her get beneath his guard, beneath his skin.

Kristine watched him as he stood half-turned away from her, a taut expression on his face. He hadn't shaved that morning even though Mr. Nickols had offered to lend him a razor, because he'd been in too much of a hurry. The dark beard added a dangerous look to his appearance that made him even more attractive in her eyes.

She remembered her surprise when she had awakened that morning from the forgetfulness of sleep to see his face looming so close to her own. Her first instinct, even despite the shock, had been to lean close and press inviting lips to his.

She felt as though he was waiting right now for her to say or do something, but she was at a loss as to what. A very disconcerting idea began to take root in her brain. From the corner of her eye, she watched Tucker enter the bathroom and shut the door. Her knees gave out all at once, but fortunately the bed was right behind her. She sat down with a bounce.

She had admitted to herself that she was in love with him. Could he have fallen in love with her, too, and not be aware of it? And could that account for the heavy, tense atmosphere between them just now? If so, what should she do about it? She couldn't let him walk away from her in a few hours. Yet something told her he wasn't ready to admit to having any special feelings for her. She was certain he cared about her, but did he love her?

Tucker closed the bathroom door, ripped the shirt from the waist of his jeans and removed boots and socks. And all the while, he stared at the cream-colored floor tiles as though they were alive and he was planning to put an end to that. All he could think about was the fact that it should be easy—staying out of Kristine Stevens's reach. Their time together was nearing its end. She'd go her way, as they had agreed, and he'd go his. What could be simpler than that?

The white-painted door across the room from Kristine flew back on its hinges. Tucker stood there, bare from the waist up, his shoes and socks missing and the top snap of his jeans unfastened.

Kristine's astonished eyes moved from his head down to his bare toes and back, taking note of the clenched fists and flared nostrils, before meeting the tense expression in the turbulent gray eyes.

"It isn't going to work, is it?" His voice sounded resigned. "We're both wondering what it would be like—especially since last night."

She couldn't answer, all she could do was look at him, so handsome, so virile, so in control. Just once, she would like to see him lose that control. For a few moments last night, he had, but only the control over his body's physical reactions. She wanted to see him lose control of his emotions.

In silence he held one hand out to her, the right hand. It was as though he knew that to offer the one encircled by the token of another woman's love would drive her away.

Kristine was on her feet, moving across the carpet without consciously making a decision. Her heart knew, if her mind didn't, that she could no longer refuse this man anything. Perhaps this would make him admit to the love she was certain he was at least beginning to feel for her.

Inside the tiny bathroom, Tucker leaned back against the closed door and stared at her. She looked like a street urchin, a very sexy one. Moving past her, he adjusted the dials on the shower and pulled her inside the enclosure. They stood under the spray, still dressed, staring at each other.

Tucker was the first to move, no longer able to restrain his need to touch her. Placing a hand at either side of her neck, his thumbs resting along her cheekbones, he tilted her head back under the shower's spray. Kristine closed her eyes against the pulsing warmth of the water and felt his lips at her throat. With lips, tongue and teeth, he lifted the moisture from her skin while his lower body, radiating heat like a furnace, pressed against hers.

The urgency with which he touched her sent shivers racing along her spine. She felt the caress of his tongue move up over her chin and cheek and finally around to her mouth. His lips were hard and searching on hers, and they demanded a response she found herself eager to give.

The warm water flowed over their joined heads and down their clothing. In seconds they were both soaked to the skin. Kristine felt the material of her shirt cling to her breasts, making the nipples stand out hard against it. Tucker's hands found the puckered nipples and he rubbed them gently between forefinger and thumb, his body plastered down the length of hers.

The sound of her moans, heard above the noise of the water, filled his ears, causing his heart to jolt against his ribs. As he roused her passion, his own grew hotter, and desire, like a coiled spring, lay tight in his loins.

Kristine's hands moved from his waist to his back, up across moisture-slickened skin, across the muscles of shoulder and back, kneading gently. A painful ache was growing between her thighs as she pressed into him, feeling him harden against her belly.

Tucker trailed kisses from her collarbone down over the wet shirt she wore to one nipple. Taking the nipple, shirt and all, into his mouth, he suckled gently, rubbing the tip of his tongue against the tight bud. Kristine gasped and took hold of his head in both hands. She couldn't stand much more of this—her stomach was churning, and her knees felt weak.

Bringing his face back up to hers, Kristine tasted his lips, touched her tongue to his mouth and felt it open. His tongue stabbed at her lips. She opened her mouth with a small whimper and felt his tongue move into her mouth with an urgent thrust. Kristine molded herself to him, wanting more.

Tucker explored her lean curves beneath the shirt with one hand and, lifting the hair aside, lowered his face to nibble at a sensitive spot below one ear. Kristine shivered and drew him closer, pressing a leg in between both his and rubbing gently.

After a moment of exquisite torture, Tucker drew back. His hands going to the buttons on the shirt she wore, eyes locked on hers, he unfastened them one at a time until none were left.

Kristine watched with bated breath as his eyes, dark with passion, moved down over the exposed skin of her shoulders to the narrow valley between her breasts. And then she closed her eyes and dropped her head back against the wall as his tongue began to stroke at the delicate, quivering flesh.

She was beautiful, exquisitely made, and he wanted her so badly he could hardly contain his need. But he'd promised himself that this time he would go slow, would make it good for both of them.

Kristine's heart fluttered, then began to pound erratically as his bewhiskered cheek gently abraded the tender skin. With a hand at the back of his head, threaded through his dark hair, she pressed him to her. She gloried in the feel of the heat of his driving desire throbbing against the muscles of her belly while her blood raced through her veins like liquid fire.

Her knees became weak and she grabbed at his slick shoulders for support. His lips traveled slowly back from her breasts to her lips. With shaking hands, he lowered the shirt from her shoulders and dropped it to the floor. Drawing her breasts against his chest, the chest hairs tickling her skin, he simply held her, letting the emotions, like the water, spread over and envelope them.

They were both panting now, the small enclosure filled with the sounds of their uneven breathing. The fires they had built in each other raged nearly out of control. She was at the point of begging him to put an end to her agony when he suddenly pulled back and tore at the remaining clothes and the package she had strapped on her body. Then his hands quickly worked the wet denim from his own. Hauling her into his arms, with her legs wrapped tightly around his waist, he entered her with a sharp thrust.

With both hands cupping her buttocks, he pressed her back against the wall, his lips burning her mouth while his body claimed her for his own.

Kristine's arms encircled his shoulders as she rode the tide of his passion. Throwing her head back and moaning in ecstasy, she soared higher and higher as she attained peak after peak of pleasure.

The sound of Tucker's excitement filled her ears, and the tempo of the rhythm increased abruptly. A slow tremor began somewhere deep inside, passing from one to the other. Neither knew where it began, and it seemed as though it would never end, as the hot tide of passion consumed them both until finally, slowly, it came to an exquisite, awesome, shuddering climax.

When it was over, Kristine hung there, suspended between heaven—and Tucker—her back pressed against the tiles of the wall. Gasping, panting, she felt him release her slowly, sliding her legs down his hips till her feet touched the wet floor of the shower drain.

And he stood with closed eyes, head pressed against her shoulder, chest heaving, feeling himself at the point of physical exhaustion.

Drawing away from her at last, his eyes avoiding her glance, he stepped out of the shower enclosure and grabbed a towel. Handing it back inside to her, he took another and quickly dried himself on it. He had to get out of there and fast. Because he knew that what he was feeling would show on his face and he couldn't take the chance of her seeing it.

Kristine switched off the shower and wrapped the towel around her aching body. When she stepped out into the room, it was to see Tucker's back disappear around the door. She followed him slowly, stopping in the room as she saw him fasten his denims and grab his jacket from the chair by the door.

"Where are you going?" she asked softly in a bewildered voice.

"I need a breath of fresh air," he told her without turning around. "I'll bring some coffee back and something to eat." He paused for a moment at the open door as though there was something more he wanted to say, but left without another word.

Her eyes went automatically to the clock radio beside the bed. It was not yet noon, but she felt as though hours had passed, whole days, since they had left the farmhouse in Illinois earlier that morning.

Kristine reentered the bathroom and quickly finished her shower, then towel-dried her hair. Time passed and with every sound heard from outside, she expected Tucker to reappear. And when an hour had passed without his coming back, she crawled, bare, beneath the covers and huddled there. She had been a fool to think their making love would change Tucker's attitude toward her. Tucker Winslow was a man being haunted by his past. And Kristine feared she had no chance with him at all until the ghosts were laid to rest and he was freed from their influence.

* * *

Tucker tracked his brother down at the fourth precinct station house shortly before noon. Two men, a black man and a Chicano, directed him to his brother's desk, located in a corner of the long, narrow room. Tucker passed down the aisle of desks, phones ringing in the background, until he came to the one flanked by a window on one side and a tall green metal filing cabinet on the other. No one was there, so he sat down to wait.

It was only a couple of minutes later that the medium-tall, red-haired man entered the room with a sheaf of papers in his hands. Someone stopped him, and he listened to what the man had to say with his eyes on the floor. But almost immediately his head snapped up, and he looked toward the back of the room, a grin breaking across the pleasantly homely face.

"Tuck! By God, you're here!"

His voice boomed down the room as he hurried toward the man waiting with open arms. They hugged unashamedly, slapped each other on the back and hugged again.

No one would have taken them for brothers—there was no similarity in build or feature—but those who knew them understood why they were foster brothers. Tucker's own family had disappeared before he was old enough to know anything about them.

"Tell you what," Bob was speaking. "It's almost one, and I haven't had lunch yet. Let me see if I can get out of here for a while and we'll go to my place for a bite to eat."

"You still hate restaurants?" Tucker asked with a grin.

Bob's face turned a brilliant shade of red, he glanced around, then nodded. "Yeah, I still spill anything that isn't fastened down. Wait here, I'll be right back," he told Tucker, and hurried off.

Tucker watched the other man go with a feeling of pride. The other detectives and some of the uniformed men called out greetings, and one or two stopped him to have a few words of conversation. Bob was the kind of guy you liked instinctively. Or if not right off the bat, then shortly thereafter. Tucker knew, because he had fought the other man's good nature and caring for almost a year as an adolescent.

The first ten years of Tucker's life had been spent creating havoc in one foster home after another, until the age of ten, when he was placed in the home of Madeline, and Robert Linton. They were the parents of one child, Bobby, aged eight. The two boys fought like the proverbial cats and dogs.

Tucker was a wild one, a hellion, he'd never known love and he loved no one. And then one day, Tucker stole some money from Mrs. Linton's purse and spent it on candy, which he refused to share with Bobby. Bobby waited until he was out of the room and took some for himself. His mother caught him with it. And by that time she had discovered the missing money. She laid the blame for the theft at her own son's door in view of the overwhelming evidence of his guilt.

Bobby could have ratted on Tucker, but he didn't, and he took the other boy's punishment, as well. When Tucker learned what had happened, he kept his mouth shut. He didn't thank the other boy, and he didn't own up to being the guilty party, but gradually the whole family noticed a change in him. And by the time his eleventh birthday rolled around, the four were a family.

"You ready?" Bob had returned without Tucker hearing the man's quiet approach.

Tucker looked up and nodded, for a moment still seeing the freckle-faced, carrot-topped boy of a lifetime ago.

"If it's all right with you, we'll take my car and leave yours here for now," Bob said.

Tucker agreed, and they were speeding toward his brother's apartment on the east side of town in a matter of minutes.

"You look peaked," Bob commented as he turned a corner on two wheels, making Tucker grab the door rest for support.

"And you still haven't learned how to drive in town. You think you're still on the open range in Texas, where there isn't anything but cactus and cattle for miles and miles."

In a few minutes they pulled up to a duplex, in a No Parking Zone. Bob stuck a sign stating Official Business in the front window, and they climbed out of the dark blue sedan.

Tucker looked around the modestly furnished, tastefully decorated apartment before following the other man into the kitchen.

"Not bad," he commented, gesturing around the kitchen with all its modern appliances. Bob was a weekend chef. He loved to putter in the kitchen and was an excellent cook.

"Thanks."

"But from the looks of the place," Tucker added, "I'd say you either aren't on the take, or you've got a numbered Swiss account."

Bob turned from where he was placing a casserole in the microwave and studied the other man in silence for a moment. Then without comment he turned back, set the timer and pushed the button. Taking a pitcher of iced tea from the refrigerator, he poured a glass for himself and one for Tucker.

"You said you were traveling with someone—someone in trouble."

Bob gestured for Tucker to sit down at the small round table. He removed two plates, forks, knives and napkins from a cupboard and placed them on the table.

"You want to tell me what's going on?" he asked when Tucker stared down at the place set before him without speaking.

"It's a woman, she was married to a guy back in Texas, a man named Spinelli—"

His brother made a sound and Tucker's eyes jerked to his face. "You know the guy?" he asked with a narrow-eyed glance.

"Not personally." Bob shrugged. "But about six or seven years ago, he was making a name for himself by doing dirty little jobs for the higher-ups in the mafioso. How the hell did you get mixed up with this guy's woman?"

"She isn't his 'woman,' or his wife," Tucker cut in with razor-sharp tones. "She's his ex, and she's in trouble because she took something that could put the guy away for a long time, maybe life, before she left."

"Damn! If she was married to the guy, she has to know these guys play rough. She crazy or what?"

"She's—" Tucker hesitated, at a loss for words to describe her. How could he possibly explain all the things that went into the making of a woman like Kristine? She was a mixture of guts, determination, stubbornness and an odd kind of vulnerability, along with other, more personal characteristics he couldn't bring himself to mention to the other man.

"You care about her?" Bob asked softly.

Tucker's eyes darted to his brother's face and then away again. "I have no interest in her—except in helping her out. I don't like the hired help Spinelli has following her—a guy named Morrell."

"Carl Morrell," the other man supplied as he sat down across from Tucker. "He's another particularly nasty piece of work. He likes to carve people up with knives, especially women. I got to know about him, too, when I was working on the police force in Dallas.

"We had him cold on a rape-murder charge, but something happened to the evidence and he was let go for lack of same."

"Lord!"

The timer went off and Bob placed an appetizing dish of meat, potatoes and vegetables in the center of the table. Adding hard rolls and butter, he told Tucker to dig in.

"You said she—"

"Kristine," Tucker supplied. "Kristine Stevens." He'd never called her that to her face, but he liked the sound of it on his lips.

Bob nodded, his mouth full, swallowed and continued, "You mentioned evidence?"

Tucker stood up and left the table to go into the other room. When he returned he was carrying a scarf-wrapped bundle. He laid it on the table, and they both looked at it for a long silent moment. He'd taken it without Kristine's knowledge. It wasn't that he really thought she'd object, but because at the time of his leaving, he couldn't bring himself to share a conversation with her. He'd just given a part of himself he'd thought long dead and buried, it was too much to expect conversation from him, too.

"You know, she'll either have to change her name and move somewhere far away, or look over her shoulder every minute of the day for the rest of her life once this has been officially accepted," Bob told him.

"I know, but I don't think she realizes that—yet," Tucker added in a low voice.

Bob reached for the packet and opened it carefully. For the next twenty minutes, he didn't touch his food as he read what was inside. And when he put it down, he'd hardly skimmed the surface of what it held. Whistling, he shook his head and looked at his brother.

"This is dynamite stuff. The man must be nuts. It reads like a journal, listing every illegal activity he's been involved in, along with the names of the others involved, since he began with the organization.

"It looks as though he wanted a little insurance of his own. This is enough to get him killed if word should leak out about it to his superiors.

"Not only will Spinelli face a long prison term, but so will a whole lot of others who at the moment appear to be lily-white. And you know, your friend isn't safe even with Spinelli out of the picture. The heads of the organization will want her dead just because she had this in her possession—you too, if it becomes known you had it."

"I'm glad it's finally in your hands and out of mine." Tucker chose to disregard what he'd said about his own safety.

"I'd like to meet this woman," Bob said as he fastened the papers into the envelopes from which they'd come.

"I would like for you to meet her—in fact, I hope you won't mind seeing that she's okay after I leave. It will take some talking on your part, to get her to agree to having her name, her identity, changed."

"I'll see what I can do," Bob promised. Picking up his fork, he pushed the uneaten food around on his plate.

Tucker watched him for a moment, then chided, "Don't play with your food. If you have something to say, say it."

Bob raised worried blue eyes to Tucker's face. "What about you? What are your immediate plans? You're not still planning to go to Chicago?"

A stubborn glint he was familiar with, burned in the gray eyes, turned on his face. Bob knew that look, and it boded no good for whoever was trying to interfere in Tucker's plans.

"You're going, aren't you?"

"Yes, I've waited five years—"

"But what good will it do? We couldn't prove what he'd done five years ago and we still can't prove it. He'd have to stand up in a court of law and admit his guilt before we could get him now."

Tucker rose from the table, his chair scooting halfway across the floor with the abrupt movement.

"I want to confront the bastard just one time—one last time, before it's finally and irrevocably finished."

Bob didn't like the sound of that. Tucker had never been one to forget what was done to, or for, him. If he received kindness, then he gave it in return. But if anyone crossed him . . .

"Are you sure it's Jack Arnold you're going after? Or is it Sylvia?"

Chapter 8

"Look, Bob, I know you don't approve of my going to Chicago. But as the saying goes, you haven't walked in my shoes. You didn't spend the last five years of your life rotting in a stinking jail cell for a crime you didn't commit," he lashed out heatedly. "While someone else reaped the benefits of your life's work."

From the look of unease on Bob's face, Tucker realized he'd better cool it. He was getting too upset for Bob to believe he only wanted a personal interview with Jack Arnold, a chance to denounce him face-to-face. He hated lying to the man seated beside him. They were brothers in every sense of the word except by blood. But some things couldn't be helped no matter how much you regretted doing them. A picture of Kristine standing in the bathroom doorway just before he'd left the motel flashed into his mind, but he shoved it quickly aside.

"I understand more than you think," Bob muttered softly.

Tucker's glance sharpened on the other man's face. Bob knew him better than anyone else, but even Bob couldn't know what he was planning to do in Chicago.

But whether Bob suspected there being any more to Tucker's visit to the Windy City or not, he changed the subject, and they discussed incidents from their childhood. The elder Lintons had passed away almost ten years ago, within months of each other, but both men remembered them with love.

When their meal was finished, Bob told Tucker regretfully that he'd have to get back to the station. He looked forward to meeting the woman Kristine Stevens, and he'd be certain the information in the packet he took with him now reached the proper hands.

The two men parted company outside the police station with a final handshake. Bob promised to keep him informed about what was happening with the information and let him know as soon as he heard anything concrete. However, he warned, it might take a couple of days to get any feedback on what was being done on the Dallas end of things.

That wasn't welcome news to Tucker. He wanted to get Kristine settled as quickly as possible—now more than ever. Memories of their lovemaking drifted through his mind. He'd done his best to choke them off since leaving the motel. He assured himself that they had both wanted it, had both known down deep inside shortly after first meeting that somewhere, sometime, it was bound to happen between them. Well, it had, and that was all there was to it. It was over, and now it was time they got on with their separate lives.

But forgetting was a hard thing to do. Because making love to Kristine was the only thing he'd known worth remembering in more than five years. She was the first woman he'd made love to since Sylvia.

Sylvia. She was one of the most beautiful women he'd ever seen. Even after all this time he could picture her as he'd seen her last, her long jet-black hair swept back from the haughty, regal-looking face and left to flow in loose waves halfway down her back.

She had eyes the color of violets and a figure that outclassed any of the models' displayed on the covers of popular fashion magazines. She possessed a sensuality that was an essential part of her, seemed to hover in the air around her, and she fired his blood as no other woman ever had.

Except for Kristine. What was he to do about Kristine?

The drive back to the cabin where they were staying took more time than was strictly needed, because he traveled the long way around and drove slowly. He was trying to figure out what to say to Kristine once they were face-to-face again.

There was no way he could explain what she had done for him, and it wasn't only the sex. She had given him back a part of himself that had gone missing while he was in prison. In there, he had not been a person, but a faceless number acknowledged only when it was time for roll call or time to take up his work duties. He filled his days and nights with two thoughts and experienced two emotions—hate and revenge.

Kristine had reintroduced him to life, made him suffer through feelings of anger, fear and concern for another human being. She'd taught him to care again. And if things had been different . . .

He couldn't let anything he'd begun to feel for her stop him, not now, not when he was so close. They had shared an exciting adventure together, but the adventure was over. She would be safe under his brother's protection and that of the law. It was time he walked away while he still could....

Damn it! He hadn't had all these doubts before he'd met her. He was doing what was right, making the guilty pay. Ever since he'd accepted the fact that the law either couldn't or wouldn't do anything to rectify its mistake in convicting him of something he hadn't done, he'd planned this. Not even his brother had been able to help him. The law didn't recognize his innocence—or Jack Arnold's guilt.

But Tucker Winslow did. And he intended seeing that justice was served. He couldn't do anything about the wasted years spent in prison, but he could do something about the man who'd put him there. He was judge and jury, and he would be executioner, too. He'd extract one decade from Jack's life for every year of the sentence he had served. Five years, five decades—fifty years—the rest of Jack Arnold's life.

The sign for the cabins came into view, and Tucker turned onto the driveway that wound back to the very last one. His palms began to sweat, and he experienced a feeling of tightness in his chest. Facing Kristine was going to be hard because he sensed she was not the kind of woman to make love with a man she didn't have deep feelings for.

The cabin had two entrances, just like a house. Tucker drove the old blue truck around to the back and parked. He sat there for a few minutes, getting his emotional bearings and taking a careful look around. Because even though his brother had the evidence Kristine had carried with her from Dallas and for all he knew, Morrell might think the two of them were dead, he was still being cautious. Things looked quiet, no different than when he'd left.

He entered the cabin softly, thinking Kristine might be asleep. He needn't have worried though, she was sitting at the mirrored dressing table, brushing her hair. At the sound of his entrance, she turned hastily toward the door.

"Where is it?" Her voice sounded high-pitched, almost hysterical.

Tucker looked puzzled for a moment until he realized she was referring to the information he had given his brother.

"Don't worry." He closed and locked the door. "It's in safe hands. My brother has it—that's where I've been."

Kristine faced the mirror in relief. She didn't want to admit that part—most—of her anxiety had been on his behalf. She'd assumed immediately upon finding the packet gone that he'd taken it to his brother. Her big worry, the one that had grown almost out of proportion as time passed and he didn't put in an appearance, was that he'd done what he'd promised and then gone on—without her.

Would he see the knowledge of how she felt about him in her face? Staring at her overbright eyes and trembling mouth in the mirror, she could see it. Surely he would, too.

Tucker came to stand beside her, looking for a moment at the two of them reflected in the mirror.

"Your hair is lighter," he commented inanely.

"Yes," she agreed, with her eyes on the image of her white fingers gripping the brush.

"I like it better blond." He hadn't intended to say anything personal, but she looked almost scared, and he was trying to reassure her that things were going to be getting back to normal for her shortly. Or as normal as her life would ever be after this, he amended slightly.

Kristine's glance drifted upward, encountering his. Even in the mirror's duplication, his eyes were every bit as compellingly beautiful as when viewed directly. She couldn't tear her glance away.

The room became very still, a waiting quality permeated the air around them, and an invisible web of electrically charged energy began to draw the two closer together.

How could this be? Tucker asked himself, resisting the desire to pull her up into his arms. How could she lure him so completely under her spell with so little effort? She was nothing at all like the type of dark-haired beauty he had always preferred. She didn't reek of sophistication and expensive perfume. She didn't exude feminine wile. Nevertheless he found his hand on her shoulder, exerting pressure to turn her toward him, into his arms.

All the fine thoughts of keeping her out of his life, keeping her from becoming any more involved with him than she already was crumbled to dust when those large soft eyes met his. All he could think about was the reality of making love to her, the soft sound of her sighs as she breathed warmth and life back into his cold heart and barren soul.

His chest felt tight and his breathing became labored. He wanted to make love to her. It had only been a few hours since they had made love for the first time—and he knew he had to have her again, right now.

Kristine closed her eyes at the feel of his palm hot against her shoulder, searing her flesh through the material of her shirt. She'd promised herself she wouldn't let this happen again—not until he had been honest with her.

Not until she knew where she fit into his life—and who Sylvia was, what she meant to him.

She could feel his power flow from his fingertips into her shoulder and throughout her whole body. Despite her misgivings about the other woman, her promises to herself, she wanted him. She wanted him to make love to her again. She wanted to experience the thrill of his body covering hers, filling her with his seed. Her heart stopped at the thought, then jerked in her chest and pounded riotously. She couldn't seem to breathe properly.

She was supposed to be keeping him at arm's length, she was thinking as he lifted her gently from the chair and hauled her almost roughly into his embrace. At arm's length, she almost moaned aloud as she met his brilliant gray glance and felt his breath fan her forehead, cheeks and mouth....

Closing her eyes, raising her hands to his chest, she felt him draw her up onto her toes to meet his kiss. The world stood still as his arms slid around her shoulders, pulling her closer, while her own arms moved up around his neck. His breath filled her mouth, her breasts were crushed against the straining muscles of his chest, the blood sang in her veins. Their fevered breathing filled the silent room—and the phone rang.

Kristine jumped and opened dazed eyes. Tucker shook his head as though coming out of a dream, his eyes already becoming distant as he looked toward the phone.

Putting her away from him, he answered it on the fourth ring. Kristine followed him with her eyes, fighting disappointment, and listened to his side of the conversation, a curious frown wrinkling her brow.

"Yeah?" Tucker scowled. "Damn! Okay, thanks. Yeah, I will. Bye." He replaced the receiver with an impatient curse.

"What is it?"

"A guy from one of the other cabins. He said he saw a couple of teenage boys fooling around the truck just now. Said he yelled and asked what they were doing and they ran off but he couldn't tell if they'd vandalized it.

"He said there's been a gang stripping cars around here lately and they could be part of it."

Moving around her, he headed for the door. He couldn't get out of there fast enough. He'd almost blown it again. If the phone hadn't rung, they'd be in bed by now, and that road could only lead to more heartache and trouble for her.

Kristine didn't watch him leave. She was dealing with a bitter sense of disappointment and an overwhelming relief at the same time. She wanted him, but she wanted truth and trust between them first. He knew her worst secrets—she knew only his name, that he'd been in prison and that he had a foster brother who was a cop. Not a whole lot to know about the man you—loved.

Something heavy thumped against the door. Tucker must have forgotten to take the key. And for just a second she wished she didn't have to let him back inside. What were they going to say to each other? How could she make love with him if he didn't trust her enough to tell her about his past—his present? What about the gun?

Shrugging her shoulders, knowing she wouldn't find the answers to her questions by hiding, she turned the latch and began to open the door. Something pushed from the other side, and Kristine fell, staggering backward halfway across the floor.

She looked up in shock to see Tucker topple forward into the room—and the forbidding figure of Carl Morrell follow close behind. Tucker lay crumpled on the floor just inside the door. Kristine hardly spared a glance for the other man, giving instead all her immediate attention to Tucker.

"What have you done to him?" She was on her knees beside his still figure in seconds.

But Morrell wasn't having any of that. Grabbing her by the back of the collar, he hauled her to her feet and threw her into a chair beside the bed. Telling her to stay put if she knew what was good for her, he then lifted Tucker as though he were a featherweight and dumped him face-down across the bed.

He quickly removed Tucker's belt and tied his hands behind his back, rolled him over onto his back and stood grinning down into his unconscious face.

"How did you find us?" she asked when Morrell looked up at her silently.

The grin widened. "Easy. I ran his license number." He nodded in Tucker's direction. "Or rather, Mr. Spinelli did. You see, I have the advantage of modern technology at my disposal—a telephone in my car." He laughed.

"Very smart, though I admit I'm surprised. I didn't think you had the brains to dial one."

The grin on Morrell's face turned to a menacing glower. "You'd be surprised at what I can do, baby," he murmured insinuatingly. "But don't worry, you're going to get the chance to find out. Now, where is it?"

Kristine shrugged. "I don't know."

And she wasn't lying, though she wasn't strictly telling the truth. The last time she had seen the packet of information, it had been here. Tucker said he'd given it to his brother, and that meant it could be anyplace right at this moment.

"You can do better than that." He moved closer to the chair where she sat. "You had better do better than that," he threatened in a soft voice. "I didn't spend the whole damned day sitting in a parked car outside your boyfriend's brother's house, waiting for him to show up, to listen to this crap. Now where is it?"

"I told you, I have no idea where it might be. So what are you going to do? Kill me?" she asked in a tone of contempt.

She sounded brave, but it was false bravado. She knew without a doubt he was capable of murder—but not until the package was safely in his hands.

With lightning speed, Morrell was beside her. Drawing his hand back, he slapped her hard across the left side of the face. Kristine's head snapped back, she gave a startled cry of pain and tasted blood on her tongue.

Refusing to give him the satisfaction of seeing her cower, she straightened in the chair and glared back at him with watery brown eyes, her hands firmly gripping the chair arms.

"You can beat me till I'm black-and-blue, and I still won't tell you where it is—I can't—I don't know."

When Morrell reached toward her face, she couldn't help but flinch away. The touch of his fingers made her skin crawl.

"Maybe I could get the information another way." His fingers played across her cheek, down her chin to the neck of her shirt and below.

Kristine squirmed away from his touch, felt her stomach lurch and finally couldn't keep from shoving his hand away. But he wasn't going to let her get away with that. Grabbing her by the chin, he twisted her face up to his and pressed wet, fleshy lips over hers.

Kristine fought him, jerking her face back and forth. His fingers tightened their hold, forcing her to be still, bruising her chin. Her lips, already sore where he'd slapped her, throbbed beneath his punishing mouth.

Holding her breath, feeling the room spin, she moaned. The nails on her clenched fingers bit into the palms of her hands as she tried to restrain her desire to punch him.

Finally she could stand it no longer. Whatever the consequences, she refused to be mauled by this animal. Bringing her heel down as hard as she could across his instep, she used her clenched fists to shove him away at the same time.

Morrell stumbled back, arms flailing for a moment before regaining his balance. Cursing fluently, his face twisted in a mask of hate, he reached a hand into one pocket.

"How about if I take a few tucks here and there," he whispered softly. The hand reappeared with a black-and-silver object grasped firmly in its fingers. A light touch with one, and an evil-looking blade sprang into view. Apprehension showed clearly in Kristine's eyes as she followed the movement of the long razor-thin blade waving back and forth in front of her face.

When the time came, he was going to go slowly with her. He deserved a little enjoyment after the trouble she and the bastard on the bed had put him through. It made him madder than hell to think that if Winslow hadn't interfered and helped the bitch, this would all be over. And he would be back in Dallas, where he belonged, going about his business.

Kristine eyed the blade with trepidation. Dear God, how she wished her own knife was in her hands right this minute and not in the pocket of her jacket hanging in the closet.

The tip of the knife touched the skin of one cheek below her left eye. Slowly it traveled around to the edge and then down the side of her mouth to a point just below her left ear.

"Well, what do you say? Are you going to tell me what I want to know—or—" He exerted a small amount of pressure, and the knife pricked delicate skin.

Kristine held her breath, afraid to breathe in case it caused the point to go deeper or slip—

As if sensing her inability to speak, Morrell backed off a few inches, but kept the blade clearly in view.

"Go ahead, do what you must, I still can't tell you something I don't know." She swallowed thickly, praying she was right in figuring he wouldn't kill her until he had what he'd come so far to get.

Anger darkened the dun-colored eyes and knotted the veins on his forehead. She knew he wasn't a very stable character, but she was still betting on the fact that he needed her alive.

There was a sound from the bed, and they both glanced in that direction. Tucker had stirred, on his way back to consciousness. A sudden light sprang into Morrell's eyes. Taking his time, knowing she was following his movements carefully, he walked over to the bed. The knife loomed suddenly into view, the blade lying across Tucker's Adam's apple.

"No!" Kristine half rose out of the chair.

"The package."

"It isn't here," she whispered in a hoarse voice.

"Where is it?"

She started to shrug, but Morrell made a slicing motion with the knife and, following it with her eyes, she murmured, "The cops—they have it—he—" she motioned toward the helpless man lying beneath the knife's silent threat "—gave it to his brother—the cop."

"Damn!" Morrell cursed loudly. Well, there was only one thing to do. If he was lucky, the cop would still have it in his possession—or stashed somewhere at his home.

Keeping a close eye on the woman, Morrell left the bed, removing his belt as he approached her. Hauling Kristine to her feet, he tied her hands behind her back and shoved her down into the chair. Then he went to the bathroom, took the plastic ice bucket, filled it with cold water and moved back into the room.

Enjoying it immensely, he dumped the icy water over the unconscious man's head. Tucker jerked beneath the freezing deluge and shook his head, spluttering and choking.

"Bastard!" Kristine spit at him.

Morrell glanced at her with a wide grin. "There are times when I really love my work—this is one of them."

Tugging the man to the side of the bed, Morrell told the two they were all going to take a nice ride in the car. He would drive, and they would ride in back—way in back—he laughed.

"Are you all right?"

"You okay?"

They spoke at the same time, ignoring Morrell.

"I'm okay." Kristine nodded and tried to grin, but her lip and cheek felt stiff and sore.

Tucker, seeing her difficulty, looked closer and saw the swollen lip, a spot of blood at the corner of her mouth and the bluish red tint to her cheek.

Head swiveling in Morrell's direction, he snarled in a deadly voice, "You low-life son of a—"

Morrell grabbed the neck of his shirt and jerked Tucker's face up to his. "I don't have to take that from you, con.

"I know all about you," he sneered, "so where do you get off thinking you're something special? Just shut your stinking mouth." He laid the point of the knife against the skin below Tucker's chin. "Or I'll shut it for you—permanently."

Shoving Tucker away, Morrell watched as he fell to lie sprawled across the bed on his back, a look of pain spreading across his angry face as his shoulders were nearly wrenched from their sockets. He didn't have to take lip from this bozo. And at the moment he didn't know which would give him more satisfaction—taking the woman or killing the man—when the time came for it.

Either way, he would fix them both so they didn't give nobody else any more trouble. He'd take real good care of both of them—it would be his *pleasure*.

Chapter 9

It was close to being dark when Carl Morrell hustled his prisoners outside the cabin toward the woods, where his car stood parked in the cover of trees. Though early evening, the overcast skies made it appear much later, and he was glad for the cover of darkness to help hide the true nature of his purpose.

He walked with an arm around Kristine's shoulders, the knife out of sight just below her chin, while his other arm rested around Tucker's shoulders. If anyone was watching, it might appear as though they were old friends. But they couldn't hear the whispered threats falling on Tucker's ears about what could happen to Kristine's pretty neck should he attempt to cut, and run.

A stiff wind blew sheets of rain into their faces as they trudged down the muddy track leading into the woods. Kristine felt goose bumps ruffle the exposed skin along her face, neck and arms. She shivered convulsively as rain soaked the thin shirt and denims she wore. Morrell hadn't taken the chance of loosening her hands to enable her to put her jacket on. Tucker was in better shape only because he'd been wearing his jacket when Morrell hit him from behind after luring him outside on the false pretext of his truck being vandalized by teenage boys.

Kristine kept trying to see around Morrell's hulk to Tucker's face. She was concerned about him because he appeared dazed and had since regaining consciousness. His eyes had a glassy look to them, and he moved stiff legged, as though his coordination might be affected. She knew head injuries could be very serious and wished for the opportunity to examine him.

Stopping at the rear of the car, Morrell took his arm from Tucker and shoved his hand into the pocket of his topcoat, extracting a set of keys. Unlocking the trunk, he grinned at the pair.

"Well, ain't this going to be cozy for the two of you?"

Kristine looked from the yawning cavity to the big man's face. "You aren't planning to put us in there? There isn't enough room, and it's freezing—what about air?"

"Don't worry." He laughed. "We'll make room for both of you, and you can keep each other warm. And as for breathing, you won't need to worry about that for very long." He chuckled softly at the double meaning of the words.

Tucker was shoved, unresisting, into the trunk first. He landed facedown against the floor, and Morrell pushed impatiently at his long legs, trying to get them twisted up inside the narrow space beneath him. And all the while, he muttered curses beneath his breath, shooting quick looks behind, knowing that he was wasting precious time. Knowing, too, that he couldn't afford to have one of the other guests getting curious, perhaps coming to see why the three had walked off into the woods alone in this kind of weather. It wasn't exactly the kind of day one would pick for a leisurely stroll.

Morrell finished stuffing Tucker inside and then turned a dark glance in Kristine's direction. There was just enough light left for her to see the menace in the scarred face looming over hers.

"Okay, baby, don't make this any harder on either of us than it has to be. I can still ram this pigsticker into the boyfriend here, if you give me any trouble. And need I add that I won't hesitate—would in fact, enjoy, doing it?"

Kristine gave him a fulminating look that spoke volumes, but moved to do his bidding. Climbing up onto the edge of the trunk, she sat teetering for a moment, twisted sideways, half-facing the still figure already inside. Before she could decide how to go about getting inside without the use of her hands for support, Morrell gave her a sharp shove and she pitched sideways, landing heavily on one shoulder and hip.

Her cry of pain was muffled in the cloth of Tucker's jacket as her face lay buried against his back. She felt her long legs being roughly pushed aside, and then the world went suddenly black as the lid closed, locking them inside.

Riding in the trunk proved to be not only frightening but uncomfortable, as well. The car lurched forward, and the occupants of the trunk were tossed from side to side as Morrell turned in the narrow space. Then they bumped up and down as the car traveled the dirt track leading from the woods to the highway.

Kristine fought against panic as thoughts of what might happen to her and Tucker, should they be involved in an accident, filled her mind. But a groan and the stirring movements of the man lying partially buried beneath her quickly drove them out again.

"Tucker—are you all right?"

She was shivering so hard that all her limbs were jerking and she had lost all sense of feeling in her fingers and toes. Sliding her face along the soft jacket, she lifted her shoulders and worked her way off him, but didn't go far, because she craved the heat his body was giving off.

"Can you hear me, Tucker? How is your head? Do you have a headache? Any pain?"

She hoped he hadn't fallen into unconsciousness. Morrell had been more brutal with him than he had with her. And Tucker hadn't shown any will to oppose him at all. She had always considered herself to be a pacifist, not inclined toward violence of any kind. But when Tucker had fallen into the motel room earlier and she had for an instant thought him dead, all feeling had drained instantly from her body. And in its place had grown hate and a fierce desire to kill the man towering over Tucker's motionless body with her bare hands.

"Ow!" Tucker groaned when Kristine accidentally jarred him, causing his head to slam into the side of the trunk. She was trying to move over and give him some room to maneuver onto his side.

"Sorry!" she murmured anxiously. "Did I hurt you?"

"No—I'm okay," his voice sounded muffled. "What about you? What did that Neanderthal do to you while I was out?"

"Nothing—he just tried to make me tell him where the information was—that's all. I'm sorry, but I had to tell him that you'd given it to your brother—"

"It's all right," he assured her. "He must have been following me and that's how he found you. He probably suspected I'd given it to him, anyway."

"If I make myself very small, can you manage to get into a more comfortable position?" she asked.

"There is no comfortable position folded up in a trunk with your hands tied behind your back," he told her wryly.

"Why, Mr. Winslow," she chided, "is that a sense of humor I hear lurking in your voice? Are you trying to completely destroy my concept of you as a hard-bitten, humorless swine of a man?"

There was a definite grin in her voice and Tucker identified it with a feeling of surprise. He could find little to smile about in their present circumstances. But he had no way of knowing she used humor to mask the escalating need she felt to release her fear in an all-out bout of screaming hysteria.

Tucker began to move slowly, carefully rearranging his pretzel-shaped body into a more comfortable position. This was one hell of a situation to be in, but he hadn't given up the fight yet. Morrell was racking up points against himself, and Tucker was keeping the score.

When he finally found the right position, if there was such a thing, he found himself face-to-face with Kristine. Closing his eyes, feeling her sweet breath blowing gently over his face, he imagined for a second that they were someplace else, and this was the prelude to a night spent in making love.

And suddenly Jack Arnold's face intruded into his thoughts, along with the question that had been growing in the back of his mind for some time now. Was putting an end to Arnold's life worth what he would be giving up? Was it worth his own life? A possible future spent with Kristine?

But what about Sylvia? With all her faults, she still haunted him. The memory of what they had once shared, their plans, their dreams of a future together still plagued him. Could he turn his back on that—on the woman?

What if, as he had thought in the beginning, when he'd first been confronted with accusations of the crime he hadn't committed, Sylvia was as much a victim as he had been—still was? What if it hadn't been her choice to leave him?

Kristine couldn't help uttering a painful murmur as his shoulder jabbed her in the ribs and his knee butted hard against her shinbone.

The sound brought Tucker back from his musing thoughts and he murmured an apology. Somehow they would get out of this, and when they did, he would have to make a decision—no, the decision was already made. He would have to stick by it and bring the past to a close. But at what cost to the woman beside him, a part of him questioned, causing him to feel a wrenching knot in his gut.

Kristine shivered and drew her legs up as close to her chest as possible for warmth. Somehow they would get out of this, she had to believe that. And when they did, she would find a way to help this man—this troubled man whom she had fallen hopelessly in love with.

"We'll be all right—I promise you that." He felt her shiver and moved closer to her. "Are you cold?"

"Y-yes—f-freezing. I didn't have t-time to get my c-coat—" Her teeth were chattering.

"Come here," he whispered. "Move as close as you can and burrow beneath my jacket. It's big enough for both of us."

Kristine squirmed closer, used her head and her teeth to pull the edge of his jacket back and tucked herself in against his warm broad chest as best she could. In a few moments his body heat began to warm her up considerably.

"Th-thanks."

"It's my pleasure."

Kristine heard the words murmured barely above a whisper and had to turn her face aside for fear he would see the tears on her face or hear her uneven breathing.

And I promise you, my darling, that if we get out of this alive, she vowed silently, *I'll help you find whatever it is you're looking for—no matter what it is.*

"I thought you were badly injured when—*he* dumped you on the floor of the motel, and when you appeared so out of it walking to the car just now," she spoke when she could.

"It doesn't do to let your enemy know your strength if you can help it."

So he'd only been attempting to throw Morrell off, make him think he'd incapacitated him more than he really had.

"Kristine?"

"Yes?"

"Talk to me—tell me about your childhood in Illinois."

Detective Lt. Bob Linton finished filling out the report on the homicide he and his partner had been called out on just after lunch and placed it in the outgoing file tray. Now maybe he could spend a few minutes going over the papers Tucker had given him. From what he'd already read, it looked as though there was some pretty powerful stuff contained on the written pages. Enough to blow the lid off organized crime in the Dallas area, maybe in the whole southwestern region of the country.

The information was still in his possession because he hadn't yet been able to get hold of the police chief. And too, he wanted to talk with the woman Kristine Stevens. It wasn't that he didn't trust his brother's evaluation of the woman, her motives and the extent of her own involvement in Vincent Spinelli's criminal activities. He just needed to form his own opinion of her before sticking his neck out by handing this package of dynamite over to his boss.

Tucker was a great guy, the very best, but Bob wasn't impressed with his track record when it came to women. So far his tastes had run to the shallow, sophisticated kinds looking for a way to climb the social ladder to a better, more expensive, style of life. And any man they could use, drop and then step over to reach the top was fair game.

Sylvia Arnold, née Reynolds, was just such a one, possibly the worst of the lot, because she had almost taken Tucker to the altar to achieve her goal. She had ridden the wave of his success, and when it looked as though he might be cresting, she'd bailed out—gone on to bigger game. Or she had been a part of the scam Jack Arnold pulled on Tucker, from the very beginning.

Bob dialed the number of the motel where Tucker and his female companion were staying and asked for their room extension. He tapped the eraser end of a pencil against the top of the metal desk as he sat waiting, but no one answered. He figured they must have stepped out for something, maybe a drink, and hung up, determined to try again later.

The afternoon wore on and Bob got busy with other things. It was almost six before he tried to reach them again. But once again the phone rang and rang without being answered. Finally, replacing the receiver with a frown, he decided that maybe he ought to go on over and see what was going on. And if they still weren't there, it might be a good thing to take a look around.

Bob signed out, hurried to his car and drove across town to the Cabin in the Woods motel. He turned down the winding gravel road to the last cabin at the end of the row. The old blue pickup Tucker had driven to the station house earlier that day was parked behind the cabin a few yards from the back door.

He parked beside it, got out and walked around to the front of the truck. With a hand on the hood, he stared at the lighted windows of the cabin. The engine was cold, obviously the truck hadn't been driven recently. He pulled the collar of his coat up around his ears against the frigid wind and made his way through the mud to the door of the cabin.

As he walked, his sixth sense telling him something was not as it should be, he loosened his topcoat, reached beneath his jacket to the shoulder holster and withdrew his .38 police special. Whatever was going on, he was going to be prepared for the worst.

He made his way quietly to the cabin window, careful not to stand directly within sight of anyone inside, and peered between the gap in the curtains. From where he was standing, he could see a good portion of the room and the door to the bathroom, standing open across the room. Nothing stirred. It looked as if the place were empty.

He moved to stand at the side of the door and knocked loudly, waited and knocked again. There was no answer. He called out to his brother, but his only reply was silence. The gun cocked and ready, he tried the door handle, still keeping out of range of gunfire should any one open up from inside. The handle turned easily beneath his touch. He pushed it open slowly, darted inside and, from a crouched position, bobbed this way and that with both hands on the gun to steady his aim should firing be necessary.

He looked inside the bathroom, the closet and under the bed. The place was deserted. His brother's jacket, the one he had worn when they had met earlier that day, was gone. But another one, a red one, one that would fit a small woman, hung on a wooden hanger in the closet.

Where the hell were they? Where would they go on foot? And why would the woman leave without her jacket in this weather? He could hear it beginning to rain again and knew from the sound that it had more ice in it than water. He gave the room one final glance around and left.

Outside, he used a flashlight and searched the ground from the cabin door to the truck. There were footprints, plenty of them, but they were too overlapping to make heads or tails of. However, there were tracks that led beyond the truck and into the woods. He followed them until he came to a set of car tracks. Here was his answer to what had happened to Tucker and the woman.

Someone, possibly Carl Morrell, had parked here, waiting to catch Tucker and the woman by surprise. It was anybody's guess where they were now.

A few minutes later, Bob left the motel office, knowing he hadn't much time to find his brother and the woman. It seemed the people in the cabin nearest to Cabin 12 had reported a car coming in through the woods at the back of the motel grounds. They thought maybe it was someone trying to sneak into one of the cabins without paying. They had apparently been staying there a while, and this wasn't the first time someone had tried using one of the cabins without paying.

But the motel manager had assured Bob that the cabins were all filled with paying guests. That's why he hadn't bothered to brave the foul weather and check out the report. He figured it was only someone visiting one of the guests, probably the people in Cabin 12.

Bob drew the collar of his coat tighter around his chin as he slid behind the wheel of his car. This was not the kind of a night to be out without a coat, he thought, remembering the jacket hanging in the closet in the cabin.

He would have an APB issued on Tucker and Kristine Stevens, but he had little to go on. He didn't even have a description of the woman. St. Louis was a big city, and there was always the chance they had been spirited away. But he would bet they were still here, because that's where the information the syndicate wanted was—still in his possession.

Chapter 10

Carl Morrell drove past the white stucco duplex three or four times before he was completely satisfied that no one was at home. It wasn't as dark outside as he wanted it to be, but he couldn't take the chance on waiting around until the cop returned home. He needed to get inside, see if the stuff was there and get out again.

At first his idea had been to leave the two in the trunk, but then he decided they might be more useful to him inside. He had no idea what the package he was searching for looked like. The woman could have tied it up with pink ribbon for all he knew, so that made it expedient to take them with him.

He drove around to the alley and parked in the covered carport provided for the residents. After first checking out the lay of the land, he moved to the rear of the car and removed his passengers, hustling them toward the back entrance to the duplex.

It took him exactly thirty seconds to breach the lock on the door.

"Tsk—tsk—" Morrell grinned at Tucker. "And your brother's a cop. He ought to know better than to have these dime-store locks on his doors. He could get himself robbed—or something worse," he added with dark meaning.

Tucker kept his mouth shut, but his eyes were very vocal in what he thought of the other man's poor attempt at humor.

Morrell held his knife at Kristine's throat and sent Tucker in ahead of them. He followed close behind, on the alert for the presence of someone hidden, waiting for them. But he searched the two-bedroom apartment thoroughly and found it to be empty. Convinced they were alone, he shoved the two into a closet, locked the door and made his way back outside.

Morrell knew a strange car parked for too long in someone's driveway these days could mean trouble for the owner. What with TV encouraging people to spy on their neighbors, you couldn't be too careful.

He drove a few blocks down the street, parked the car inconspicuously and walked, grinning, swiftly down the street toward the duplex. He was a professional, and he was good at his job. And it looked as though this one was turning out to be a piece of cake after all.

"Well, at least it's warmer in here," Kristine mumbled from somewhere near Tucker's shirtfront. The closet was quite small, and they were sandwiched into the tiny space like sardines in a can.

"Yeah," he agreed. It was very warm indeed. Even in a situation as desperate as this, he was still aware of Kristine's feminine attributes. Especially since they were pressed so tightly against his chest and thigh.

"What do you think he plans to do with us when he gets back?" she asked timorously.

"Probably make us help him look for the goods," he answered in a strained voice.

He had one hell of a headache, and his left wrist felt as though broken glass had been ground into his flesh. He was having to battle against a feeling of dizziness, and he wasn't certain if it was a result of the blow to the head he'd received or because of the close proximity of Kristine.

"Tucker—you asked me all about my childhood, while we were in the trunk—and I told you. And you know all about the fiasco of a marriage I had in Texas." She hesitated. "But I still know almost nothing about you. All I'm certain of is that you have a brother—"

"My past isn't important—"

"It is to me," she whispered, her face raised near his chin. She couldn't make out his features, but imagined the gray eyes under thick black brows frowning down at her. "Please—this might be the last chance we have to—"

Bending his head, he cut her words off with his mouth. But he wasn't completely convinced he'd done it just to keep her from asking any more questions.

The kiss sent the pit of her stomach into her toes as she raised herself, parting her lips, to deepen the kiss. His mouth moved over hers, devouring its softness. The small space became filled with the sound of their uneven breathing. Tucker's mouth left hers burning with fire and moved down to her neck, to the pulsing hollow at the base of her throat.

"Kristine—"

The closet door was thrown suddenly back, and Carl Morrell stood in the doorway.

"Well, well, ain't this cozy. I just can't leave the two of you alone for a minute without you getting up to something naughty, can I?"

Tucker bit out a curse and Kristine cringed back against the wall in fear. Morrell had pulled the blinds and turned on a small light before coming to let them out. And in its glow, she saw the cruel glare in the glance he turned on Tucker.

Yanking him out of the closet, Morrell slapped him, causing his head to snap back against the wall. Tucker jerked upright immediately, fighting the other man's hold, and lowered his head as though about to charge him.

"No!" Kristine screamed, "Please—don't!"

Tucker halted abruptly, turning to look back at her frightened face and pleading eyes. He was angry enough not to give a damn what the other man did to him, but he knew that if Morrell killed him now, Kristine would be alone and at his mercy.

Facing the taller man, Tucker gritted from between clenched teeth, "Another time, Morrell, and I'll see you in hell."

Morrell shook with laughter as he shoved Tucker into the center of the room. Then he pulled Kristine from the closet, planted a goading kiss on her mouth under Tucker's deadly glare and shoved her to stand beside him.

"Okay, it's time to get down to business. I want that package, and you two are going to help me find it."

From the holster at his side, hidden beneath his jacket, he drew a long-barreled gun with something attached to the end of it and pointed it at Tucker's chest.

"Now this, baby, is a gun." Morrell drew a loving finger down the blue-black barrel. "And this—" he tapped the black cylinder affixed to its end "—is a silencer. Either of you do anything I don't like, and the other one gets it—right between the eyes."

He looked from one to the other. "You both got that? I'm going to untie your hands so you can help me search this place. But this is the only warning I'm gonna give either of you. So remember, each of you is responsible for the other's life." Motioning with the gun, he said to Kristine, "Come here."

She stepped forward slowly, her eyes glued to the monstrously huge gun in the man's hand.

"Turn around," he directed.

In a moment, Kristine was stepping back to her former place, watching as he motioned Tucker forward. When Tucker was standing with his back facing the other man, Morrell pressed the end of the silencer hard against his temple and looked across the room at Kristine.

"Bang, bang." He laughed. "You're dead."

Kristine saw Tucker's jaw clench, his whole body tauten. Her eyes begged him. After a moment she saw him relax ever so slowly.

"Good boy," Morrell whispered. "Your girlfriend wouldn't look so pretty with a big hole between her eyes. And this gun makes a real mess, believe me.

"Now, get busy, you two. I want results, and I want them fast, before little brother gets home. We wouldn't want to have to use this on the cop," he taunted Tucker, "now would we?"

It was half past nine when Bob Linton drove down the street to his apartment. He had turned the package over to the captain at the station, told him about his brother's disappearance and placed an APB out on him and a female companion—no description of her. The two were to be picked up and brought in if spotted.

After five years in prison and all the unhappiness he'd faced, Tucker deserved some peace. Thinking back to their childhood, he wondered why it was that trouble, like a shadow, seemed to follow the other man around.

He was almost home, having reached no conclusions, when he happened to spot the black Cadillac parked at the curb, four blocks from his place. He slowed and drove on past. A few blocks down the street, he made a U-turn and came back.

Could this car possibly belong on his street? He doubted it. His neighbors' automobiles ran more to small foreign compact cars and an occasional Ford. But nothing like the opulence of a Cadillac. The hair stood up on the back of his neck. His sixth sense, one that all good policemen developed over the years, was on the alert again.

Passing the car at a leisurely pace, he looked it over carefully. Tucker had mentioned that Morrell was driving a black Cadillac when he sliced his tires. A coincidence? As a cop, he'd learned to discount coincidences. A coincidence had to first be proved to him before he believed. Things happened because one person or another made them happen.

A block away from the long black car, he pulled over to the opposite curb and parked. Taking the radio receiver into his hand, he called for backup and warned them to come in silence. Perhaps a new neighbor *had* moved into the neighborhood without his knowing it—one who was the proud owner of an expensive Cadillac, but he doubted it. And you could never be too safe.

In a few minutes, he had been joined by four patrolmen from two squad cars. Two men staying in the front and two going along with Bob to the back, they separated. The patrolmen awaited a signal from Bob to move in.

The apartment had been thoroughly ransacked, and they had found nothing. Morrell was angry and becoming more abusive with each passing moment. Tucker was worried, because he seemed to be directing his anger and abuse more and more toward Kristine.

The man was a nut case, there was no doubt about that, and he seemed to thrive on violence. Tucker watched as the other man slicked long, greasy hair back away from his forehead with one hand, while the other one gripped the gun tightly. Was he mistaken, or had he seen Morrell's hand shake? It looked as though he was losing it.

Maybe now would be the best time to make his move, before the other man became so skittish he began spraying bullets at random. It would be taking a chance, he knew that, but at least he could gain some time for Kristine. If he could draw the man's fire, she could get away.

Gearing himself up for the move, he refused to make eye contact with Kristine even though he felt her trying to reach him with her eyes. There was no question in his mind but that she would know immediately what he was about to do, and she'd be certain to give the game away.

Morrell was standing with his back toward the doorway to the kitchen, his eyes on Kristine standing over by the couch. The gun he held was pointed toward Tucker. There was a mean look in the mud-colored eyes turned on Kristine, and Tucker saw the gun begin to waver ever so slightly in her direction.

Now—

The rear door, opening from outside into the kitchen, rammed back against the wall. At the same time, the front door did the same.

"Down!" Tucker yelled to Kristine, making a dive in her direction. "Get down onto the floor!"

They connected and dropped, Tucker's body shielding hers. Morrell looked on in amazement as two cops in blue uniforms stood squarely in front of him, each holding a gun pointed at his head. And from behind, a voice told him to bend over and place the gun flat on the floor or else the owner of the voice would be forced to put a bullet into the back of his brain.

Morrell's head swiveled slowly in the direction of the threat. Bob Linton's blue eyes met his. And there was no doubt in Morrell's mind but that this cop would shoot without a second's thought. Bending slowly, his eyes locked on Bob's face, he placed the gun on the carpet.

"Now kick it toward me," Bob directed, "carefully. We don't want any accidents." His voice dripped ice. "Do we?"

Morrell straightened slowly and pushed the gun with the toe of his boot in Bob's direction. In a few minutes handcuffs in place, Morrell was led from the building in the custody of the officers. Kristine stood beside Tucker, her hand in his, and watched him leave. A feeling of relief spread through her.

"Well, little brother, looks like you got here in the nick of time." Tucker smiled.

Kristine gazed up at him in amazement. So that's what he looked like without the cold glitter in the gray eyes and the hard line to his mouth.

"Somebody had to," Bob answered cheekily. "Remembering back a few years, it seems as though I did a heck of a lot of nick-of-time arriving."

His face sobered as his eyes moved over the woman standing at his brother's side. So this was the reason the captain was turning handsprings at headquarters and why his brother had nearly gotten himself killed.

"Hi, I'm Bob Linton." He stepped forward. "It seems this guy isn't going to introduce us, even though Mom did a better job than that of teaching him manners."

His voice was neutral, but he held his hand out to her, willing to give her the benefit of the doubt.

Kristine placed her small hand solemnly in his, gripped it and gave it a firm shake. Then, meeting his eyes, she grinned widely up into his homely face. She liked this one. He had an honest, open face. And right now, he was worried about what kind of woman had conned his brother into almost getting himself killed for her.

"I'm Kristine Stevens. And I want to thank you for your help just now. I was getting worried that your brother here might be planning to do something heroically stupid and get himself shot."

Bob's face broke out into a smile that stretched from one side to the other, and the blue eyes twinkled down at her in a friendly manner. Looking at Tucker, he said, "Now this one I like."

Tucker glanced up from where he was rubbing his left wrist and looked from Bob to Kristine and back.

"Yeah, so do I."

The belt used to tie his hands together had caused the gold ID bracelet to cut into the flesh, bruising it and making it sore. Kristine saw him rubbing his wrist and walked over to join him. Seeing the red angry-looking welts and the spots of blood dotting the skin beneath the bracelet, she reached out to him.

"Here, let me unfasten that so you can put something on your—"

"No!"

Tucker jerked his wrist from out of her grasp. She looked startled at first and then hurt. The bracelet, always the damned bracelet. He didn't even want her to touch it. Biting her lip, eyes filling with tears, she met his stony glance.

Now he'd done it. Morrell couldn't make her cry, no matter how badly he'd treated her, and the bruise on her cheekbone attested to the fact he'd been plenty nasty. But he could. Tucker saw that he could hurt her enough to make her cry with just one word. It was time for him to go—time to let her get on with her life—without him.

Moving away from her, he crossed to his brother's side. Bob was giving him an enigmatic look, but Tucker refused to acknowledge it. He had more important matters to discuss than his brother's obvious disapproval of him.

"Where's the evidence?" he asked.

"It's in the hands of Captain Lewis. It's being processed, and copies are being faxed to Dallas," Bob answered expressionlessly.

"And Morrell? Will you be able to make the kidnapping charges stick?" he asked.

"Plus a few others, like breaking and entering, and possession of an illegal weapon. Don't worry, we'll put him away for a long while. Not even his expensive lawyer will be able to get him out of this one."

"Good." Tucker pivoted to face Kristine. "Good," he repeated. "It's over," he told her, his eyes locked on to hers. "You're safe now, and it's all over."

There was a tone, a sound of finality to the words. She knew he was talking about more than her being chased halfway across the States by Morrell. More than the nightmare of her marriage and divorce from Vincent Spinelli.

He was telling her goodbye.

Chapter 11

Kristine twisted restlessly from side to side in the wide double bed. She should have been asleep by now, but every sound that drifted to her ears caused her to jerk instantly awake. It had been over six months since she had first become aware of Vincent Spinelli's illegal activities and confronted him with her knowledge. Six months since the terror had begun—and now it was all over. But her mind couldn't adjust to that fact so easily.

She had finally drifted off into an uneasy sleep, but the sound of loud voices in the living room had awakened her again. She tried not to listen to their conversation, but it was impossible not to.

Tucker was supposed to be sleeping on the couch and Bob in the recliner. Bob had assured them both earlier, when they had each protested the arrangements, that he spent more time sleeping in the recliner than in the bed.

Kristine had thanked him kindly for use of the bed, borrowed a pair of his pajamas, taken a shower and retired for the night. She was physically exhausted and was fast reaching the point of mental exhaustion, as well. She hadn't asked for the chaotic turn her life had taken a year ago, nor for the recently added disturbing influence of Tucker Winslow. From the little that had been said in her presence and what she had overheard earlier as she was coming from the shower, she knew Tucker's influence was about to pass out of her life, because he was leaving for Chicago in the morning.

Bob had tried to dissuade him, told him he needed to stay around to give testimony about Morrell. But Tucker had been adamant. They didn't need his testimony, they had Kristine and all that damming evidence she had brought with her from Texas. He was going, and that was final. The subject had been dropped abruptly as Kristine wandered into the room.

But apparently the conversation wasn't over, had only been put on hold until now. "It's Sylvia, isn't it?" she overheard Bob ask. "She's the real reason you're going to Chicago—isn't she? It isn't Jack Arnold you want to confront about what happened five years ago, it's her," he accused.

"Tuck, damn it, the woman is a vixen. She threw you over when she learned you weren't after the big money. That you were, in fact, more interested in advancing modern technology here in the States than in putting a row of zeros behind the balance in your bank account.

"She had to know what Arnold was doing. She worked in the business, too, didn't she? And the two of you shared the same house. Damn it, she married Arnold while you were being sentenced to spend time in prison. What does it take to make you see—"

"Maybe I want to hear it from her own lips," Tucker interrupted him, his eyes resting on the bracelet still encircling his swollen wrist. "Circumstances change, people change, sometimes it's beyond our control. Look at Kristine. She wouldn't have chosen to marry Spinelli if she'd known all there was to know about him."

"We never know all there is to know about a person," Bob interjected, thinking about the man across the room from him lying on his back staring up at the ceiling.

"Maybe not," Tucker agreed, "but I still need to have *her* tell me what her reasons were for doing what she did. I have to hear it from her own lips," Tucker repeated in a low voice.

"And Kristine? Where does she fit into all of this?"

"She doesn't."

"Damn it!" Bob slapped his fist against the arm of the chair. "I knew it! I knew it was too good to be true, that you'd finally found a woman worth having and were smart enough to realize it."

"Hush!" Tucker darted a quick glance back toward the bedroom door, then changed the subject. "In the morning I want you to talk to Kristine about this witness-relocation program you told me about. She thinks that now that the bad guys are behind bars, things will be the same for her."

In the bedroom Kristine turned to face the wall. She knew about the relocation program from watching TV and reading about it in books. It meant that she would be given a new identity and have to live someplace else. She would never be allowed to contact anyone from her old life—could never be the same person ever again. It would be like being reborn—it would be like being sentenced to live the rest of her life in hell if it didn't include Tucker.

And she wasn't about to consent to it. Sitting straight up in the bed, hands clenched at her sides, she thought about what the future would be like without Tucker

Winslow as a part of it. It was not a future she wanted to contemplate living. She loved the man, and she was going to fight for him. He might *think* he still wanted this Sylvia person, this woman now married to another man, but he loved *her*. She knew it! And she had to stay with him until *he* knew it, too.

If all he wanted was to talk to Sylvia and Jack Arnold, then why the gun? And suddenly, fearfully, she knew the real reason behind his buying the gun. It hadn't been out of fear of being robbed while on the road. It was because of Jack Arnold and what he'd done to him in the past. And what Tucker planned to do to *him* in Chicago.

He was going to kill the man. And as sure as she knew she loved him and would do anything to try to stop him, she knew that if he succeeded with his plan, his own life would end the moment he pulled that trigger. Even if he got away, it wouldn't matter, Tucker wasn't a killer, he wouldn't be able to live with what he'd done.

Somehow she had to stop him, to make him see that nothing, especially revenge, was worth wasting his life on. She was quickly coming to the conclusion that things like what had happened in her own life were best forgotten, buried deep beneath remembered good times. She knew she and Tucker could find happiness together, make new good times together given the chance. But first Tucker had to be convinced of that, and to release the hate inside of him, so there would be room for the love to grow—love for her.

And as for Sylvia, she belonged in the past, too, over with and forgotten, that was the label she should wear. And if Kristine had her way, that's how it would be. She hadn't missed the part of Bob's conversation about Tucker and the woman having shared a house together, and the thought caused her to be eaten up with jealousy.

How could the stupid woman have gotten that far with Tucker and thrown him over—and for money?

The next morning Kristine sat at the breakfast table and dutifully listened to Bob explain how important it was for her safety to allow them to relocate her. Because though Spinelli and Morrell would be in jail, unfortunately, that didn't mean they would be cut off from the rest of the world. They could still strike at her from behind bars—the crime syndicate could reach her practically anywhere, any time.

The idea frightened her all right. But not nearly as much as facing the rest of her life without Tucker. She could not buy her safety at the cost of Tucker's freedom, possibly his life. And she couldn't betray this man's trust in his brother and solicit his help by telling him what she suspected his brother was up to.

While Tucker showered and changed into fresh clothing Bob had somehow managed to acquire on short notice for him, Kristine promised to give his words careful consideration. She retired to the bedroom to do so. But once inside, she began to compose what she would say to him when the time came, because she had already made up her mind.

At ten o'clock Tucker and Bob said their goodbyes. And then they went to look for Kristine. She was nowhere to be found inside the apartment. Tucker panicked and went tearing outside, fearing that Spinelli had somehow managed to get to her, even here under their protection.

He pulled up short when he found Kristine sitting in the seat of the pickup, parked next to Bob's green four-door sedan.

"So I see you're ready at last," she greeted him calmly. He couldn't know how shaken she felt inside.

Bob stood back, looking from Tucker's grim face to Kristine's nervously determined one. This was one time he suspected his big brother had met his match. As much as he wanted to keep this woman safe, to see that she went someplace far away from harm, he knew she was the best medicine his brother could have found to cure him of the sickness his past had infected him with.

"Get the hell out of that truck right now!" Feet planted firmly on the ground, hands on hips, Tucker confronted her angrily.

"Not on your life, buster!" she came back. "Just think of me as an added fixture that comes with the truck. 'Wither it—and you—go, so do I,'" she misquoted.

"I'm not joking, Kristine, I told you to get out of the truck and I mean it. I'm going to Chicago, but you're not. You don't realize how unsafe a city that size would be for you now.

"Didn't my brother tell you how dangerous it was to give evidence against the crime syndicate? They'll crush you like a bug if given half a chance and never think twice about it."

Raising a stubborn chin, she looked him right square in the eye. "What about you? You helped me, doesn't that make it unsafe for you, too? I'm certain Chicago could turn out to be a very dangerous place for you, indeed." She continued in a suddenly lowered tone, "If you understand my meaning." Pointing a finger at him like a gun, she lowered her thumb slowly as though firing at him. "It's a long way to Chicago from here. Don't you think we had better get going?"

Grabbing the door handle, Tucker jerked the door open and reached for her. Kristine slapped her hand against his jacket pocket—the one with the gun in it.

"Are you sure you want to do that?" she asked in deliberate tones as his hands fastened onto her shoulders.

"I don't know what you mean—" he began stubbornly, eyes trying to hold her glance, lips compressed firmly into a hard line.

"Yes—" she ground the gun into his hipbone "—you do."

Grasping her wrist in a punishing hand, he pressed it steadily away. "You don't know what you're doing," he warned, out of his brother's hearing.

"I know all right. I'm trying to stop a fool from making a mistake that might cost him the rest of his life."

"Get out!"

"No!"

"I don't want you with me. Even if I leave here with you, I'll force you out at the first stop sign I come to," he promised in uncompromising tones.

Though her eyes showed hurt at the threat, her voice remained strong and steady. "And if you do, I'll go to the first pay phone I come to and call your brother and tell him all about what you have in your pocket. I don't think it will take much imagination on his part to come up with what your plans are for it."

"Bitch!"

"Sticks and stones," she murmured, fighting the need she felt to cry. She didn't want to make him hate her, she wanted him to love her. This was coming out all wrong.

"All right," he gave in abruptly. "But I want you to understand one thing, our time together is finished. And—what happened between us before—" He looked at her meaningfully. "Well, it won't happen again.

"You're only going along because I don't want my brother involved in all this. I don't want you involved in it, either, for your own good." He paused, hoping she would see he wanted only what was best for her. And going with him to Chicago was the worst possible thing she could do. But he could see by the implacable look in her dark eyes that she wasn't about to budge.

"All right, but if you get caught up in something that is way over your head—well—you were warned," he finished ominously.

He backed away from the open door, allowing Kristine to close it. Bob had hung back, giving the two privacy for their conversation. But now things seemed to be resolved between them, and he moved forward, coming to join them.

"Well, what's it going to be?" he asked Kristine. "Are you staying?"

"No." She shook her head.

The black rinse had almost completely left the blond strands, and they glistened in the sunshine, creating a nimbus around her small head. Bob thought she looked like an angel, an angel with sad eyes and a determined chin. He hoped she was up to the challenge he was certain his brother would present for her.

Taking Bob's hand in both of hers, Kristine held it warmly. "I appreciate all that you've done for me. And I know you're only thinking of my welfare when you urge me to enter the witness-protection program. But I'm thinking of my welfare, too," she told him earnestly, hoping he'd understand her true meaning. "And it just doesn't include something like that—not now."

Bob leaned in the window and planted a kiss against her soft cheek. "Good luck," he whispered. "He needs you, whether he knows it or not." Backing away from the truck, he watched Tucker climb stoically inside.

"So long, little brother," Tucker said, "you'll be hearing from me."

The truck backed out of the carport and moved slowly down the alley. Bob watched it go with a kind of knot twisted in his gut. Everything wasn't all that it seemed. It never was where Tucker was involved.

Tucker and Kristine headed out onto Interstate 55 in silence.

"Are you going to drive the whole way to Chicago without ever speaking to me?" she asked after a few miles. When he didn't answer, she continued, "Or looking at me? Look, I'm sorry I had to do this—"

"That's just it," he bit out. "You didn't have to do this. My life has nothing to do with you." Taking his eyes off the road long enough for a quick glance in her direction, he asked, "What about our deal? Remember that? I helped you, and we agreed that once you were safe, it was quits. What about that?"

Kristine bit her lip in chagrin. She had agreed to the deal—sort of. He had coerced her into it—nevertheless—

"I'm sorry."

"I don't want an apology. I want you to live up to your part of the bargain."

He was waiting for her to agree, and when she did, she knew he would stop the truck and put her out. Already she could feel it slowing.

"I'm sorry," she repeated in a low voice.

The truck picked up speed. "Keep your damned apologies. I should have known better than to trust the word of a woman."

"You called me Kristine—"

"What?" His head swiveled in her direction, a frown drawing his brows down over the gray eyes.

"In the closet—and in the trunk of the car—you called me Kristine," she explained. "Why? Why did you travel halfway across the country with me and never speak my name—and then—twice in a few hours—why?"

Tucker clenched his jaw and gripped the steering wheel without answering. She was a thorn in his side, a burr in his flesh, he had to keep reminding himself of that. He was taking her along because she had forced the issue, but he didn't have to like it. And he wanted her to know he *didn't* like it.

If she thought he had changed his mind about her—and if she thought she could change his mind about what he was planning to do in Chicago—well, she had another think coming.

His course was set—it had been for over five years. Somehow he'd always known it would come down to this—him facing Jack Arnold alone, just the two of them.

He knew now that he'd never expected the law to take care of Jack's punishment. All along he'd known it would be himself who meted it out. And whatever the cost to himself, he was prepared to accept it—and to go all the way with it.

But what about the cost to Kristine? His eyes slid in her direction. She was gazing morosely out of the window. She didn't seem to be very lucky in her choice of men. He looked back at the road. What was he thinking? He wasn't her man. He had no idea what might happen to her in Chicago, but whatever, it was on her own head.

She was an added liability he didn't want, couldn't afford. Then why had he taken her along? He glanced in her direction again, noticed the sunlight dancing in her hair and knew the truth of it.

Somewhere down inside, he wanted her with him, didn't want to be parted from her before it was absolutely necessary. He didn't understand his feelings about her or about Sylvia, was in fact thoroughly confused by them. Maybe he was just one of those men who went through life constantly tripping over women who would only mess up his life.

He couldn't let her know it, didn't even want to admit it to himself, the thought made him angry, but at this moment he was glad to have Kristine's slight figure sitting beside him.

Chapter 12

The next four hours passed slowly in a seemingly never-ending procession of monotonous scenery. When they finally came to the outskirts of Chicago, Kristine was bone weary, headachy and suffering silently with an upset stomach. She had eaten very little that morning before leaving St. Louis. She'd been too worried about what would happen when Tucker learned she was going to insist upon accompanying him. And on the road she had drunk only coffee, unable to even contemplate food in the face of his obvious displeasure at her continued company.

After her first attempts at conversation had fallen short of the desired results, she hadn't attempted to make any more. It seemed Tucker was determined to keep the troubled atmosphere intact between them. He kept his morose attention focused strictly on the road, leaving Kristine with nothing else to do but watch the flat, treeless countryside, gray and dull in its winter guise.

In Chicago, Tucker chose the motel without asking Kristine's opinion. And when he stopped before the office and climbed down from the truck, she gave no sign that she wanted to go with him, not that he would have allowed her to go in any case. He was torn between regret for what had already passed between the two of them and what was still to come. And he was angry: at her for prolonging their relationship past the agreed limits; at himself for not being strong enough to get rid of her at any cost; but most of all, he was angry with the man who had caused this whole situation by his actions over five years ago.

The closer Tucker got to his quarry, to the sure knowledge of the coming of Jack Arnold's day of retribution, the more other feelings, other thoughts and considerations were being pushed aside. It's how he wanted it. He wanted to be able to concentrate on nothing but the means whereby Jack would pay for all he had put Tucker through over the past five years. He would have to meet Tucker face-to-face and explain, if he could, why he had sent him to prison—sent him to hell. And then he would have to pay for it all—the pain—the humiliation—and Sylvia.

With dragging feet, Kristine entered the motel room behind Tucker. Standing in a pose of weary dignity, her mind a fuzzy haze, she glanced up and around the room. It looked the same as all the others she had seen on this trip. No—not quite the same. There were two beds this time, one on either side of the room. Tucker was making it clear to her that he had meant his words of that morning. There was to be nothing more between them—no point of contact, either of a physical or an emotional nature.

Making her way around his stationary figure, she headed for the bathroom. She had to get out of his presence and seek privacy before releasing some of the unhappiness she was feeling. Once behind the locked door, she pressed both hands over her eyes and felt the tears start.

After a good cry, she blew her nose, took a deep breath and pushed the hair from her eyes. What she needed, she decided, was a long, hot soak in the tub. She would have liked to have been able to fill the tub with some exotically scented bath salts that would remind her she was an attractive woman—one who had plenty to offer some man—but plain hot water would have to suffice.

She removed her clothing, climbed into the tub and lay back with a sigh. The only trouble with having plenty to offer a man was that the only man to whom she wanted to offer it apparently wanted someone else.

When she left the tub, she donned the same clothes she had traveled in, for the simple reason that she had nothing else to wear. A change of clothing hadn't been high on her list of priorities recently. But perhaps it was time to change that, she contemplated, as she left the bathroom. She still had most of the money she'd been paid for the sale of the wedding ring.

Tucker glanced up from the magazine he was leafing through as she entered the room, gave her a penetrating look and asked, "You all right?"

"Just tired," she answered. *Please don't be nice to me, don't treat me like a friendly stranger,* she begged him silently. That would be the crucial blow to her fragile feminine ego.

"Feel like getting something to eat?"

"No—not just now. But if you're hungry, why don't you go on without me?"

He stood up, hesitated, gave her a narrow-eyed look and stood his ground. "I could simply go out and not come back. You do realize that, don't you?"

Kristine dropped down onto the bed nearest the door and removed her sneakers. She hadn't put her socks on after her bath, and she stared at her bare toes without immediately answering.

Her wet hair clung round her face in tight curls, making her look the kid he had once dubbed her in an attempt at keeping a distance between them. It hadn't worked then, and it didn't work now. He had firsthand knowledge of just how much of a woman she really was.

"Did you hear me?" he asked, moving a step in her direction. Why didn't she answer him? He didn't want to feel sympathy for her or to notice the lost, fragile look in the dark eyes she tried to keep hidden.

At last she looked up at him from beneath the fringe of hair almost obscuring her eyes, and still she didn't say anything.

"What's the matter? Cat got your tongue? You sure had plenty to say this morning at my brother's place. Did you feel safe there? Think you could get away with it because he was there to champion your cause? Whatever the hell that is.

"Don't think I didn't hear him telling you that I needed you." He was breathing hard in agitation, the anger building to a point all out of proportion to the situation. "Well, I *don't*! I don't need anyone." Wrenching his eyes from her blank face, he started toward the door.

"If you don't come back, I'll call your brother, I swear I will. I'll tell him—" Jumping to her feet, she fisted her hands and said with forced calm, "No, I'm not going to keep threatening you like a mother threatens a recalcitrant child to make him behave.

"Do whatever you want to do. Leave if you want." She swept an arm toward the door. "Right at this moment I don't give a damn what you do. Go on—do it—" she added wearily, plopping down onto the bed. "Just go ahead and do it," she whispered. "I don't care." And lying back, she turned her face to the wall and closed burning eyes.

She did care, she didn't want him to leave, she didn't want to call his brother. But she needed peace, just a little peace. There had been a scarcity of that commodity in her life in recent months, and she was reaching a breaking point. She had never felt so empty, so hollow in all her life as now. She needed rest—and sleep—for now, she only wanted to sleep....

Tucker made as though to leave, it's what he fully intended doing, but he didn't. He sat back down into the chair and simply stared at the sloping contours of her back for a long, long time. And as he watched, he saw the tension gradually seep out of her limbs. Her shoulders relaxed, her breathing became shallow and regular.

When he was quite certain that she was asleep, he stood and advanced toward the bed. Taking a blanket he found folded at the foot of the bed, he covered her with it. He stood looking down at her for a long moment, then moved back to his chair. The shadows in the room lengthened, unnoticed by him as he continued to watch her sleep.

Kristine murmured softly, turned onto her back and began to surface slowly toward consciousness. A sharp sound caused her eyes to pop open, and she looked around the room in confusion. Where was she? Morrell! She felt all her muscles tense, and then she remembered. Chicago, she was in Chicago—with Tucker.

They had been fighting—again—and she'd told him to leave.

All at once she sat straight up in the bed and glanced hurriedly around the room into deep shadows. It must be getting on toward late evening, unless she'd slept the clock around. Tucker! With a sinking sensation in the pit of her stomach, she saw he was gone, and then a sound came from the bathroom. The door opened softly, and Tucker stepped out.

Their glances met across the room, and it was like lightning striking both of them right through to the heart. Tucker dabbed at spots of shaving cream dotting his cheeks and neck and felt his heart hammering beneath his ribs.

"You're awake."

"Yes—you didn't leave," she blurted.

"No."

"Does that mean—"

"It only means—I didn't leave—yet."

The uneven beat of her heart began to steady, she pulled her eyes from his, pushed aside the cover he must have placed over her, sat up and bent to find her shoes. He was here for now, couldn't she take it one step at a time? One hour at a time. She found her shoes and slipped them on.

"I'm hungry now—can we go eat?"

A couple hours later, after they'd eaten in a seafood restaurant near Lake Michigan, he asked if she would like to drive around the lake, and she agreed. Neither one wanted to go back to the motel any sooner than absolutely necessary. The atmosphere there reminded them too much of the cabin in St. Louis and what had taken place between them there.

It was near nine when they drove down Lake Shore Drive, past the older brick apartment houses. Red carpets extended from the main doors of many, down the steps and across the sidewalk to the curb. Liveried doormen looking smart and slightly foreign in their fancy uniforms stood at attention, ready to help arriving and departing guests into their limousines.

Kristine watched as a limousine pulled up to one such apartment house, and the doorman dressed in red and gold opened the door and extended a white-gloved hand to assist the occupant to alight. A tall, elegant woman clad in mink slid out onto the sidewalk then turned to wave at whoever remained seated in the back of the long, black limousine. Light from the covered portico fell onto her face.

Kristine caught her breath in silent admiration. This woman was one of the most strikingly beautiful she had ever seen. Tall and chic, she carried herself with a model's poise. Her raven-black hair was swept back from high cheekbones and fastened with diamond-studded combs. The fingers of the hand she fluttered at her companion were beringed with large sparkling jewels. She literally dripped wealth from her head to the tips of the rhinestone-studded heels she wore on slender feet.

"Have you ever seen anything like her?" she murmured to the man beside her. And when he didn't answer, she transferred her gaze from the woman now entering the building to the stunned look on Tucker's face.

"My God, it was *her*! That was Sylvia, wasn't it?" she asked in a strangled whisper.

Still without answering, Tucker moved out into traffic. He hadn't expected to see *her* tonight, and he was reeling under the blow of her breathtaking loveliness. The years had not changed that.

"Take me back to the motel," Kristine breathed. She was defeated and she knew it. There was no way she could compete with a woman as beautiful as that.

At the motel, Kristine sat down in a chair across from Tucker and stared at the floor. Now that the shock of seeing the woman had worn off a bit, she was getting her equilibrium back. There was no denying the woman's great beauty, but if what she'd heard from Bob was correct, then her beauty definitely was only skin-deep.

Tucker deserved better—he deserved Kristine. And she was going to do her level best to make him see that.

"Are you planning to kill her, too?" she asked abruptly into the silence that had fallen between them in the truck and followed them back to the motel.

Tucker's eyes shot to her face. "W-what?"

"I said, are you planning to shoot her, shoot that woman, too, when you go to kill her husband?"

Pulling his eyes from her face, he jumped to his feet and strode around the room. "Don't be ridiculous."

"Then you aren't planning to kill her—just make her a widow. And then what?"

"Leave it alone, Kristine."

Kristine, he'd used her name again. Her heart leaped at the sound of it on his lips. Even spoken in anger, it made her feel all warm and melting soft inside.

"No, I won't leave it alone," she answered in a resolute tone of voice. "I want to know what you plan to do after her husband is dead." It hurt to voice the next question, but she had to. "Are you going to ask her to run away with you?

"Do you honestly expect her to do it? To give up the limousine rides, the jewels, the furs? To live a life on the run from the law?" There was no mistaking the skepticism in her voice.

"Who said I was going to shoot anyone?"

"I'm not a fool, you know. You wouldn't have brought that gun along if you didn't intend to use it."

"I think you should keep your mouth shut about something you know nothing about." He paused in his pacing, directly in front of her seated figure, and met her glance.

"I would," she whispered, with her eyes locked on to his. "I'd live with you—run away with you."

Grasping her by the shoulders, Tucker drew her to her feet and shook her. "Stop it, you don't know what you're saying."

"I know that I lo—"

"Be still!" He threw her away from him, back down into the chair and took up his pacing once more.

After a few taut, silent moments, Kristine spoke again. "Tell me what happened with you—and her."

"It isn't any—"

"Of my business, I know. Tell me anyway."

Tucker probed her dark eyes with his. Suddenly, coming to a decision, he took a seat in the chair across from her and began to speak.

"If I'm going to tell you about us—her—whatever, then I guess I should start from the beginning. I met Sylvia at a computer company where I worked for a while after college. She was a secretary there.

"When Jack and I formed our own company, I asked her to come to work for us. I knew she hadn't been very happy in her old job—"

"Why," Kristine broke across his words with her question.

"Why?" He frowned. "Why, what?"

"Why wasn't she happy at her old job?"

He couldn't remember right off. Then, "Oh, some rumor had been started by a couple of the other secretaries about her and Mr. Patterson, the owner."

"What was it about?"

Tucker shrugged. "They worked together a lot at night, and with a little help from the gossips, his wife got the wrong idea." Kristine raised a brow and he defended the other woman. "Come on, you've seen Sylvia. Naturally another woman, one who was nowhere near to being as—attractive—as her would feel threatened, especially if her husband was spending a lot of time in Sylvia's company. She was his secretary." He dismissed the whole thing with a shrug of his powerful shoulders. "There was nothing to it."

"And then she became your secretary, and the two of you worked closely together," Kristine murmured softly. "How long before she got you to pop the question?"

"Look, what does this have to do with anything?"

"How long?" she persisted stubbornly.

"Four weeks, so what?"

"How long did you know her before, at the other company?"

"Three or four years."

"And did you—go out?"

"No—we didn't travel in the same circles at that time."

Kristine raised a brow and nodded. "I see."

"What," he asked. "What do you see?"

Shrugging a shoulder negligently, she met his glance and murmured, "She wasn't interested in small fish, only the big ones. She probably was fooling around with her boss—but he was married—then you came along. You were starting your own company, that meant you must have money—and best of all, you were single. She sounds to me like a woman with an eye out to the main chance—''

''That's enough!'' Tucker thundered. He climbed to his feet angrily, grabbed his coat from the bed and marched to the door without another word or glance. The windows rattled under the force of the slammed door.

Kristine watched him go with tears in her eyes, but there was a slight smile on her lips. He was angry with her, but she'd given him something to think about. No matter what he said to the contrary, she sensed that he wasn't quite certain that Sylvia wasn't as greedy and grasping as she appeared to be when Kristine had pointed it out to him just now.

Tucker was gone two hours, and when he returned he brought coffee along with a blast of cold air as he opened the door and came inside. He had been upset when he left, because Kristine was putting into words questions he'd been asking himself over the past few years and coming up with the same unpalatable conclusions he had.

He wasn't certain what had upset him the most, the slurs on Sylvia's character or the fact he appeared to be one of the biggest fools alive for having believed in her. And did he still believe in her? He didn't know. All he knew for certain was that he had to see her again to ask her, himself, what had gone wrong five years ago.

Kristine was sitting up in bed, wearing one of the shirts Bob had given Tucker before they left St. Louis, pretending to watch a movie on TV. She kept her attention focused on the screen and didn't deign to notice his presence until he stood beside the bed and cleared his throat.

Getting her attention at last, he held out a cup of coffee to her silently. His glance skittered over her and away again as he sought to dismiss the tantalizing sight of a soft ivory shoulder bared almost to the tip of a firm jutting breast. He didn't want to remember how those same breasts, feeling as smooth as satin, their nipples drawn tight, had stood out beneath the wet material of her shirt or how it had once felt to make love to her beneath the shower's warm spray.

He could feel his lower body pulse with heat and begin to strain against the confining material of his jeans. He had to put a stop to this, and right now, or else he would soon be in bed with her, putting lie to all he'd been telling her about how there was to be nothing between them from now on.

Talk, that's what they needed to do—talk. Taking a seat in the chair farthest from the bed, he sat hunched forward, holding his cup in both hands and began to speak.

"I didn't finish answering your questions earlier. I never got around to telling you what really happened in Dallas, why I spent the last five years of my life in prison."

"I didn't think you wanted to talk to me about it."

Tucker shrugged, darted a glance at the shadowy hollow visible between her breasts and took a hurried sip of tepid coffee. With his eyes on the scuffed toe of one boot, he began to speak in a voice that sounded like rusty nails, cleared his throat and began again.

"I told you already that Jack and I went into business together, I didn't tell you what that business was. We sold computers and their components. And I headed a research department for furthering the advancement of their abilities.

"Ever since graduating from college, I had been working on developing a newer, smaller microchip that could hold more information and process it faster than anything on the market at that time.

"After years at it, I finally came up with the right combination, and I was able to design a microchip that could store billions of bytes of information and process it ten-to-one hundred times faster than the systems that were presently in use."

"But that's fantastic," Kristine said admiringly. She drew her knees up beneath the covers, rested her chin on them, wrapped her arms around her legs and encouraged him to continue.

"Take a look at your thumbnail. You see how small it is? Well, that's the size of the microchip I developed." He was getting excited just thinking about the possibilities of what his discovery could mean, to the field of medicine, for instance. Diagnosis of terminal conditions could be made faster and in volume, allowing the treatment to begin before the illness had reached the point of no return.

Leaning forward he continued. "The reason my discovery was possible, the reason it was so revolutionary, was due not only to the ability it had to outwork the present solid-state systems, but because I designed the microchip to work with gas."

Kristine frowned. "Gas? But—"

"I know, gas has no form, no ability to retain a shape. And that is exactly why no one had used it before now. But you see, I applied genetics to my theory—and it worked."

"Genetics?"

"That's right. I injected one of the denser gases with DNA, creating a form of pseudolife, giving the molecules a working blueprint of what to do.

"You see, the trouble with today's solid state is that it can only work in a set and ordered pattern. It does what it's made to do. It works forward and backward, but it isn't versatile, it can't, say for instance, move from side to side.

"Now look at your thumbnail again. You can move it back and forth, and side to side. It moves as your finger moves—that's versatility. And besides that, gas takes fewer atoms, and that makes it possible to store and carry more information."

"I think that's wonderful. But—" she looked across at him "—if you developed this five years ago, hasn't that been long enough for it to be on the open market by now?"

She didn't know a whole lot about computers and microchips, but surely something as innovative as that would have been featured in magazines and would have rated a story on one of the TV news programs.

Tucker crushed his coffee cup in his hand and threw it with unnecessary force into the trash can located beside the mirrored dresser sitting across from the foot of the bed.

"Yeah, it's long enough," he answered from between clenched teeth. "And the reason you haven't heard anything about it is because Jack Arnold, the son of a—stole it from me. Then, when questioned about its existence, he lied. I spent five years sitting in prison because he lied.

"You see, while I was in Washington, D.C., selling the damned thing to the U.S. government, Jack was back in Texas, selling it to a foreign power."

"My God!" Kristine breathed softly. So that's why Tucker had come after the other man and brought along a gun. She wasn't quite certain now herself that the other man didn't deserve to get exactly what Tucker had in mind to give him.

"Yeah." He met her look of indignation and continued, "The deal I had made with the government had gone through, the papers were signed, all I had to do was make delivery—and I couldn't—because the prototype, all the blueprints and the formulas for making it work were gone. Stolen by Jack Arnold."

"Didn't you explain?"

Tucker laughed, but it wasn't a humorous sound. "Oh, yes, I explained. But, you see, the federal government doesn't buy explanations—it buys product, not words. I was told to produce the microchip or go on trial for trying to defraud the government out of millions of dollars."

"Millions?"

"Oh, they weren't paying me millions for it—but it had the potential to make that—and I'm sure much more than that—for them. You see, I was more interested in the technological benefits to mankind at the time."

"How could he do that? How could your own partner get you sent to prison?"

"I had refused to sell my invention to the highest bidder. There are countries with lots of money, but little technology. Their people are poor and undereducated. The money stays in the hands of greedy rulers who would rather buy their technology from other countries than to help educate their own people to develop it.

"They don't want their constituents getting too smart, they might come to realize that despite all their promises, their rulers are really only concerned with furthering their own interests and lining their pockets with gold. Anyway, I wanted the advantages of my discovery to be utilized here in the States before it went overseas. That was the important issue as far as I was concerned."

"And Jack Arnold had no compunction about stealing it and selling it to the highest bidder," Kristine theorized.

"Apparently not," Tucker admitted wearily. Suddenly he was tired of the whole thing. "When I went on trial, they questioned him about my claims of having left the prototype in his possession while going to Washington. He denied ever having seen such a thing, or ever talking to me about the development of it."

"Surely you had something," Kristine asked. "Some papers, notes, something to prove him wrong? What about your other employees?"

Tucker shook his head.

"You couldn't redesign the microchip? Make another one?"

"Have you any idea what is involved in developing something like that? Sure I remember some of it, but not years of work, years of trial and error—" He shook his head again, rubbed a hand over his face and sat back in the chair, his chin sunk onto his chest, his legs sprawled out before him.

Kristine looked at his shoulders slumped in dejection and dared to ask the one question that was burning a hole in her brain.

"Why didn't Sylvia tell them the truth?"

He heard the question all right, but his lips remained firmly sealed. For the simple reason that he didn't know why. He couldn't imagine why the woman he loved, who professed to love him, would sit on the witness stand and deny knowing anything, anything at all about the proceedings.

She was only a secretary, she had told Tucker's lawyer under cross-examination. She didn't have anything to do with the development of new products. His lawyer suggested she should know more than that after having lived with Tucker for several months. He suggested that surely she had heard him discuss his work now and again. But she raised tearful eyes to the jury and explained that they were having problems in their relationship. She said she had been walking around in a daze for weeks, nervous and upset, fearing she had made a terrible mistake in agreeing to marry the defendant. But she was afraid of his brooding moodiness, afraid to ask him for a release from her promise.

Even now, he could feel the sudden pain of a knife twisting in his gut, just thinking about her words and the effect they had had on the jury. Why had she lied? They had made love the night before he left for Washington, and there had been no sign of any hesitation or nervousness on her part. On the contrary, she had been as passionate as ever.

"Well, are you going to answer me?" Kristine asked loudly. He was thinking of her, she could see it in his eyes. And she was eaten up with jealousy. How could he want someone who had calmly sat by and allowed him to go to prison for something he didn't do?

Tucker looked up, met her glittering eyes and shrugged. "I can't, I don't know the answer."

"And still you want her?" she dared to ask.

The gray eyes hardened. "You are treading on dangerous ground." Maybe he'd made a mistake by telling her all that he had. He was supposed to be pushing her away, not drawing her deeper by involving her in his past.

Kristine wanted to throw something at his head, to pound some sense into him. How could such an intelligent man be so stupid, so blind, about a woman like Sylvia Arnold?

She had to get out of the room before she told him exactly what she thought of him—and the treacherous bitch he still wanted after all this time.

Kristine threw the covers back, forgetting that all she wore was the shirt. But a quick glimpse of Tucker's face as he caught sight of her bare limbs soon reminded her. Her abrupt movements slowed, and she took the time to deliberately smooth the material down over rounded hips, giving him a careful glance from beneath lowered lids. He might be confused by the past and the other woman's part in it, but he was here with her now, and she realized he was nowhere near to being immune to her attractions.

Tucker kept his head lowered after that one glance, but couldn't help following her with his eyes as she passed him on the way to the bathroom.

"We've got to get you some clothes," he muttered in barely audible tones.

Kristine pretended she hadn't heard him and passed into the room, closing the door. When she came out a few minutes later, an extra button had been unfastened across her bosom. Maybe she hadn't been going about things the right way. Perhaps the only way to get Sylvia out of his head was to drive *him* out of his mind—with desire for herself.

Tucker was sitting exactly as when she'd left moments before, but now his eyes were glued to the television screen. He didn't even look up when she paused beside his chair. However, she knew he was aware of her presence, because she could see a slight tension in the flexing muscles of throat and jaw as he swallowed. And when she touched his cheek, he flinched and quickly looked up at her.

"What are you doing?"

"I was only gauging the temperature in here." With a soft, inviting look in the dark eyes holding his, she whispered, "What did you think I was doing?"

"Don't start something you can't finish, Kris."

Leaning nearer, letting him get a clear view of her breasts loose beneath the shirt, she asked, "What makes you think I can't finish what I start?"

Something stirred in the depths of the gray eyes. He raised a dark brow and allowed a bold, assessing stare to drift to her breasts, then slowly raked the whole of her body with it. Without warning, he caught her arms, jerked her sideways onto his lap and covered her mouth with his while shoving a hand beneath the gaping shirt to roughly grapple a breast.

The pain squeezing Kristine's heart at his careless handling far outweighed the pain on lips and breast.

He released her abruptly and, seeing the raw hurt staring at him from out of her eyes, left her in the chair while he got to his feet.

"You asked for that! Don't beg for something you don't want, you just might get it." His meaning was clear.

"It's *her* you want, isn't it?"

Running a hand through his hair, Tucker lashed out at her from over his shoulder. "Don't start that again—"

But she wouldn't be put off. "You want her! You want to kill her husband so you can have her!" The tears fell from her lashes and ran down her cheeks, but she didn't notice. "She's what you've been after all along. Your brother was right when he accused you of coming to Chicago just to get her. You don't care about the time you served in prison, or that Jack Arnold stole what you worked all your life to develop. You want her! You want her so badly you would kill another human being to possess her—"

"What do you want from me?" he asked harshly. But she only stared at him, her dark eyes swimming in tears.

He knew, he knew what she wanted. And the very fact that he knew, that he couldn't give it to her, made him even angrier. She needed a man who loved her, who would give her children—someone with a future—someone who had it all in front of him— Damn it!

Dragging her into his arms, he crushed her to him, his kiss angry. But Kristine twisted and turned in his arms, fighting to get free. This wasn't the way she wanted it to be when he held her, kissed her.

Finally, with a wrenching twist, she tore out of his grasp. "Stop it! Let me go! I hate you—" With a gulping sob, she threw herself facedown onto the bed, her body racked with pain that came not from bruises but from the heart.

But Tucker wasn't through with her yet. He flung himself down beside her, maneuvered her over onto her back and managed to subdue her with both her hands held in one of his, above her head, against the mattress.

Kristine kept her eyes tightly closed at first, she didn't want to look at him. She hated him, hated herself for caring about him, but most of all she hated Jack and Sylvia Arnold for what they had done to make him act the way he did.

She felt the harsh, uneven tenor of his breathing as the muscles of chest and thigh pressed into hers. She sensed movement, then felt the hair being pushed back away from her damp, hot cheeks and forehead. Surprised at the gesture, she opened her eyes and stared up into his face.

Her throat tightened immediately at the swift change of expression she saw taking place there, from one of unbearable tenderness to total confusion. He was as mixed up as she was about what was happening between them.

"I don't want to hurt you."

"Then get off me," she told him uncompromisingly. She wasn't forgetting, if he was, that this situation had been created because he wanted another woman, one who had betrayed him both for money and with another man.

The gray eyes hardened, a dark expression moved over the set face and grim mouth. Suddenly he leaned over to reclaim her lips with harsh intent. Again and again he kissed her, holding each kiss longer, probing her lips with his tongue, seeking entrance against the tight barrier of lips and teeth.

Kristine fought him in the only way she could. She was no match for his greater strength, but she could deny him any pleasure in his conquest. Like a statue, she lay beneath him, unresponsive, ungiving, lifeless.

After a moment longer, the assault on her lips ended, allowing her to breathe a sigh of relief, because she had felt her defenses weakening. The heat radiating from his body, the hardness pressed firmly and insistently against her softness was becoming an intoxicating lure she was finding it increasingly hard to resist.

And then she felt his lips against the side of her neck, the silky wetness of his tongue as he tasted the delicate skin below her ear before placing a soft kiss in the pulsing hollow of her throat. Kristine strained away from him, twisting her head aside. But that only gave him a larger scope for his ravishment as the shirt she wore parted, revealing her shoulder and one of her breasts to his fevered glance.

"Oh, Lord, Kristine—" he murmured, pressing the shirt farther back with his nose. His rough cheek rested against the top of her breast, and with the tip of his tongue he stroked her nipple lightly.

Kristine shuddered and tried to jerk her hands, still clasped above her head, from his hold. "Let me go!" she begged.

"I—can't," he answered, sliding up till his face was even with hers. A large hand cupped her cheek and turned her gently to face him. Their glances met, hers filled with hot anger, his with hot, repressed passion.

The gray ones asked a question that the dark ones stubbornly refused to answer. Slowly, his glance still locked with hers, he lowered his face until his mouth touched, then moved gently against hers before covering it softly. After a brief moment of contact, he drew back, his breath feathering her face.

Again he allowed his head to descend slowly, his caressing mouth planting slow, drugging kisses against her unresponsive lips. Until all at once, he felt her lips part, and with a soft moan, she began to kiss him back.

The hand at her wrists loosened, moved down over her shoulder, to waist and hip. And then, in a slow caressing gesture it moved up the inside of her thigh, beneath the hem of the shirt. Gently he smoothed back and forth across the satin skin of belly and thigh while his mouth built a raging need in her for more—for total possession.

Kristine felt passion rising in her like the hottest fire, clouding her brain, fragmenting her thoughts, as Tucker's hands and lips continued their hungry search of her body. And as his ardor mounted, the response he had awakened in her became a white-hot demand for fulfillment.

And when that time came, when she could no longer resist the funnel of fire that had begun as a tremor inside her, she gave in to it, feeling it spread from heated thighs and groin until it reached and filled the very core of her body. As gusts of delight shook her, she heard Tucker's own groan of release join with hers.

And then it was over. They lay looking at each other in silence for a long moment. She could see the darkness of regret in the gray eyes, almost hear the words forming on his lips before she turned away. She didn't watch him move off the bed or stalk toward the bathroom door; she was too busy fighting the choking need once more to cry.

Where would this all end? How had she become so entangled in the life of this man? She went back over in her mind the time they had spent together from the day they met to now. There was no denying that he had intrigued her from the very first, with his touch-me-not attitude.

Everything about him fascinated her. From the controlled way he spoke to her to the way he could make her feel inept or gauche with just one look from those cold gray eyes. She always had the feeling that if he wanted to, just by wishing it, he could make her disappear without a trace.

He had treated her with arrogance and suspicion yet he had helped her escape death at Morrell's hands. He'd made her angry enough to bite nails in two and made her heart pound with passion. He'd frightened her and coerced her and once even made her wonder if he was quite human.

But he had also made her fall in love with him.

She'd seen the hurt pride, the wounded anger and the pain he carried around deep inside. And she had experienced his caring, seen him labor under the weight of his feeling of responsibility toward her.

After all that, could she let him go? Could she just walk away as he wanted her to?

No, the answer was no. She loved him, he was locked into her mind and into her heart for all time. At this moment, tiredness lay like an invisible net covering her body. But tomorrow she would get her perspective back. Tomorrow, after some much needed rest, she would figure out what to do, how to help relieve Tucker of the combined burden of guilt on her behalf and confusion on behalf of Sylvia Arnold.

Tomorrow she would come up with an answer.

Chapter 13

Tucker eased his arm from beneath Kristine's head and slid across the small space to the side of the bed. Once on his feet, he stood for a moment gazing down on her sleeping face. What beautiful black fans her lashes made against the creamy paleness of her cheeks, and what a contrast to the blond hair.

How ripe and full her lips looked, a kiss-me suggestion to the way she held them even in sleep. He remembered nibbling on the lower one while they had made love the night before. Even after the fiasco earlier in the evening, when he'd been so rough with her, when he'd locked himself in the bathroom and vowed he wouldn't touch her ever again, in the middle of the night he'd crawled from his bed to hers. And she hadn't denied him.

A voice inside bade him to reconsider his immediate plans. It bade him to climb back between the covers and bury himself in this woman's warmth. It told him to forget his memories of the past, the idea of revenge, and to think only of Kristine, the present and the possibilities of a future with her.

He knew how much she wanted him. She had refused to worry about her own safety, the possibility of being at the head of the crime syndicate's hit list. She had followed him to Chicago, to try to talk him out of his plans to waste the rest of his life for a few minutes' satisfaction from pulling the trigger and ending Jack Arnold's life. Wasn't that proof of how much she cared?

But it had always been as hard for him to accept love as it was for him to give it. All anyone had to do was to ask his brother, Bob. He'd tell you just how hard it was living with Tucker. How hard it was on those who loved him.

It was with deep regret that he left her that morning, but he knew he had to go. His plans were made, for good or bad. There wasn't any place in them for Kristine. And when he'd finished with his work, she wouldn't want to be a part of them anyway.

When Kristine awakened later that morning, Tucker was gone. She found a note on the bedside table and a handful of money. She read the note, but the money stayed where it was. It felt too much like being paid for services rendered.

Had she been wrong in thinking she could persuade him of his true feelings for her by making love with him? It seemed she had been wrong about everything else in recent months; maybe she was wrong in this, too. But how could she deny him when she wanted him so?

In the pit of her stomach, the knot of dreadful anticipation, with which she had lived since learning of Tucker's purpose in coming to this city, was growing. How long before he set out to fulfill his reasons for being there?

* * *

Tucker sat in the blue pickup two blocks down the street from the apartment where he and Kristine had spotted Sylvia the night before. The time was close at hand and he was ready.

He climbed from the truck and began to walk. There was a hint of snow in the air, and the streets close to the lake were at least ten degrees colder than those a few blocks farther away. At intervals, strident gusts of bitterly sharp wind whipped his hair and stung tears to his eyes.

Pulling his collar up around his neck, he hunched his shoulders inside the sheepskin jacket and pushed his hands deep into the pockets. He quickened his stride, staring straight ahead. People passed him on the street, but he paid no attention to them, his one purpose in being here was to get a grip on the problem of how to go about gaining entrance to the apartment building.

For the next two hours, changing positions on the street, not staying in one area for too long, Tucker watched the doorman and his habits. He needed to find a pattern and then discover where he could fit himself unobtrusively into the pattern without anyone being aware of it.

After a while, snow began to fall in big airy flakes, and feeling the bite of the cold clear to his bones, Tucker sought shelter in a small restaurant across the street from the entrance he watched. The room he stepped down into had windows on a level with the sidewalk. The small booth the hostess showed him to was beside a window that looked out onto the street directly across from the building's entrance.

The lighting in the dining room was dim and cozy, and as Tucker sipped from his coffee cup, he wished for just a moment that Kristine was sitting across from him with her wide smile and dark, expressive eyes. And then thoughts of the woman who lived in the building only a few yards distant forced Kristine from his mind.

Sylvia Reynolds—no, Arnold now, was more beautiful than he remembered. He needn't have wondered about how the years would have affected her. He couldn't forget that though she belonged to Jack now, once she had promised to be his wife. Jack had stolen everything from him. Well, he hoped he'd enjoyed these past few years, because he was about to meet justice head-on and have it all taken away from him, just like he'd taken it away from Tucker.

As he drank his coffee and watched the scene across the street, he noticed that at 4:00 p.m. exactly, the doorman stepped inside and disappeared from view. It was ten minutes later before he reappeared, and then Tucker realized it was a different man. Apparently the shift had changed, and he realized that for ten minutes admittance had been open to anyone who dared to enter.

So the coast would be clear for ten minutes at the shift change. Time enough to allow him to get safely inside before the new doorman came to take up his post. What he might find once inside the building was another thing altogether. There he would just have to take his chances.

As he continued watching, he assumed that the men who worked there had a room downstairs in which to change clothes, because a little later, the man who had been replaced left the building, dressed in street clothes. Waving to the man now on duty, he walked off down the street.

He'd seen what he came to see, so he paid his tab and left the restaurant. The shifts lasted eight hours, so that meant that midnight would present a good opportunity for what he had in mind. Now all he needed was to learn the movements of the pair he sought out. And before long, he'd be ready to put his plan into action. Once and for all, the pair who had damned his past as a lie and stolen his future would be confronted and made to pay for their deeds.

Tucker returned to the motel at about six in the evening. Kristine was watching a news program on the television. The story involved the arrest of several men believed to be key figures in the Dallas branch of the Mafia.

A tall dark-haired man with his hands covering his face was being led from the courthouse steps by police officers when Tucker came to stand beside Kristine's chair. He watched her face as she watched the screen, and he knew suddenly that he was seeing Vincent Spinelli. The realization went through him like wildfire. This was the man she had been married to not so long ago.

A tumble of confused thoughts and sensations assailed him. He didn't like the idea of her having been married, but he had no right to either like or dislike the idea. That's the way he wanted it—wasn't it?

"The ex-husband," he observed coldly, hard gray eyes riveted on her face.

Kristine met his glance almost defiantly. "Yes," she answered coolly. She had nothing to be ashamed about. She wasn't the only one in this room who had made the mistake of thinking herself in love with the wrong person.

"Well, it looks like they're putting him where he belongs—behind bars."

Getting to her feet, she switched the television off and made as if to leave the room. But Tucker caught her arm with a detaining hand.

"Any regrets?" he ripped the words out impatiently, immediately condemning himself for feeling the need to voice them.

"About what?" she asked without inflection. But her dark eyes burned into his.

"Do you regret last night?" he asked softly, a mocking light entering the gray eyes. They both knew he had had her full cooperation both times. He touched her, and like a match set to tinder, she went up in flames.

"I think we both should back off a little," she replied, still in that cool tone of voice. She didn't know for certain where he'd been all day, but she had a pretty good idea.

"Do you?" he murmured quietly.

The hand holding her arm drew her around until she stood facing him. He stepped close, placing a leg between both of hers. His denim-clad knee rubbed against her inner thigh. The hand at her arm slid down to her wrist and, drawing her hand to lay against his chest, held it there. His other hand moved around to the small of her back and, pressing against her hips, he pulled her fully against him.

A little while ago, Kristine had been certain she could resist him if he attempted to make love to her again without first explaining what his feelings were toward her—and Sylvia Arnold. Now she wasn't quite so confident.

He met her eyes with that maddening hint of arrogance she recognized, and she wanted to throttle him. At the same time she couldn't deny the dizzying feeling of being in the right place, the place where she had longed to be all day and all evening, even as she had wondered where he was and who he was with.

"Where have you been?" She fended him off with words as his face drew near to hers.

The descent of his head halted abruptly. The gray eyes that had been intent on her mouth encountered her gaze.

"Out."

His head began once more to descend. But Kristine was determined not to be played for a fool. She would not be his plaything by night while he sought the company of another woman during the day—and evening.

Twisting in his arms and arching her body, she struggled to get free. "Let me go. I won't be used—"

"Used!" His laugh raked over her like nails down a blackboard. "I—use you?"

"Yes."

"If you want to discuss being used, then how about the way you used me? Didn't you climb into my car while on the run from your husband? And to escape Morrell?"

Kristine's eyes widened in shock on his glowering face. But shock quickly gave way to anger, and her nostrils flared in fury. She opened her mouth to scream at him, then closed it in silence.

He was right, she had used him—perhaps it was only fair that he use her in return. But surely her use of his protection had not brought him the pain that his use of her love was wringing from her.

Pulling her roughly, almost violently to him, he swept her up into his arms. Kristine buried her face against the thick cords of his throat. She couldn't watch his face as she asked the one question she couldn't keep from forming on her quivering lips.

"Were you with her?"

Tucker faltered in his step. Though he held Kristine, wanted her with every fiber of his being, he couldn't deny that the thought of another woman lay buried in the back of his mind. The arms holding her tightened fractionally, but his answer, when it came, was firm and strong.

"No," he whispered deeply as he came down onto the bed beside her.

For the next two weeks, the days followed the same pattern as the first one. Tucker was gone all day, returned sometime during the evening or not until late at night. When he returned, he would climb into bed beside Kristine and, if she was asleep, awaken her. And then he would make wild, passionate love to her in an attempt to drive from his mind the demons that plagued him.

Kristine hadn't the strength of will to refuse him or to leave him. Somewhere, she kept telling herself, deep down inside, he needed her. And if she persisted, continued to be there whenever he sought her out, he'd eventually recognize that need for the love that it was.

Each time he made love to her, she hoped he'd forget himself, loosen the tight bonds he placed on his feelings and whisper words of love to her. But her hopes were in vain. The words remained unspoken, and the hours between sunset and dawn grew longer and colder.

Several times she asked to accompany him on one of his jaunts, but he only looked at her and shook his head. And when she attempted to discover what it was that he did while he was gone, her questions were met with a stony silence.

By the end of the second week, Kristine was at her wits' end. She loved him, she was certain of that, but the certainty she had maintained up to now, that he loved her, too, was in grave doubt. He was destroying her with the long silences, the desperate, almost angry lovemaking.

He wasn't violent or rough with her, but the turbulence was there just below the surface, like a volcano getting ready to erupt. And it frightened her. He had never in so many words told her he planned to cold-bloodedly take a human life, and she hadn't really believed that, when it came down to it, he would be able to. But as the tension mounted, so did the doubt in her own ability to gauge his intentions correctly. Or the motivation behind them.

Perhaps hate was indeed stronger than love. Perhaps Tucker's need to find release for his anger was greater than his need for love—for her.

Or perhaps, the love he needed was not a new one, but one that had begun years ago, before she had met him. Perhaps the hold Sylvia had on him extended much further than the piece of jewelry he wore on his left wrist.

Was Tucker planning the demise of his partner because of what he'd taken from him and the stigma he'd left him with of having spent five years in prison? Or because when Jack Arnold left, he had not gone alone?

Many times in these past few days, Kristine had felt the cold touch of the bracelet against her skin and been revolted by it. She had almost asked him to remove it before making love to her—but she hadn't. When the bracelet came off, if it ever did, it would have to be his decision, and his alone, to remove it.

The days passed with little for her to do. She found a small shopping center within walking distance and bought some necessities, including a few inexpensive items of clothing. She also bought some crossword puzzle books and spent the days in switching from puzzles to television to taking walks around the immediate area.

She awoke slowly and knew instantly that she was alone in the bed. He was gone—again. That afternoon, unlike most of the others, he had returned to the motel to share dinner with her. Once the meal was finished, they had gone back to their room. And as the door closed behind them, Tucker swept her into his arms and made fierce, passionate love to her. Kristine had felt her hopes flowering once more. Was this a sign that his true feelings were at last making themselves known to him?

But they had soon fallen asleep, and now she was once more alone. She decided a shower was what she needed and upon coming out of the bathroom, switched on the television. She had no real interest in watching it, but it would be company. There was no telling how long Tucker would be gone tonight.

Kristine stared at the television screen. The late news had been off for over an hour. A detective show that she tried to get interested in began, but it was no use. Something was telling her that this night was different.

Getting to her feet, she paced the floor, stood at the window and stared at the black covering over the empty pool, blowing in the wind, then dropped the curtain and paced some more. It was almost one in the morning. Where could he be?

Her eyes darted toward the dresser where Tucker kept the gun tucked away in an extra pair of socks. Was it still there? It had been when he left before. A couple of times recently she'd looked just to make certain.

Why didn't she look now? What was stopping her?

Adrenaline pumped through her system, making her knees feel shaky and her hands cold and clammy. This was ridiculous, of course the gun was still there. What made this night different than any of the others?

She stared at the television screen, saw the moving figures without understanding what they did or what they said. Her eyes, drawn as if by a magnet, kept finding the second drawer in the dresser, the drawer that held Tucker's things.

The gun was there, she was positive of it, tucked away in his socks. There had been no indication that Tucker had finished with whatever he did day after day and was ready to take action against Jack and Sylvia. The gun was there.

The staccato sound of gunfire drew her abruptly to her feet. She twisted about, looking toward the door and window, her heart in her mouth. She turned toward the television and allowed her tense shoulders to droop in relief. The sound had come from there, someone was firing an automatic weapon on the screen.

She felt unbelievably foolish, but knew there was only one thing to do, she would take a look at the gun. Once she had reassured herself that it was where it should be, where it could do no one any harm, she'd be all right.

It wasn't as easy as it sounded. She didn't want to look at it and think about what it could do to Tucker's life—and to hers—if he used it. The idea of the gun hadn't bothered her perhaps as much as it should have. But for a long time she had only thought of it as protection against Carl Morrell.

Now her hands shook as she placed them around the handles on the drawer and pulled. The drawer stuck and she had to pull hard. It flew back without warning, almost knocking her off her feet.

Regaining her balance, Kristine stared at the corner where the sparse bundle of socks normally rested. Everything that had been in the drawer belonging to Tucker was gone. Including the gun.

Chapter 14

Tucker parked the truck on a side street a few blocks away from the apartment building and walked the distance to within a block of it. The wind was blowing directly off the lake, and a light dusting of snow powdered the ground beneath his feet. Keeping his hands in his pockets, the left one wrapped around the handle of the gun, he paused at the place he'd picked out earlier that day and slid into the concealing shadows of the doorway.

It was almost midnight, time for the doormen to change shifts. At that moment, he looked up and saw the man he recognized from his recent casing of the place walk round the corner and trudge toward the lighted entrance. Right on time, Tucker thought with satisfaction.

A few minutes later, he followed, glancing up and down the street before darting from the shadows and into the unmanned revolving door. He found the elevators right away, but passed them by for the door marked Exit. He would use the stairs, no sense in taking a chance on anyone questioning his presence in the building at this time of night.

On the eighth floor, he paused to peer through the glass panel at the top of the door, looking in both directions before stepping from the stairwell onto the plush red carpet of the hallway. The coast was clear. There were only two doors visible, and both were tightly closed.

He had watched a taxi driver carry bundles upstairs for Sylvia one day and learned from the driver that the Arnolds lived in the penthouse suite. The man had told him all he knew about the place for a ten-dollar tip. And for another twenty had given him the address of a former second-story man he knew who just might have a few tools for sale left over from his former trade.

It hadn't taken Tucker long to get what he needed and now he was ready. For over two weeks he'd been shadowing the couple. He knew when Jack left the apartment in the morning and where he went. He knew the location of his favorite restaurant for lunch and even his favorite item on the menu. And he could tell you what nights of the week Sylvia was likely to return late from an evening out, spent with or, more frequently, without her husband, Jack.

At night, when he returned to the motel, he couldn't stop himself from making love to Kristine. He kept telling himself it wasn't right, it wasn't fair to keep her on a string that way, but as much as Sylvia's beauty fascinated him, Kristine's warmth drew him like a moth to a flame. He needed her even though he paid for his actions with deep feelings of shame. And his confusion over the real reason for his seeking Jack Arnold out became worse with each passing day.

And now soon the confusion would be over. The penthouse suite loomed just ahead. A strange cold excitement began to fill his whole body. He could hear his heart thundering in his ears and taste the sharp, almost bitter, taste of fear on his tongue.

The door was locked, as he'd known it would be. But he'd come prepared. He reached into his pocket, darted a glance back over his shoulder toward the stairway door and withdrew a small thin tool from his coat pocket. Inserting it into the lock, he jiggled it, felt it resist then heard a small click as the lock was forced open.

Removing the lock pick, he returned it to his pocket, grasped the doorknob and made his way silently inside. If Sylvia followed her usual pattern, tonight she would be out until after one o'clock. But he wasn't quite certain about Jack. It had been hard to pin down his movements at night with any regularity.

With a small flashlight, another item he'd kept in his pocket, he made his way slowly through the empty rooms. Jack was obviously not at home. There was no denying the apartment's elegance. It was what he had expected from seeing the couple's obvious wealth as he followed them about town.

Renewed anger sliced through him at the thought of all this opulence, bought with money made at the cost of his own freedom. Fingering a silk dressing gown lying across the bed, he bunched it in an angry fist and threw it across the room. Apparently Sylvia hadn't suffered overmuch in his absence. It had been made clear to him as he followed her these two weeks that she had everything she wanted, but it was never so clear as now. She was virtually living the life of a queen. And now that he thought about it, wasn't this the kind of life-style she had always talked about wanting?

Tucker found his way back into the living room and sat down on the couch in front of the fireplace. He laid the gun across his lap and waited. He had no idea how long a time he sat there, almost in a daze. There was no sound to warn him of a presence, the noise must have been muffled by the carpet, but a slight movement of the room's air current brought to his nostrils the sensuous aroma of perfume. He knew without a doubt whose face he would soon see.

There was a startled gasp as soft light sprang from the lamp sitting beside the door, and two huge blue eyes met Tucker's over the barrel of the gun he held pointed in her direction.

She was even more beautiful seen up close than he remembered. Her beauty was such that each time you saw it, it was with a sense of shock at such perfection of face and figure. The black hair was swept back from her face, revealing the sparkle of diamonds in her ears. And the hand she placed at her throat in a gesture of self-defense appeared to be almost weighed down by the huge sapphire adorning the third finger.

What was *he* doing here? Jack had assured her he would be in prison for at least another two years. They were supposed to be safely in Europe before he got out, yet here he was sitting in their living room, for God's sake.

Sylvia recovered quickly from her shock, much quicker than Tucker recovered from the surprise of meeting her face-to-face for the first time in over five years. And she instantly recognized the dazed look in the gray eyes for what it was—the old hunger she had always been able to inspire in him. Taking a step into the room, she opened the silver mink and, in a graceful move, allowed it to fall from her shoulders. She placed it carefully across a chair and turned fully to face him.

Tucker couldn't contain a slight gasp as the dress beneath was revealed to his yearning gaze. Made of silver lamé, the bodice of the gown barely existed, was in fact little more than a minute strip of the shiny material that barely covered each nipple. The skirt fell away from her narrow waist and clung to every curve of hip and thigh. It was slit up both sides and revealed long, shapely legs covered in expensive nylon with each step she took closer to the couch. Whoever said it was more provocative to leave something to the imagination hadn't seen this woman in this gown.

"Well, Tucker, isn't this a—nice surprise." With the gliding sway he remembered from old, she closed the gap between them and held one hand out regally, making him feel as though he should bow and salute it with a kiss.

"You're alone?" His only response to the gesture was to stand.

"Why, yes, did you expect to see someone else?"

The low, sexy tones reminded him suddenly of Kristine and the way her voice sounded after making love. Resolutely he pushed the memory aside, she had no place in his dealings with this woman. "Let's not play word games," he answered in a dark tone of voice. "I know you and Jack are married, have been for quite some time now. You know why I'm here, so where is he?"

Still maintaining that air of cool poise, she made a slight fluttering movement with the fingers of one hand and shrugged a delicate shoulder. "Obviously not here."

"Obviously," he echoed sarcastically.

"What do you want with him?" she asked softly, moving a step closer, continuing to ignore the gun as she had since first entering the room and seeing it.

"Let's just say—I have a present for him."

His voice sounded cold and inflexible, but she recognized the hot look in the gray eyes. He wasn't any more immune to her now than he had been when they were engaged. A step closer and the gun barrel was pressing against her bosom. She dropped a violet-eyed glance to the offending object, then looked back up at him from beneath long, mascaraed lashes and whispered, "Do you really need that?"

Long red-tipped fingers pressed against his inner thigh and moved slowly upward. She almost had him under her spell, he could feel that old magic causing his senses to spin. The familiar scent of her perfume brought to the surface memories of the many times they had made love.

"Have you forgotten our time together?" she asked seductively. In her heels she was almost as tall as Tucker, and all she needed to do was angle her head and then she was pressing her mouth hotly to his.

Tucker was a normal, healthy male, and the feel of a half-naked woman in his arms stirred him in the normal healthy male way—for approximately thirty seconds. And then he was wrenching his mouth from hers.

"What's wrong?" she asked in a stunned voice. No one refused her favors—no one—not ever.

Tucker was reeling with the knowledge that she hadn't moved him. He'd held her, felt her lips beneath his and expected to feel as he had in the past. He reached down deep inside of himself to find the passion she had always been able to stir and found only emptiness—and shame.

Thank God, Kristine hadn't seen him just now in the arms of this cold, avaricious bitch. How could he have thought he still wanted this woman, who was willing to betray not only him, but the man she had married in his stead. It was fitting that his future not include Kristine, he didn't deserve a warm, giving, loyal woman such as her.

"What about Jack?" he asked, wondering how far Sylvia was willing to take this.

She smiled that slow, catlike smile he recognized, quirked a fine brow and shrugged that elegant shrug.

That's what he'd thought. Raising his empty hand, holding her gaze, he deliberately drew the back of the hand slowly across his mouth. He saw the violet eyes flicker and knew she understood the significance of the gesture, as he had understood her shrug.

There was a long, tense moment, and then Sylvia shook the dark hair back over one shoulder with an uncaring flourish and crossed the room to the fireplace. She took a cigarette from a small enamel-painted box, picked up a jeweled lighter lying beside it, snapped it open and touched the flame to the end of the cigarette.

Then she took a long drag, filling her lungs with smoke, and released it slowly. Smoothing a hand down the slender curve of her hips, she looked up in Tucker's direction and met his eyes. Gesturing toward the sofa, she invited, "Sit down. It appears as though you want this to be a business discussion—very well, let's talk business."

Tucker took a seat on the couch once more and waited for her to continue.

"Five years ago, when you were trying to sell the microchip to the government here in the States, Jack was working on a deal with a foreign government for ten times the amount of money you were willing to settle for.

"He sold it, too, and made more money than we could ever have expected to make in two lifetimes if you had had your way."

"The chip was not his to sell. I developed it, it was in our contract that any new developments made would remain my property and mine alone. He was only entitled to a portion of the sale money—that's all."

"Well, it's done, he sold it. I really don't see what you're getting so steamed up about." She turned to grind out the half-smoked cigarette in the ashtray.

"The technology was supposed to stay here in the U.S., that's why I developed the chip," Tucker told her from between clenched teeth.

"Well, don't get so upset, it is going to stay here. Jack sold the chip twice," she told him admiringly. "He downgraded its abilities and sold it here about six months ago."

"What? Jack doesn't have the knowledge to downgrade it—"

"No, he doesn't—but the man he hired does."

"Wait a minute, how can Jack sell the chip here if he's already sold it in Europe? That is called fraud, a term you and he should be pretty familiar with considering the circumstances. And surely by now the government here knows that I was right—I wasn't trying to defraud them—"

Sylvia glided across the room and took a seat beside him on the couch. "They know."

"Then why was nothing done about my false imprisonment?" he asked coldly.

"The government doesn't like to admit to making mistakes. And you did get out—early—didn't you?

"Look." She laid one small hand over his larger one and moved closer. "There's enough money to go around. I know Jack would just as soon have you in the business again, as to have you as an enemy."

Tucker gripped the gun tighter, he didn't trust her. There was no longer any question in his mind that she had been a party to Jack's plans from the start. Money was everything to her, he finally realized.

"We're planning to move the business to Europe this spring. Just imagine what it would be like to live on the continent. You and me on the French Riviera. We could find any number of things to do—together." She pressed closer, her thigh sliding against his, the slits allowing the skirt to fall away, revealing a long, dangerously high expanse of bare skin.

"You remember how you used to spend so much time working? You left it up to Jack to take me to plays and to dinner—

"Well, Jack is very involved with the business just now—he wouldn't be any the wiser—no one would get hurt."

Tucker's eyes lowered to the enchanting proportion of voluptuous breasts made visible as she leaned closer. He could admire the beauty of the display and still see the woman for what she was. A two-timing schemer who cared about only two things in life—herself—and money.

Had that greedy gleam always been this evident in the violet eyes? Why hadn't he seen it before now?

Five years ago, she had probably said something similar to Jack. No one would get hurt—but Tucker had—he'd lost five years of his life—five years he could never regain.

Kristine searched the whole room, looking for the gun. But it was nowhere to be found. Tucker must have taken it. Dear God, what should she do? She couldn't let him kill this Jack Arnold, he'd go to prison again—if he was lucky. Premeditated murder—did it carry the death penalty in Illinois?

Throwing herself across the bed, she stared at the ceiling. What should she do? If she called the police and sent them to the apartment, Tucker would know she'd been the one to do it. He'd hate her for that.

But could she stand silently by and watch him throw his future away for the sake of revenge?

What should she do? Jumping to her feet, she paced the room furiously. Even now, he could be pulling the trigger while she dithered here, undecided about what to do.

Tears burned her eyes. She loved him, she couldn't stand to see him throw his life away in such a stupid fashion. Seating herself beside the telephone, she stared down at it for a long time in indecision. She couldn't call the police and blatantly turn him in. But there was one thing she could do, and it involved making one of the hardest decisions she had ever had to make. Tucker would see it as betrayal, she saw it as an act of love.

Finding her jacket, she removed a piece of paper and sat back down at the phone. She dialed quickly, before she lost her nerve, and listened to the phone ring on the other end. When no one answered, she hung up and called the St. Louis police station.

When Bob Linton came on the line, she told him she had expected to find him at home at this time of night. He told her that the homicide department didn't know whether it was day or night. People killed people at any hour of the day.

"That's what I called you about—murder."

"What?" he asked in surprise.

"It's Tucker—the gun is missing—and I know he took it. I've been expecting it—he's acted so strangely lately—"

"Whoa! Slow down and back up a bit. What's this about a gun?"

"Tucker bought a gun, in Dallas, I guess. He's had it since we met—I think. He's going to kill Jack Arnold with it—"

She could hear the curses coming down the line at her. After a moment, Bob asked, "Where is he now?"

"I don't know for sure. When I awoke he was gone. But I'd guess he's at the apartment where this guy Arnold lives. I know he's been following them around—at least that's what I think he's been doing. He wouldn't let me go along when he left here—day or night."

Gripping the phone in both hands, she said, "You—we've got to stop him before he does something foolish. He's throwing his life away, and for what?"

Dashing the tears from her eyes with one hand, she listened as Bob began to speak. "I have a friend in the Chicago police department. Dan Connors is his name. He's familiar with the case against Tucker. He's kept an eye on Jack and Sylvia for me since they moved there from St. Louis a few years ago.

"He'll know how to handle this discreetly, without involving anyone else in the department. I'll call him as soon as we hang up—he'll take care of Tucker—"

"I'm going along just to make sure," she informed him determinedly.

"What? No way—"

"Look, I go with your man, or I go alone. Either way, I'm going."

"Okay, I'll tell Connors to come by and get you. But I don't like it, and he won't, either."

They hung up, and Kristine dressed in record time. And when she was ready, she placed a call to the Chicago police department herself. She was told Detective Connors was at home, but they would have him call her. She told them it was a life-or-death situation and to make him understand that.

Within minutes of hanging up, the phone rang.

"Dan Connors here, who's this?"

Kristine explained who she was and that she was going along with him to the apartment. He objected, she had no place in a situation as potentially dangerous as this, he told her. It would mean his badge to involve a citizen.

Kristine told him fine, she'd see him there. Before she hung up, he'd agreed to meet her at the front of the building.

She replaced the phone, quickly called a cab and sat back to wait. It was done, for good or bad, the authorities were going after Tucker—and she was the one who had put them onto him.

Could she learn to live with his hate, if he couldn't understand or forgive her for making the choice she had made?

Could she have lived with herself if she had acted differently and he killed the man? It was his whole future he was throwing away—and perhaps hers, too.

Chapter 15

Jack Arnold shouldered his way through the revolving doors, shaking the snow from his shoulders. It was coming down hard now, and it looked as though they were in for more than the predicted flurries. Nodding briefly in reply to the greeting from the elderly doorman standing just inside the building, he continued without stopping to the elevator doors.

As the doors closed on his figure, a tall black man in a dark gray suit and topcoat and a young woman in a red ski jacket and jeans entered the building. Within moments they were on their way up to the penthouse suite.

Tucker had disengaged his hand from Sylvia's grasp and gained his feet when they heard the sound of a key in the lock. Drawing the gun from his coat pocket, he motioned for the woman to keep quiet and moved back a couple of paces, out of her reach.

Jack Arnold dropped his overcoat onto a chair inside the living room door and looked from the immobile woman to the tall, stern-faced man holding a gun in his hand.

The two men observed each other for a lengthy moment, and it was Jack who finally broke the silence.

"It's been a long time." He spoke calmly without giving the gun a second glance.

Advancing into the room, he strode up to Sylvia and gave her a peck on the cheek. "Good evening, darling, I trust you've made our—guest—welcome in my absence."

"But, of course, dear," she answered sweetly, clasping his arm in both of hers.

"Well, aren't we the loving couple?" Tucker sneered.

Jack spared him a glance before disengaging his arm and turning toward the corner of the room. "I suppose you don't mind if I fix myself a drink?" He walked to the bar without waiting for an answer.

Tucker saw the arrogant tilt to his one-time partner's head and followed him with the gun. He could see no sign of remorse or regret in the man for what he had done to him. White-hot anger surged through him.

"You stole my life's work. You lied under oath and sent me to prison for something I didn't do. You left me to rot in a jail cell for five years, knowing full well it was you who belonged there, and not I."

Jack turned to face him, took a sip from his glass and shrugged his shoulders. "Am I supposed to beat my chest and tell you how sorry I am? Sorry that I took the chance to become a millionaire and ran with it?

"Well, if that's what this little charade—" he motioned with the glass of amber liquid "—is all about. Then I'm afraid you're in for a disappointment. If I had the chance, I'd do it all again. I'd take the money, the woman and run." He grinned at Sylvia, but sobered as his glance encountered the cold gray eyes fastened onto his face with murderous intent.

"You admit everything?" Tucker asked deeply.

"Admit it? Well, of course I do. But who's to know outside this room?" Carrying his drink with him, he sat down in a chair before the fireplace and spread his legs comfortably.

"I certainly won't tell anyone, and neither will Sylvia. And as for you—well, who's going to believe a convicted felon over me?"

"You arrogant bastard, that's exactly the attitude I expected you to take." There was cold purpose in Tucker's voice as he stepped closer. "And what is to stop me from putting this gun to your head and pulling the trigger?"

"I don't think you'll do that. And I think you've forgotten something. There are two of us, and only one of you. Can you count on shooting both of us before one of us can get to you?"

"However," he continued softly, "I don't think that will be an issue here." He looked over the top of his glass at Tucker. "For the simple reason you haven't the guts to kill me. Now, in your place, I could." Jack rose to his feet. "I would find it no hardship at all to kill you."

"Jack," Sylvia gasped in protest, hurrying to stand between the men. "Not murder. I draw the line at murder."

"Oh, do be still, Sylvia. You didn't show such concern five years ago when we plotted to send the man to prison. He could have been killed there—it happens all the time. I had rather hoped it would in our friend here's case, too."

Tucker looked from the woman to the man and back again. As much as he regretted having to admit it, Jack was right and he knew it. He could not cold-bloodedly kill him. He hadn't the stomach to kill, not even two people he despised as much as he despised this pair. They belonged together—obviously theirs was a match made in hell—and he wished them well of it.

Tucker backed away. Even though he was the one holding the gun, he felt uneasy. There was nothing, he realized this pair would not sink to. And his death would be the icing on the cake for them, so to speak.

And he had been willing to throw his life away for this—the whole of the rest of his life wasted on these two. They weren't worth it.

He had a future, and he knew exactly what he wanted to do with it. Whether the authorities ever cleared his name or not was suddenly unimportant. The only real thing of any importance was Kristine. She had stuck by him even through these past two weeks when he had treated her so badly. Would she be willing to listen to an apology from him?

All at once he wanted very badly to get out of this place, to breathe fresh air uncontaminated by Jack and Sylvia. Let them go on with their machinations, he wanted no part in them. He would make his own way in life—there were still challenges in the computer field, and he would be around to meet them, and with Kristine at his side if he was lucky.

"For once you're right," he told Jack. "I haven't the stomach for killing—not even someone who deserves it as much as you. The two of you are beneath contempt—and I won't waste my life by ending yours."

Even knowing he still hadn't gotten the proof he needed to see them where they belonged, behind bars, he was leaving. Tucker was backing toward the door when the door burst open and a black man built like a wrestler charged in. He was carrying a gun in one hand and a badge in the other.

Dan Connors faced the three people in the room with a slight smile on his dark face. "Don't anybody move, please. As you can see, I'm carrying a badge.

"You—" he motioned with his gun toward Tucker "—bend over and place that weapon on the floor—nice and easy."

When Tucker had complied, Dan told him to move away from it, then turned a little to face the other two.

"Don't be alarmed, folks. I heard everything from outside the door. Oh, and in case you're wondering—" he patted his pocket "—I do have a search warrant, right here. Everything is nice and legal."

Kristine stepped inside and looked at Tucker. Tucker drew heavy brows over dark gray eyes and glanced questioningly at the cop.

"Go ahead," Dan told him. "I figure I can trust you, I know your brother. Just don't leave the premises." Dan leaned over and picked the gun up from the floor.

Tucker stepped around him, hearing him begin to fire questions at the man and woman he'd placed side by side on the couch. Taking Kristine by the arm, he drew her none too gently outside the apartment and into the hallway.

"What are you doing here?" he asked in a cold, angry voice. Not her, too, he was thinking, please let it be some kind of a coincidence that she happened to be behind the cop.

"I—I couldn't let you do it—Tucker—I couldn't stand by and watch you ruin your life—"

"You turned me in?" he asked incredulously. "You called the cops on me?"

"No! Not exactly—"

"Then what—exactly?"

"I called your brother—"

"You did what? You took it upon yourself to bring my brother into this, even knowing I didn't want him involved? By what right?" All thoughts of how much he had come to admire her—come to love her—were swamped by the flood of disappointment—the sense of betrayal he felt at what she'd done.

"Tucker—" Kristine held on to his jacket lapel. "I love you—I couldn't let you go to prison again—"

"And just what do you think is going to happen when your friend in there takes me in for possession of a handgun? They aren't going to let me go simply because you ask them nicely. I'm a convicted felon just out of prison. This could send me back—"

He was so angry he wanted to tear things up with his hands. Closing taut fingers over her hands, he dragged them from his jacket.

"Get out of my sight! I can't bear to look at you. I thought you were different—I thought I could trust you—But you're like all the rest—"

"No—Tucker—please—listen to me—" she pleaded, tears running down her cheeks. She had known she was taking a chance on this being his reaction when she'd made the choice to call Bob. But she had thought that she would be able to make him listen—make him see the sense of it.

She had been wrong. Not in what she'd done—if she had the choice to make, she'd make the same one again. It was too bad she hadn't had enough faith in him to know he'd do the right thing. She had been listening right along with the cop, Connors. She'd heard him tell Jack and Sylvia he wouldn't waste his life in killing them.

Should she have waited? Trusted him more? Was he right when he said she was like all the others?

Fighting her own guilt as well as the feelings of hurt his accusations caused, Kristine watched him turn away from her in disgust and walk away. She'd give him time to calm down, and then she'd talk with him again.

Kristine sat staring at the vast brown-and-yellow desert. It was June, and the hot sun made heat waves dance in the distance. She had been off work for all of thirty minutes and barely had time to remove her shoes when the telephone rang. Working in medical records was tiring, but not as tiring as standing on her feet all day would have been if she was still a practicing nurse.

She lowered herself onto the chair beside the phone, facing the wide picture window, and answered it on the third ring.

"Hello, is that you, beautiful?"

The familiar deep tones rang down the wire. "Yes, it's me, who else would it be?" She grinned tiredly. It was unbelievable how much she had come to look forward to his phone calls in the past six months.

"How are you?"

"Fine, just fine." Easing swollen feet up onto the ottoman, she relaxed back with a sigh. This was pure heaven, now all she needed was a tall, cool drink and a long nap. She always needed a nap these days. Must be the heat.

"Are you liking Arizona any better?"

"It's okay, I guess it kind of grows on you."

"Was that a pun?" Bob asked laughingly.

"No, no pun intended. I'm just feeling old and grumpy. When am I going to see you again? It's been almost four months."

"I don't know—we still have to be careful, you know," he reminded her. "I have something to tell you."

"Tucker?" she asked fearfully, sitting up so fast her head literally swam.

"He's fine—honestly." He paused as if searching for the right words. "He's been asking questions. I finally had to tell him that you had agreed to the witness relocation program. That seemed to satisfy him for a time, but—"

Kristine's heart pounded, and the hand holding the phone began to shake. "Did you tell him why?" she asked dry mouthed.

"Not exactly—that is, not all of it. I did tell him about the attempt on your life after you returned to St. Louis and went to work."

"And?"

"He's looking for you. Not long ago we had the first big argument we've had since we were kids."

"And?" she prodded again.

"He threatened—"

"Bob—did you tell him where I was?" Please, she was praying, please, please say you—

"I debated calling you for a long time," he hedged. "I didn't want to upset you. In your—"

A heavy fist fell against the front door and seemed to rattle the whole house. Kristine dropped the phone and turned to stare at the door with wide frightened eyes.

"I know you're in there, so you might as well let me inside before I break this damned door down."

"Oh, no," she whispered, looking around the room with worried eyes, seeking a place to hide.

"Open up and let me in!" A fist thudded loudly, and the air turned blue with curses.

Kristine knew there was nothing to do but open the door; otherwise, her neighbors would no doubt call the police and that would be another thing he would never forgive her for. Scooting forward, she got to her feet and ambled toward the door.

Taking a deep breath, pushing the hair back from her hot forehead, she gripped the door handle and pulled it open.

"Hello, Tucker."

His eyes, still the same silver gray as she remembered, slid from her hair, a few inches longer than when he'd last seen her, to her waist, and halted abruptly.

"My God," he breathed softly. "My God."

Kristine placed a protective hand over her rounded belly and stepped back a pace.

Meeting the almost defiant light in her dark eyes, he asked, "When?"

"Do you mean when did I get pregnant, or when is the baby due?"

"Both—I guess." He sounded dazed.

"I'm not sure when I—conceived—neither of us did anything to prevent it." She wanted him to know, if he resented the fact of the pregnancy, that it was his responsibility as well as her own. "As for when it's due to be born, September." She smoothed a gentle hand over the warm mound and repeated, "September."

"May I come in?" he asked softly, his eyes hungrily devouring her face, her figure.

Kristine stepped back and allowed him to enter the room. When he had taken a seat, she saw he was staring at the phone on the floor and blushed hotly. Sounds of a voice bellowing her name could be heard coming from it.

She bent to pick it up, but Tucker was there before her and handed her the instrument deferentially. He continued to look dazed, slightly confused. Neither expression nor the gallant gesture seemed somehow to be in his line.

Kristine placed the phone to her ear and said, "I'll call you back later." And without further ado she hung the phone up and took a seat across the room from him. In silence she put her feet up, crossed her hands over her stomach and looked at Tucker.

"So," she began when he still didn't speak, not knowing what to say but feeling compelled to say something. He looked so good, not at all as though he'd been pining after her. "How have you been?"

"Fine, just fine." Tucker laid his hands on his thighs and looked around the room. He'd never felt this awkward in his life. Not even on his first date. What did you say to the mother of your child, whom you hadn't seen for nearly six months. Whom, in fact, you had refused to see out of stubborn pride.

"I guess you must have gotten your microchip back?" Kristine ventured into conversation. Why had he come? It didn't appear as though he regretted the way they had parted, he hadn't even mentioned it.

Tucker's glance darted sharply to her face. "You don't know?"

Kristine frowned in puzzlement. "Know what? I haven't heard anything—"

"You talk with my brother regularly," he stated almost accusingly.

"Yes," she agreed, "but we don't discuss you."

The fingers on his thighs flexed. "You don't discuss me? What do you discuss? The weather?"

"Sometimes," she answered equably. "And sometimes we discuss my health, or my job—or his—"

"All right," Tucker said, getting to his feet restlessly. "I get the point. You talk about everything but me."

Whirling suddenly to face her, surprising a look of pain on her face, he asked, "Why is that? Why don't you ask about me?"

He waited in mental agony for her answer. He loved her so much—he had never stopped—not even when he was angry over what he'd considered her betrayal of his trust. For weeks now, ever since he'd gotten off probation for possession of the gun, he'd been trying to get Bob to tell him where she was.

It had taken a while for him to get over his anger with her, but when he had, when he'd looked around and realized she was gone—really gone—he'd been driven nearly crazy with worry.

Bob had told him about the incident when a man had followed her home from work one night and tried to break down her door. And, when that hadn't worked, he'd fired a blast from a shotgun through the door. Kristine had called the cops, but a neighbor who kept a gun in the house for protection ran the man off before they arrived on the scene. That had apparently made her decide to become a part of the relocation program.

Though Bob didn't tell him this, by that time, Kristine had known she was carrying Tucker's child and she determined not to take any chances on losing the baby. She might never have the man, but she would have his child to love and to raise.

Kristine stood up now and turned toward the window to stare with unseeing eyes at cactus, rock and sand. What did he want from her? How was she to answer him? Did he want to hear how she had lain awake at night crying that first week after his confrontation with Jack Arnold and Sylvia? An emotional wreck because he refused to either see or speak to her. Did he want to hear how her money had run out and that had left her with no option but to call Bob and ask for his help?

Or perhaps he wanted to hear how she had been both wildly ecstatic and deeply depressed to learn she was carrying his child. Should she tell him of the horror of being shot at through the door with a shotgun? Or the loneliness of giving up an identity and moving to a place she had never been, to try to start a brand-new life alone, when all she wanted was a man who apparently didn't love her enough to forgive her for saving his life.

"No," she answered slowly, meeting his eyes directly. "I didn't ask about you. You didn't want to know about me, remember?"

"And my child? Were you going to bear my child without telling me about him?" There was pain evident in the gray eyes, but his voice was even.

"I don't know," she answered honestly.

Clenching her hands together at the crest of her protruding belly, she stared at the floor. His pain hurt her. It made her feel guilty, and she should have no reason to feel that way. He had sent her away, not the other way around.

"Oh!" She jumped and spread her hands out over her belly.

"What is it?" he asked anxiously. "Are you all right? It's too soon for the baby—isn't it?"

"I'm fine," she assured him with an enchanted smile. "He just kicked me, that's all."

"And you can feel it that strongly?" he asked in amazement. "Does it hurt?"

"No, of course it doesn't hurt, silly—oh! He did it again."

Tucker moved closer, his eyes glued in fascination to her belly. Had he seen a slight movement just then? Could you see a kick from outside?

"Please—" He looked from her face to her belly and back.

"You want to feel it?" she asked gently. And then, not bothering to wait for an answer, she took his big hands and folded them around the precious mound.

"I felt it!" He sounded like an excited boy. "Good Lord, he's strong." He sounded awed.

Kristine placed her hands over his, pressed them to her and closed her eyes. He wasn't wearing the gold identification bracelet. She'd never seen him without it before. It was too good to be true. She couldn't possibly be standing here with Tucker, enjoying such a private, tender moment as his child's first movements, and learning that the shackle he had willingly worn, binding him to another woman—to another life that did not include her—was gone.

"Kristine? Are you all right?" His eyes were on her face, a worried expression in their depths. One hand left her belly to cup her cheek tenderly.

"Yes." She smiled and couldn't help the tears that glistened on her lashes. "I'm fine—now. But I do feel a little—light-headed."

Tucker took her into his arms and held her to him, his face against the soft hair at her neck. She smelled so fresh and sweet—he'd remembered that about her all the time he'd been without her.

"I love you," he breathed against her soft skin. "God, how I love you."

"Tucker, did Bob tell you I was pregnant?" she asked abruptly, pulling out of his embrace to look up into his face.

He tensed a moment and then relaxed. His eyes met hers clearly, nothing hidden in their depths. "No, he didn't, I practically had to beat the information that you were in Arizona out of him. But that's all he would tell me."

"And how do you feel about this? About the baby?"

"How do I feel? I feel like a man who just learned he's going to be a father. How am I supposed to feel? I feel surprised, awed, thrilled—humble?"

"Oh, Tucker." She grinned and raised a hand to his face. "I love you, too."

"Does that mean you'll marry me?" Nothing in his whole life meant as much to him as her answer. He could feel his insides tighten painfully as she looked up into his face without answering. And when she finally spoke, it wasn't what he expected her to say.

"Do you think we could live together and manage not to fight every day of our lives?"

"I don't know," he answered truthfully. They were both strong personalities, and neither would give in easily if he or she thought they were in the right. "But I'm willing to find out. And even a fifty-year battle is better than living without you."

Were there tears in the gray eyes looking down so intently into hers?

Nothing in his past could come anywhere near to destroying him as completely as living without Kristine would do.

"I think we deserve each other," she whispered against his mouth, feeling him shudder with relief as he held her tightly, carefully to his broad chest.

Tucker couldn't have agreed more.

* * * * *

Silhouette Sensation

COMING NEXT MONTH

ONE GOOD TURN
Judith Arnold

One summer in Washington, a wide-eyed optimist named Jenny Perrin had shown Luke Benning how easy it was to believe in yourself, how perfect love could be.

Luke never knew why she'd disappeared from his life or where she'd gone. But he hadn't forgotten the lessons Jenny had taught him, just as he hadn't forgotten Jenny. Seeing her again, Luke had to find out what had happened eight years ago. Was it too late for them?

LOVE THY NEIGHBOUR
Jacqueline Ashley

Detective Jack Spencer had a lot to learn about women. When he went undercover without listening to Emma Springer's advice, she decided to play a more active role.

Jack was pretending to be a male escort, so Emma secretly signed on as a client. She was about to discover just how perilous — and romantic — police work could be.

Silhouette Sensation

COMING NEXT MONTH

GUILT BY ASSOCIATION
Marilyn Pappano

Was Christopher Morgan a spy? His brother had been arrested but had been murdered before he could give away the identities of those he'd worked with. Could Christopher really have been involved?

Someone was quietly investigating and Shelley Evans's editor wanted to know who and why. Would Christopher Morgan talk to a reporter? Would it be dangerous to approach him?

NIGHT SHIFT
Nora Roberts

Cilla O'Roarke loved the nights when she worked as a DJ at a Denver radio station. At least she loved them until the calls started; there wasn't anything nice about death threats!

Cilla preferred to keep her distance from the police, but that was difficult with detective Boyd Fletcher. He was strong, laconic, infuriating and determined to watch over her every second — day *and night!*